Whisper Down the Years

a novel

Elia Seely

FEATHER MOUNTAIN PRESS

Whisper Down the Years. Copyright ©2012

Elia Seely

Feather Mountain Press
PO Box 85
Manzanita, OR 97130

ISBN 978-0-61580377-7

ACKNOWLEDGEMENTS

There are always a number of people to thank at the culmination of any endeavor, and I am one of those readers who actually read the "acknowledgments" page in other books, because I feel it is part of the story of the book itself. This humble section illustrates the truth that, while there is the fulfillment of dreams—no small thing—there is also the support behind the dreams—no small thing—without which dreams might possibly not come true.

To that end, I thank and acknowledge **Nancy Slavin**, for her fine friendship, her skills as a writer, editor, reader, teacher, and as a fellow sojourner. **Norma Seely, Nichelle Seely, Arlene Rife**, and **Irene Seely** are the female lineage holders of the literary tradition in my family: from them I realize it is possible to write. **Eddy Deane** gave liberally and effortlessly of his design skills, and made the whole thing rather fun. **Emily Trinkhaus** is a mentor and friend, and eagerly contributed her editing and eye to my "final" words, and is a believer that pretty much anything is possible for Saturn in Aries. **Rachel Zuses** offered me a fine retreat to push through the final edit. **Daric Moore** was there for the actual adventure of Orkney; I thank him for the tireless interest in my research, belief in my characters, and the willingness to ride a three-speed into a 100 mph wind. Run on, Magnificent Seven!

There are many others who have supported me in many ways; my life is really one wave of gratitude. You know who you are and you know I love you.

* *

This is a work of fiction. While many of the places are real, there is no Blackstone village, and the characters and events are completely figments of my imagination. I met many fine people in Orkney, and none of them seemed at all murderous.

for norma, nichelle, arlene, and irene

for daric

CHAPTER ONE

The bones fell like dominoes, a fragile menagerie no more suggesting flesh than stones or winter branches. No blood, no cry, just remnants of life scattering across checkerboard lino. Finn recognized the remains of his life, like so many ribs and vertebrae; the structure of his marriage, job, fatherhood broken, dried out, undone.

You're a gruesome bastard, sure. He bent to gather the bird and animal bones and deposit them into a bowl on the counter. Finn cursed his friend Colin's jumble of artifacts that lined every surface of the house. He tried to keep the objects in order, but his own untidiness added to the clutter of the cottage and exacerbated the claustrophobia that pressed down upon him more every day. He stood straight, forgetting the slant of the ceiling, and banged his head. He swore and yanked open the kitchen door, stepping into the force of the unceasing Orkney wind.

When Colin had offered up the cottage, Finn jumped on the opportunity. He had needed to leave Belfast, distance himself from the scenes with Nuala, his stagnating reporting career, the unsteady life that found him too often in a pub. Although Colin would be away for six months, Finn hadn't intended to stay more than four weeks in this cluster of islands flung off the northern coast of Scotland. His sabbatical had rolled by into an unbelievable four months, with nothing to show for it but one article written and less than impressive progress into Colin's library of classics. Nothing sorted between him and his wife: no divorce, no custody arrangement, no clean slice through the assets.

Finn stared east over the pasture that stretched away from the back of the house. The wind breathed into him. There was the smell of cut hay. And space, sky; a loneliness that was palpable, and in this moment, intolerable to contemplate.

Christ.

He walked back inside and into the bedroom, pacing through his emptiness. His phone vibrated in his pocket and he pulled it out to read the text. Matthew was at the pub and there was a music session on—wouldn't he come down for a drink? Finn checked the time as he clicked the phone shut, tossing it with a surge of happiness onto his bed. Nine forty-five; he'd easily be in time for an hour of music and company. There would be fags and food and Bushmill's, and maybe Venus would be there. The only woman that had really turned his head since he'd met—and left—Nuala. He strode into the sitting room and grabbed up his coat from a chair, eager to go out and leave the silence of his own circling thoughts. It didn't matter that the pub was more than a mile away down the road and in his carless state he would be obligated to walk or ride Colin's ancient three-speed.

Finn left the cottage and stood again in the insistent wind. A lapwing mewled in mid-flight, suspended in the air above the billowing grass of the field behind the house. A footpath led away through the field, now half obscured by the vigorous summer growth of the grass. He thought again about Venus and her girlish body and dark straight hair streaked with white. He hadn't seen her in a while and it would be good to see her now. In fact, he *could* walk to Blackstone village via New Farm where Venus lived with her granny Kate and invite them both to come. Finn knew the path led to the lane that ended at their farm. That route was the long way round, sure, but there was no reason not to try to make a connection with Venus, and God knew the exercise would be good for him. Tonight his expansive mood seemed to hinge on seeing her, maybe have a little flirtation. He didn't have Venus' phone number, so to see her a walk it must be. He felt a thrill in his stomach at the thought, and his loneliness and a sudden strong desire urged him over the stile and to the track and the fields.

The footpath took him over several pastures where the hay was cut and rolled into the buns that would be stored for winter feed. The ground was uneven. He passed behind Knowehouse, the nearest farm to Colin's cottage and the home of an unpleasant old woman, Morag Leach. He walked quickly to avoid seeing her. He'd had quite the run-in with her and her son, Neill, a few months back. He saw her moving in the light of a window as he passed.

Finn enjoyed the two-mile ramble over the fields, the solitude heightening his desire to meet up with Venus. He climbed over a stile that brought him to the narrow road leading to New Farm. The rain began as he started down the lane. He jogged to avoid getting soaked, slowing as he reached their stone barn, his stomach beginning to pulse with pain. A cow and two calves stood impervious to the wet but the calves skittered away as he approached. Finn walked to the dark house, suspicious that no one was home. He rapped on the door but there was silence; only the ocean breathed behind the house, the rain muttering on the roof tiles. He went through the garden gate and looked in the kitchen window; no sign of Kate or Venus. A clock on the wall read 10:42; they were out together and where else would they be but the pub?

Finn went down the old track that led away from the farm and the lane. To his left the land sloped down toward the sea. The tide was in and the sliver of beach that edged Kate's pasture was covered with water. Her old fishing boat rocked at its mooring. The unused road led half a mile downhill to a ruined churchyard that perched on the edge of the sea. He slowed as he came by a corner of the stone wall. Finn knew that Venus came here often and it was her special place as if she was still a child. He had made many trips to the church since he discovered that she came and sat among the stones and gathered the nettles that grew along the walls of the sanctuary. A sycamore grew in one corner of the yard. He had found Venus' cache of treasures—rocks, shells, bits of pottery—one day when he had come to look for her. But the churchyard was usually deserted when he arrived, as if she sensed when he would come and so avoided him.

Finn stopped and entered through the iron gate. He knew he wouldn't find her but still he went in. He wanted to lie with her in the shelter of the grass. To look at the sky above rushing with clouds and know her secrets and her simplicity. He walked among the gravestones to the wall that bordered the sea. It was crumbled in places and natural stair steps led down to a flat place among the rocks. Sometimes she swam here; he had seen her once several weeks ago and thought she was a seal with her sleek black hair shining in the sun. The water was very cold and he didn't know how the hell she swam in it.

Finn rubbed his fingers against the rough stone of the wall. A snail inched along the crevices of the rock pulling its spiral of shell. He turned and looked at the sycamore across the churchyard. He saw a shape in the twilight and his heart beat more quickly and he began to sweat. Would that be Venus, sitting there? Had she not seen him? He wove his way through the headstones toward the tree.

"Venus?" he called softly. "Venus?" Finn stopped as he neared the tree. Its branches hung low, sheltering not a woman but a crumpled body lying in an awkward parody of a devotional pose. Adrenaline hit his system and Finn felt his senses sharpen and his vision take a new clarity. As he stepped closer, he could see that it was a man who lay face down among the stones.

"Jesus," Finn whispered. "Are you all right there?" Rain swept over the grass with the wind. "Are you all right? Can I help?" Finn knew that the man would not answer when he smelled the stink of urine. The blond hair was matted with blood and the pulp of brains. A shiny gleam of cheekbone protruded from the brown smooth skin.

Finn became aware of the cold absence of life. He let the shock wash over him and recede. He had seen bodies before—shot, knifed, burnt, blown in pieces. He knelt to feel for a pulse. "Oh, aye, you're well beyond it, man." A deep coldness settled at the base of his spine. The branches of the sycamore genuflected in the wind. The broad leaves brushed the top of the battered head. Finn realized he knew the dead man.

"Fuck me," Finn whispered, drawing his hand away.

Gerard Ventoux, eminent musician and folklorist, and director of Orkney's famed Festival of Isles. A man Finn had met and interviewed four months before, of whom he had heard the whispers of scandal, yet who had exuded charm and élan. And now was as dead as a man could be.

CHAPTER TWO

"Come on then, Venus. What do you say? Give us a song."

Venus let her hair fall over her face. She heard Sammy's soft request; felt a familiar constriction in her heart.

Mary grabbed her hand. "Do. I love to hear you. It's been ages."

"Oh Mary," Venus said, "I don't know if I can—all the songs seem so hard to me now. Too close to home." She gave Mary a melancholy smile and looked away. The pub was crowded with noise and smoke. At the large corner table where she sat with her friends, Matthew and Sammy were taking a break from the first session of music.

"All the more reason to sing them. What do you fancy?" Matthew asked, and pumped air into the bag of his Uilleann pipes.

Venus glanced at Matthew's striking face. His eyes were a sharper blue than Mary's, and possessed an edge of challenge. She held his glance a moment and looked away. Though she barely knew Matthew, there was something familiar about him. Venus' skin prickled with a rising heat.

Matthew fingered a few notes, licked his lips. "Sing *Miss Brown* for me then, remind me of home."

"That's not a Scottish tune," Venus protested.

"Humor the Irish," Matthew said. "Me so far from home. I'll wager you know it—doesn't she?" He winked at Mary as he took a long pull from his pint.

"There's not many tunes she doesn't know," Sammy said, reaching for the bodhran, tapping the scarred table with the drumming stick. "She sang many a fine ballad at Mary and my wedding. Not a dry eye in the lot of us." He smiled to encourage her.

Venus' eyes burned in the smoke from cigarettes and the open coal fire that blazed, winter or summer. She knew it was light outside, despite the dark inside, and longed to be out walking by the sea. The noise of twenty voices, the clatter of glassware, a cough, a whistle, a release of laughter all rose up and over her, a ponderous, breaking wave. But she was an island there, inside. Alone. She looked up from the table as Emily's glance caught her, then flicked away.

Emily moved in her chair, angling herself toward Matthew. She laid a hand on his arm. "Do you know any local tunes, Mattie?"

Venus watched Matthew ignore his girlfriend's question. Emily drew her hand back and moved again in her chair.

"*Miss Brown*, then," Venus said.

Matthew put down the pipes and reached for his fiddle. Sammy shouted another round of drinks while Matthew tuned.

The barman arrived with a tray, setting down sloshing pints for the group, and a glass of ginger ale for Venus.

Matthew began the first mournful notes. Venus breathed in and hesitated, then released the bird of her voice. Once the tune began she had to give in to it, falling into the notes. Her eyes closed and beyond the music she was aware of the abrupt silence in the pub. Only the two of them that mattered, herself and Matthew, pulling forth the sweetness of the melody. Venus felt tears start, and her lungs bloomed with a glorious fullness. When she gave Matthew the song, she opened her eyes and focused on him, his own eyes closed, head leaning into his instrument. His fingers were delicate, and he found the notes with ease. Dark, straight hair lay on his cheek. Emily sat staring down, sadness suffusing her face. Venus lifted her gaze to the ceiling and moved into the last verse. Matthew drew out a lingering shimmer of sound as she let her voice fade on the final melancholy note.

When the song was finished there was a moment's quiet. Matthew met her eye and smiled. Like a whip he flew into another tune. Sammy came in with the bodhran, hand a blur with the frenzied tempo. Keeping time, squeezing Mary's hand hard, Venus let herself rise into the next melody, a well-known local tune. Other voices joined her, and they were united by the songs of history.

They pulled the entire pub through a cacophonous forty minutes of music, the air a chorus of shouts and song and stamping feet. The noise of the room pressed against the low-beamed ceiling. Venus felt herself small and gleaming, pressed hot between her best friend Mary and the side of the bench. It was Matthew who finally called end to the session, his hair and face dripping with sweat. Someone bought a round of whisky and the barman squeezed to their table with another tray of glasses. Venus slipped away from the group and crossed the floor to where her grandmother sat with her old friend, Peter.

"You've not sung in so long—what a treat." Kate smiled and slid over to make room for her granddaughter.

"Aye, you've a right talent," Peter said. "Wouldn't do to let it get too rusty."

Venus ducked her head and rested it on her arms. She felt Kate's hand stroke her hair as she closed her eyes.

"That Matthew's a good fiddler," Kate observed. "But his girlfriend, Emily, she doesn't play or sing at all? She doesn't seem too happy."

Venus raised her head and looked over to the table where her friends sat. Matthew and Emily were a contrast to each other. He was dark, with an intense, social personality. Emily was blond and introverted, single minded in her research of her folklore studies. Matthew met Venus' eye and put his arm around Emily. He turned his face and whispered something to her. Venus caught the look of anger that crossed Emily's face before she turned to him with a wooden smile. She seemed to cringe under his embrace.

"They don't get on well, those two," Peter said, watching the couple also. "Like as not they'll be finished before their stay here is out."

"You don't miss much, you old devil," Kate grinned and placed her hand on his. "You're too old for her—"

"And too good for her," Venus interrupted with a small smile.

Kate cackled and Peter blushed to the roots of his thatch of grey hair, dipping his gaze to his pint of bitter.

Venus sat up and leaned against the back of the bench. She tapped the table with long fingers. "I want to like her, but I don't. I'm not sure why."

Venus thought of the lightning glances that had passed between her and Emily earlier. Like with Matthew, there was emotion there that she recognized. Perhaps it was nothing more than an understanding of what it was like to be with a man who tormented you, a man who both pushed and pulled. For it was clear to Venus that things were that way between Matthew and Emily. Venus' only long-term relationship had been torturous, full of the conflicted emotions that she recognized, and disliked, in Emily. Even though four months had gone by since the painful ending of that partnership, Venus felt the draw of Gerard's personality just being on the island with him. Venus didn't like thinking of herself as submissive and fearful, as Emily appeared to be.

Kate nodded, as if reading Venus' thoughts. "Aye, well, she's *not* like you. But she reminds me of a girl I knew—well, never mind. I feel sorry for her, right enough. She's not a happy lass and that's obvious. Not like your Mary, there."

"Oh, aye," Peter responded. "But then she made a good match, even if he is a lowlander."

Venus looked at her best friend, hazy in the smoke of the room. Mary sat, small and rosy and blond, snuggled in the embrace of her husband Sammy. He was obviously taking the piss out of Matthew—the two were sparring with smiles and friendly gesturing. She could hear Mary's infectious laugh filtering through the other noise of the room. Venus looked back at Peter. His dark eyes were warm and the skin of his face brown and drawn tight against his skull, the only lines those which webbed his eyes and that led from mouth to dimple. Venus realized for the first time that Peter was handsome, despite his age. Kate's hand still rested on his arm. He was smiling at her Gran, as the old woman's gaze traveled eagerly around the room. Handsome, yes. And her Gran was still active and strong. Venus stifled a smile and rubbed her eyes. She was tired. The clock above the bar read twenty minutes to midnight.

CHAPTER THREE

Finn retreated from the body with a new wariness; it was possible the killer was still in the churchyard. But no, the body was cool and no reasonable killer—here Finn laughed without humor at his own thoughts—would remain near his own crime. He had to think, to get straight what was the best thing to do. He reached into his jacket pocket for his mobile. Of course he must inform the police, that was clear. But . . . there could be complications, ramifications, and he was keen now to end his four month stay and leave the islands. His daughter Una's face flashed in his mind, the fairy-sized freckles scattered over her nose, her fringe of carroty, fine hair, blue eyes, and soft sweet baby smell. He had to get back to her, work things out with Nuala.

"Fuck," he said as he searched his other jacket pocket and then his trouser pockets for his phone. "Where's that fucking mobile?" He scanned the cottage in his mind; after he had received the text from Matthew . . . yes, there it would be, lying on the bed—how had he forgotten it? But now surely the absence of the phone absolved him of a need to call the police. No, there would be no reason to assume the responsibility; the man was dead, beyond help in any case, and someone else would find him. Venus—och, well, that would be terrible for her. He felt his stomach clench again in indecision. "Fuck's sake," he said again and ran a hand through his now dripping hair. The clarity of moments before retreated into a paralyzing hesitancy. *Get the fuck out of here, man. You're leaving your fucking DNA all over the place.*

The realization that one hair, miniscule fibers of skin, wool from his jumper, anything at all could place him here, incriminate him, even, in the crime itself, propelled him out of the churchyard.

"I need a drink. I just need to clear my head," he whispered. He decided to make for the pub, equidistant as he was now from New Farm and the High street of Blackstone village. A mile walk down to get straight what he would do. And if Venus was there, well . . . he'd make up his mind when he arrived, had that drink.

The rain stopped as the usual tearing wind blew the squall further west. The moon, waxing full and pale appeared as the clouds split apart. Una returned to his thoughts, and a phone conversation he'd had with his mother earlier in the evening. A frustrating exchange, as usual; his ma was a great wringer of hands and crier of doom but not given to practical action. But, the call had served to finally catalyze him into action: it was time to go home, to deal with Nuala's betrayal, and to be Una's da.

He had answered the call on the first ring. "How is Una?" he pressed, "Have you seen her?"

"I've not been able to. Nuala won't return my calls and I don't feel right just going round. I told you before."

"Chrissakes, Ma, you're her granny. You have every right. Just because she's slapped a restraint order against me doesn't make any difference to *you*. If you would just–"

"Why don't you come home yourself, then, and sort it out? Think how I feel with your problems to mind as well as my own."

"Och, Ma, this isn't about you. It's about Nuala being as difficult as she can be when she's the one to fault. It wasn't me caught out shagging some Protestant bastard, a cop in the bargain, for fuck's sake."

"Then come home now. There's many that will support you as a good da. Nobody blames you. We all know what she's like. I told you not to marry her, didn't I?"

"Look, I don't think Una's safe with Nuala. She's drinking a lot, Ma. I thought I'd made that clear last time we talked. I'd a thought Una's safety–"

"Don't you start–"

"No, I won't. And don't you trouble yourself. I'll come home this week, soon as I can get myself sorted and get a ticket for the ferry." Finn had snapped the phone closed and breathed deep. His gut throbbed with pain and a slow ache had settled over his heart. He thought of Nuala, the sweep of her dark hair against her cheek, the sweet whisky tones of her breath, the weight of her breast in his hand.

Finn shivered as sweat cooled on his body and the wind beat his sodden hair against his cheek. His decision to leave Belfast and take a leave of absence from his life had seemed such a good idea at the fag-end of the winter in March, when the skies were grey, his heart greyer, and the hopelessness of divisive politics still plagued his beloved Northern Ireland as if it were 1973 instead of 2003. Now here he was, in the rain and ceaseless fucking wind of Orkney, running away from a dead body, for fuck's sake, more of the dark side of life that he couldn't seem to get away from.

Christ. I've got to get out of this place.

Finn neared the bench that marked the last descent into the village. He could see the lights of the High street and hear the waves lapping onto the small beach that fronted the main street of Blackstone. He stopped, unsure again of what he was going to do about the discovery of Gerard's body. He shivered, felt bile rise in his throat. He was ready to leave the island, needed to, in fact. Involvement in a police investigation would be time consuming, probably keep him on the island at least a few days more, possibly prejudice the outcome of what he was sure would be a long and ugly custody battle with Nuala. The last thing he needed. But could he really leave the body for Venus to find in a day or so, and the gulls to find sooner? Though he didn't know if Venus knew Ventoux, still, how horrifying to find a body, violated by man and desecrated further by nature. Or Kate, even, hearty she was but still a great age—would a shock like that do her ill?

Finn resumed walking. *Get a drink first, man. Settle your nerves. No need to hurry it.* But the wind blew in a fresh squall, and as he felt the spray of rain across his face, Finn began to run.

CHAPTER FOUR

The door of the pub banged open, the sound disappearing in the noise. Finn Ross stood, catching his breath, his eyes searching the room. His face was red, and Venus saw that one hand held his stomach. She recognized he was afraid. In her mind's eye she saw her sycamore tree, and the cool rays of summer twilight reflecting on the deep green leaves. She put her hand on Kate's arm.

Finn pushed through the pub towards her.

"Well, it's Mr. Ross. In a right rush to find you, looks like." Kate laughed. "I told you he fancies you."

"Hush, Gran. He's not here for me. I think there's something the matter—"

Finn was at the table. Venus saw pallor underneath the bloom in his cheeks. He collapsed onto the bench, as Peter moved aside.

"I need a drink, man. Jesus God." He ran a hand through his hair, the black curls hanging long against his neck in their wetness. Peter turned and signaled to the barman.

"What's the matter Finn?" Kate's smile disappeared. "You look a fright."

Finn licked his lips. Venus noticed the cracked skin of his mouth; saw the slick perspiration on his forehead. He panted and leaned forward, shutting his eyes.

"Mr. Ross, now, here," Peter put an arm over Finn's shoulders. "You're not well."

"It's me gut, gives me no end of trouble. I've just been running," Finn gritted out the words. "I just need a minute now. Where's that fucking drink?"

Venus shrank into the bench, folding her arms against her chest. She saw Kate and Peter exchange a glance.

"Get up to the bar, love, and get him a whisky," Kate said, giving Venus a little push. But the barman arrived and set a glass in front of them.

Finn reached for it and took the drink in one mouthful, letting the amber liquid linger in his mouth before he swallowed it. "I've got some—news. I think . . ."

Venus couldn't read the strange expression in his eyes as he glanced at her, but her impression of his fear deepened.

"Jesus," he said, once the whisky had reached his stomach. He breathed more evenly. "Have you got a smoke?" he asked Peter. Finn took the proffered pack and drew out a cigarette. He reached for a book of matches on the table and lit it, inhaling deeply. "I don't know—" he began to cough.

Venus wanted to laugh. The world seemed in slow motion as she watched Finn struggle to get his breath. He was like a character in a nighttime drama, pulling out the suspense for the audience; what did he have to tell? What bad news could *he* bring them? But she sensed the edge of her own dark hysteria, weeks dormant, lap at her feet like an inky pool. She saw again the waving sycamore.

Finn took another breath, steadying himself. He laid the cigarette in the ashtray. "I've been off fags awhile." He looked round the crowded pub.

Venus watched Finn's eyes settle for a moment longer on Sammy than anyone else. His gaze flicked back to her and then his hands, shaking slightly, picked up the cigarette again. He inhaled, seemed to consider. They all waited for him to speak. Kate's hand was on her arm.

Finn sighed a stream of smoke, and collapsed back against the back of his seat. "Well, I've found a man, dead—killed—I'm not sure, up in your churchyard." He nodded at Venus. "I—I was looking for you, to see if you wanted to come out and thought you might be there. Well," he inhaled deeply on his cigarette again, "I found him there under the sycamore."

"I think it's a policeman you're wanting, Finn. It's not our land there—Sammy is who you need. But who is it? Do you know him? Is it someone we know?"

Finn seemed stunned by Kate's response. Venus felt a well of fear grow inside her, backed by panic.

"Well, I do know him. I interviewed him for a story when I first arrived here. It's the Director of the Festival of Isles, Gerard Ventoux."

Finn's voice continued, but Venus couldn't hear the words. She spiraled into herself, felt all sensation slip away. She focused on a lamp above the bar, the cigarette smoke swirling around the amber shade. A fly buzzed sluggishly, beating itself upon the glass shade. The etched floral pattern on the glass blurred, and her vision faded to only the soft, far away glow of light.

Venus was only dimly aware of Kate sheltering her with her arms as Peter waved Sammy over. Sammy left after talking to Finn. The noise of the pub died away, the atmosphere of trouble penetrating the room. Though no one had been told to stay, they didn't know what else to do. Music stopped, speculation started. Venus slipped down the rabbit hole of her own shock, far away from Kate's voice explaining to Finn that Gerard had been Venus' boyfriend until a few months before. Finn hadn't known; his face was grave, apologetic. Sergeant Crombie came in to fetch Finn and take him to Kirkwall to be questioned; still the villagers sat and drank in the shock.

Kate and Venus left the pub at one. Venus blinked against the contrast of cool air against her burning eyes. She held Kate's hand as they stood in the cobbled street. Mary stood with them, hugging herself with her arms. Peter smoked without speaking, watching the sea.

"Venus, I'm sorry," Mary said again, interrupting their silent observation of the sea. "I know it was over for good this time between you, but still . . . I'm sorry." She brushed Venus' arm with her hand.

"I've got to get home, to bed. How will we work in the morning?" Venus stretched a smile across her face.

"You won't be coming in! Don't think of it. I'll manage fine without you."

"No, Mary. The cafe will be busier than ever. I'll need to work. What good will it do me to sit home? You're right. Ger—we were through. It doesn't matter he's . . . dead. It's just the shock. Because I knew him so well, because we . . ." Tears stung behind her eyes. She turned to Kate. "Let's go."

"Let me give you both a lift in the car." Peter said. "There's a fair gale blowing, though looks we're past the rain for a peedie while."

"Yes," Kate answered. "Look at the moon."

It hung like a pendulum over the sea. Venus stared at the whiteness of it, willing the light to enter her. She glanced down the small beach that bordered the high street.

Matthew and Emily stood on the sand. Emily's blond hair was white in the moonlight. They stood a distance apart; Venus could hear their raised voices but not the words. She took her grandmother's hand, rubbing her fingers over the knobbled joints. She ignored the flutter in her chest.

"Gran," Venus pulled Kate close to her.

"Go and get your car, Peter. We'll wait right here." Kate reached up to put her arm around Venus' shoulders.

Peter walked away, his stride agile for a man eighty years of age. Her Gran was like that too, so young seeming at eighty-four. What had given them so much life? It seemed strange that these two should be so alive when Gerard was dead. He too had appeared to defy time and age, handsome with a Gallic charm even in his middle fifties. Venus had never noticed their age difference, never felt over twenty years his junior. And now—she tried to imagine his face and couldn't. She realized that she didn't know how he had died.

"Venus, please don't come to work tomorrow. I'd rather you wouldn't. I can get my sister in to help."

"No, Mary, I'll need to be with you. With people, with friends. Please." Venus' throat ached from singing and smoke, from holding in tears.

She looked back to the beach where Emily and Matthew still argued. Emily gestured, obviously upset. Venus let her gaze travel away down the sand. Venus shuddered.

"You're all right, my love." Kate squeezed her arm.

"I'll see you, then," Mary said, drifting up the street as Peter approached in his car. "But give a call if you change your mind. Come in whenever you like."

"Aye. I'll be there. Come on, Gran. My throat aches." Venus looked back at the beach as she and Kate climbed into the car. Matthew was gone and Emily stood, her face in her hands. She was alone on the beach, the ocean a blue hum in the darkness.

CHAPTER FIVE

Venus lifted the tray of glasses from the dishwasher and rattled them onto the counter. She grabbed the tea-stained cloth tucked into her apron and lifted the glasses out one by one, drying and placing them on the shelf. The kitchen of the Mourning Dove cafe was dim and grey with morning light. Venus looked over the counter of the pass-through into the small dining room. Mary cleaned tables with a circular swish of damp towel. Tubs of cutlery stood out on the sideboard with a tray of mismatched teacups and saucers. She heard Mary humming songs from the night before, but her friend's face was pale, and dark circles swept under her eyes. Venus' own eyes were gritty and ached with tiredness. Sleep had come only after Kate had administered an herbal sleeping tonic for her and tucked her into bed.

"Just check the scones, would you Venus?"

Venus left her towel on the glass rack and went back to the old cooker. She pulled open the oven door. A fug of soft, brown baking enveloped her. The heat steamed her face and she closed her eyes briefly against it. She pulled the sheet pan of scones from the oven.

"Ta," Mary said, returning to the kitchen. "I'm moving slow today. What a night. I still don't think you should be here."

Venus went back to wiping the glasses. Her entire body felt dull, yet there was an edge of pain under her skin, behind her eyes. "I could barely sleep after all. What would I be doing at home? I think I must—" The kitchen blurred. She reached a hand to the counter, missing it with a stagger forward.

Mary was at her side, pulling over a stool. "Here, you're not all right. I knew it! Sit down." She held Venus' face in her hands.

"I just—I keep thinking—" Tears ran over Venus' lips, staining her tongue with salt. She began to shake. Mary held her face to her chest, stroking her hair and crooning.

Venus slid into the grief, felt the pull in her shoulders and neck as the sobs shuddered through her body. Her mind was full of images: Gerard laughing, his voice matching her own in song, his earnest desire to elevate the music of the islands, to celebrate it. Her stomach pulled in, twisting and empty at the thought of their lovemaking. But she saw also his face distorted with ugly anger and cruelty as he taunted her, physically wincing at the memory of his hand thudding against her cheek. Mary drew her closer. Venus moved her head, feeling the roughness of Mary's jumper against her skin.

"Oh here, love, here. It will pass. Let it come out, just let it come." Mary reached for the tea towel to wipe Venus' face and nose.

"Mary, Mary—he was so, so—"

"I know, I know. You don't have to say anything. He was a bastard, but it's terrible he's dead just the same."

"Oh, Mary, don't speak ill, so. Not of the dead."

"Nonsense. He is—was—what he was. And he hurt you, over and over, and I'll not forgive him for it. But if he's been killed, well that's an offense against nature and God, and whoever's done it should be found and put away."

"*Was* he killed, Mary? Murdered, like? I don't remember anything Finn said after—" Venus looked up into Mary's face, searching her friend's suddenly closed gaze.

Mary hesitated. As the wife of the one Detective Inspector on the islands, she often was privy to information that she shouldn't share. Venus knew this, never took an interest anyway in the crimes of the islands. But this was different. Gerard had been her lover for over two years, the only serious relationship she'd ever had. And he was dead now, found in her own sacred spot. She closed her eyes again, fresh tears rolling over her cheeks. How would she ever repair the damage to the energy of her special place, now that violence had been done there?

"Tell me Mary. I need to know."

Mary sighed. "I don't know much. Sammy rang about half-two to say he wouldn't be back before heading down to Kirkwall. They'd just sealed the scene—"

"Sealed? Do you mean I can't go there? But—"

"Well, yes, love, it's a crime scene. No one will be allowed, likely, for a few days at least."

"So he *was* killed?" Venus swallowed, her throat dry.

"Aye, so it appears to be. He was—there was—a head wound." Mary's eyes slid away.

"What do you mean?"

"Venus, don't bother me for details. You don't need to know and I shouldn't tell anyway. It will be out soon enough. You'd best concentrate on your own feelings and dealing with the shock of it all."

Venus wiped her eyes. There would be more tears, she knew. This was the beginning of the release. She hadn't loved him anymore. Their relationship had been one of dependency, almost of addiction. Gerard had swept her up, sharing her love of music and nature; it had seemed too good to be true. Her Gran had been wary of the age difference, of his smooth good looks, his foreignness. But Venus had found his French-accented English

25

charming. As to the age difference, it hadn't mattered. He had drawn out her elusive sexual nature with energy and skill. He was tireless, driven, so very alive. She had thrived, bloomed in this new love.

But time had revealed a dark streak in him, first in a wit that was black and sharp, then in constant criticism of everything she did. Her naiveté, which had at first charmed him, became fodder for his sarcasm and judgment. But there was the passion. After every row, every stinging slap of words, there was always the passion. Until hurting her with words hadn't been enough.

But that was over. Rough though the last months had been without him, she knew she was better off with Gerard out of her life. But who would want him dead? Her head spun with the thought of how much hate it would take to kill another human being.

Venus stood and rubbed her eyes. She took a deep breath. "Mary, you're right. I think I should go home. But I don't want to leave you."

"Let me ring my sister. I talked to her already this morning. She'll be expecting to hear from me."

CHAPTER SIX

At nine o'clock Finn pushed open the door of the Mourning Dove cafe. The small ring of the bell over the door was lost in the morning chatter well underway. He recognized most of the faces from the pub the evening before, familiar to him anyway after four months on Orkney's Mainland island. He rubbed his face and eyes, feeling the pulse of a headache over his right temple. The cafe windows were streaked with steam. He wandered to his favorite table, empty but with the debris of another's meal still pushed aside. Outside the sun blazed through a fierce wind. The walk had refreshed him and his face burned with the cold and sunlight. The cafe was humid. He took off his jumper and wool hat.

Finn looked around the room. The yellow and white paint never failed to cheer him, and he liked the old photos and children's paintings that hung on the walls. He knew Mary had started the cafe ten years before with no money to spare from start-up costs, which included renovating the derelict building. The furnishings and decor had come from jumble sales and local residents. The shabby charm reminded him of his aunts' houses in Belfast and Eniskillen; those houses that had been a kind, light refuge from the squalor of his own home, stale with the smell of drink and sadness. He rubbed his eyes again, and squinted at the chalkboard that showed the day's specials.

"Some Recovery breakfast, then, Mr. Ross?" Mary stacked the dirty plates on his table and washed crumbs away with a damp rag.

"Aye. How is Venus this morning? Have you seen her?"

"She'll be fine." Her voice was distant. "She was in this morning, but I've sent her home." Mary picked up the plates.

"I still feel so awful. I had no idea—"

"It's all right. You weren't to know."

Their eyes met, and Finn thought he read a warning there.

"Did you have to stay in Kirkwall long?"

"Aye. First your Crombie gave me a right going over and then I had to wait for a lift back to my house." He paused. Mary's unsmiling gaze was fixed on him. "I didn't know him well, Gerard. It was only that I had interviewed him when I first came away here, for a series of articles. I've not seen him since that time. Been three months or more now."

"I'm not the one you need to convince of that, Mr. Ross." Mary allowed him a smile. "And for your breakfast, then?"

"The Recovery, sure. And a pot of tea—Barry's." He watched her disappear into the kitchen. Finn closed his eyes and leaned back in the chair. It had been a long night. He had been at the Kirkwall police station for two hours or more, giving his statement to the red-eyed and suspicious Sergeant Crombie. Waiting for a lift back, he had dozed in the brittle plastic seats in the waiting lounge, interrupted by the noise of the scene of crime officers coming in, followed by DI Sammy Douglas. Black coffee from a machine and another round of questions, then Crombie had sped him home.

Once back at the cottage he had flopped on the damp sheets of his bed, the sun already burning in a partly clear sky, the wind howling around the corners of the house. But sleep wouldn't come. Finally he had walked the mile into Blackstone to eat.

Exhausted, scoured dry and fuzzy by too much smoking and drink, he couldn't keep his thoughts from Una, from her future and his own. He had moved from his house six months ago, and been gone from Belfast for over four months, tucked away on this northern Scottish isle. After the first few weeks of drinking at the pub and walking in the wind and rain he had retreated into himself, full of a tangle of longing and hatred for his wife and fear for Una. Nuala had sent divorce papers; he remembered the stormy day he had thrown them into the Eynhallow Sound. The pages had blown in the spirals of the wind, flying so long he had thought they would never descend into the sea.

After the denial came the need for resolution, and he had tried to call Nuala, her ma, old friends they had shared, anyone who might hear his side. But he'd been met with walls of silence. Those who had claimed to love him, laugh at his jokes, sing with him in the pub, took their sides. Panic had come again, and anxiety for Una's safety. Letters had arrived at last, from his sisters, from one or two colleagues at the paper. They had seen Nuala, talked with her; Una seemed fine, everyone sane. No one said they had seen Nuala with a ginger haired man, no one said that Una asked after her da.

Finn leaned his head in his arms on the table, the noise of the cafe making a soft tunnel around him. He saw Nuala on the day he'd left her, smoking in the kitchen, her dark eyes and raspberry mouth.

Finn sat up again. "Jesus, man," he whispered, and reached into his back pocket for his flask. He turned his face to the wall to drink. He let the whisky sit in his mouth. He stared into the pious face of a woman in black holding a little child. Whose relative? He let the liquid slide down his throat. When he turned away from the wall of photographs, a woman he didn't know was standing with a plate and teapot on a tray.

She barely spared him a glance and set the large oval plate down before him. The whisky burned in his throat and he felt acid rise in his stomach.

He reached for the toast on the plate as she sat it down. Without looking at him she arranged his teapot and cup, clattered down some silver.

"Ta," he said as she left the table. *Home cooking, served with love.* He laughed and cut into his egg, watching the yolk surround the tomato in a sea of yellow.

CHAPTER SEVEN

Venus walked from the cafe to the narrow high street and crossed to the beach. Small waves beat the shore and the wind whisked the water to white caps in the tiny bay. Low tide exposed the beach, piles of seaweed, and bits of rubbish. A milk jug glowed against its nest of tangled kelp. Venus strode to where it lay and picked it up. Swinging the jug against her leg, she turned for home.

She continued along the beach, inhaling the pungent smell of seaweed. Between the sliver of sand and the high street was a jagged border of rock, crisscrossed with cuts and patterns that seemed almost human made instead of the work of the sea. The rock gave way to the shell-strewn beach. Venus still loved to comb the sand for minute snail and limpet shells in all colors, most containing the subtle spiral found everywhere in nature. She had found a few of the *gruellie belkies* that the tourists loved to search for—a small, pale pink cowrie—though most of those were found on the beaches closer to Skara Brae. But now her thoughts were elsewhere, drifting on the fuzzy edge of exhaustion.

She reached the end of the beach and climbed, careful of slippery seaweed, over the rock to the path that led over the headland and away from Blackstone. The wind blew a song through the chimes that hung in the gallery at the end of the high street. Venus turned back for a look at the village. She had never lived elsewhere on Orkney, never wanted the so-called city life available in Kirkwall—itself only a village of a few thousand. She had sung with a madrigal choir in Stromness, and with a guitar and violin trio that played traditional music. She had met Gerard through music, and with him her music had gradually died inside of her. He had encouraged her, then dashed her talents, pulling her back and forth on a precipice of self-doubt. Last night in the pub had been the first she'd sung in months. And last night he'd died.

She shuddered as her eyes scanned the quiet village. Blackstone was a marvelous place to live. Open to the sea, its beach and streets welcoming the currents of weather that streamed up and around the tall, old buildings and narrow streets. A market, post office, cafe, and pub; one gallery run by a cooperative of artists, a garage . . . what else could one need? There was rarely any crime here; death was most often natural and explainable. As DI for the whole of Orkney, Sammy hardly had any case more challenging than drunken driving and the occasional tragedy that accompanied it or an accidental death on one of the outer islands. Who would want Gerard dead?

Venus continued her climb up the hill. The grass was waist high and full of wildflowers—pink ragged robin, the purple crane's bill that grew with such profusion in her and Kate's garden, a field of yellow iris. The sea was a remembering blue. The air blew over her. She wore the scent and movement like a gown, feeling the sensation of coolness like a fall of icy satin against her skin. Her steps took her over the familiar path, past the secluded bench that overlooked the beach and up to the crumbling churchyard, perched on the cliff. She stopped. This was her special place. She had come to the churchyard since she was a child, to play quietly among the gravestones, waving stalks of flowers, and nettle. One sycamore grew in the corner, and underneath she had a seat and collection of shells and artifacts, gathered since she had chosen the churchyard for her sanctuary.

Now the grass was marred by tire marks, and yellow crime scene tape snapped in the wind. She could see the sycamore over the top of the stone wall. There it was, where Gerard had been found. Finn's face flickered in her mind, replaced by Gerard's. The milk jug fell from her hand. Venus sank to her knees, groaning as dry spasms racked her body. A pair of lapwings shrieked overhead. She heard the motor of a fishing boat carried on the wind. She raised her head as the heaving passed, and saw her retriever's golden head peer around the corner of the stone wall.

"Teke!" she called weakly, relieved. He ran to her, lapping at her face as she buried her head in his soft neck. He smelled of grass and the sea. She held onto him tightly as clouds raced through the sky and birds cried their dismay over the churchyard.

"Come on, then, let's get home," Venus said, and Teke bounded up the path ahead, after a cursory sniff of the milk jug.

"Venus! Venus!"

She stopped and turned to the voice behind her. Sammy ducked under the crime scene tape and walked toward her. He still wore his jumper and jeans from the night before and his face was creased with tiredness.

"Are you still here, Sammy? Have you not been home at all?" She bent to pick up the milk jug.

"I wanted to come back by myself, without all the men here. Think a little."

They stood facing each other in the wind. Venus held her blowing hair from her eyes. Her mouth tasted stale and bitter. Sammy's eyes searched her face.

"Are you going home? Let me walk with you; I've left the car at the top of the track. Fine for the ambulance and the SOCO's van to ruin their suspension, but not our new car. Mary would have my head." He tried a smile.

"All right." Sammy seemed like a stranger now, despite his attempt at friendliness. She shrank inwardly, looking at the ground as she walked.

"Venus . . . I've not got much practice in this. I know you aren't—weren't . . . Ahh, Jesus. I'm sorry Gerard is dead. I hope it's not a burden on you." He had stopped walking and ran a hand over his pelt of dark hair. He was unshaven and his brown eyes were full of concern.

"I saw you were sick just there," he continued. "I didn't know if I should help, or—" he looked at her helplessly, once again the familiar, sentimental man she knew. Loving father, loving husband, a man who cried over the death of pet rabbits and at school programs.

"Don't worry yourself, Sammy. I don't know how I feel. It's all just shock, I think. I don't know." Teke loped back down the path, looking at her with question in his eyes. Venus read compassion in the dog's gaze; he seemed to sense her distress and sat close, leaning his head against her leg. She steeled herself for her next question, and looked out toward the wind whipped sea. "Was he killed, Sammy? I mean, did someone *intend* to kill him? On purpose, like?"

Sammy followed her gaze to the ocean. "Yes. Yes they did. Someone murdered Gerard last night, very much on purpose."

Venus literally felt the blood drain from her face. Her mouth was dry and her tongue thick. "Why?"

"Aye, that is the question. Why indeed? I don't know much about the man. And I don't know much about murder—this is my first homicide investigation, as I'm sure you know. We just have to begin at the beginning. When did he die and why, and when we know that, then we can answer the question who." Sammy began to walk again.

Venus followed by his side. Her gaze swept over the farms scattered across the land, the islands of Wyre and Rousay sitting low in the water. The tiny isle of Eynhallow alternated golden and gray in the shifting sun. She could see the tide pulling out of Eynhallow sound, waves breaking beyond the bay as the currents of the sound grappled with the North Atlantic. The Sea Mither, benign spirit of summer, reigned in the ocean now. The Mither brought calmer seas and milder weather, after her March struggle with the winter spirit's gales. Teran was bound at the bottom of the sea, and though he might shudder and roil in his watery bindings, he could not free himself until the autumn equinox. Teran would bring the rage of winter and banish the Sea Mither until she would return in the spring, strength renewed for another battle. The calm weather was indeed upon them, however much the wind and frequent rain belied that fact.

Venus inhaled deeply, then exhaled in a shuddering sigh. Orkney was so small, so special, so safe. Of course people died—drowned, crashed their cars, committed suicide. The wrath of weather was always present, the sea always a danger. But murder was rare. Again she wondered who could have hated Gerard enough to kill him. Even in their worst moments, in her bleakest pain of withdrawal from him, she had never hated him, never wished him dead.

"Venus, there are questions I'll need to ask you. You knew Gerard better than most." Sammy cleared his throat. "And I'll need to know where you were yesterday afternoon and evening, before the pub, of course."

"Where *I* was? But why? What—?" she looked at him blankly, stopping again. Teke stopped too, with a barely audible whine. The wind rushed through the grass of the pastures that bordered the rough track, made more uneven by the recent traverse of police vehicles.

"It's routine. I'll be asking everyone who knew him. You would be surprised what little thing you saw or heard can mean. Or perhaps you talked on the phone with him. Or—"

"I haven't spoken with him in over two months. I've seen him only once since we broke up." Her mind flickered over the memory. It was unpleasant, an embarrassing argument. Actions of someone she didn't want to be anymore. She looked away from Sammy's narrow gaze. "I don't have anything to tell you. I was at the cafe most of the day yesterday. Mary will confirm that."

"But after work? Did you come up here, to the churchyard? Did you see anyone? Notice anything strange?" He resumed walking. "If you'd like to talk with me tomorrow, that's fine. If you don't feel up to it now."

Venus was silent. She thought back to yesterday. She *had* come to the church, taking her usual route home. She had in fact brought a new intriguing rock to add to her collection around the sycamore. But there had been nothing. "What do you mean, strange? What would be strange?" Venus felt as if her thoughts were swimming through a thick mud.

"Anything that didn't belong, a vehicle, a bike, big objects."

"Big objects?" Venus held back a hysterical laugh. "Like what?"

"Cricket bat, golf club—"

Venus remembered Mary's remark, her slippery glance. A head wound. "Did they—was his head . . ." Her stomach twisted.

"Severe trauma to the head. His face was smashed on one side." He paused. "Whoever did this had a lot of anger in them." Sammy squinted at her.

"Or fear," Venus whispered, a sudden vision penetrating her mind. Three women, one bruised, one young, and one . . . The vision spun away into blackness as Venus felt herself fall into the tall weeds that lined the track.

CHAPTER EIGHT

Kate dusted dirt from her hands and put her palm to the earth. Her hair blew about her lined face, the thick grey strands tickling her lips and eyes. Pushing down she lifted one knee with a grunt, and eased herself to standing. Pain quivered in her right hip and left knee, but she ignored it. She looked down with satisfaction to the herb cuttings in her basket and clicked her tongue against the empty hole where a molar had been extracted, long ago. At eighty-four she was the only one of her few remaining friends with her own teeth.

She wandered to the bottom of the garden. Violet-blue crane's bill bloomed along the length of the low stone wall, encircled her miniscule greenhouse and ran up the far wall to the gate near the back of the house. Kate smiled as she looked out over the wall to the grassy slope leading down to the sea. Clouds gathered and closed in on the isle of Rousay, across the sound; soon the island would be under streaming rain, and not long after she would hear the drops on her own roof. She squinted at Eynhallow, nestled shimmering in the sound between Rousay and Mainland. Kate raised a gnarled hand and waved. The Fin-folk were in their summerland. She had never seen the fabled white summer homes of the sea people, but had always wanted to.

"Those that do are never grateful," she murmured. "Silly, silly girl." A solemn child with thick brown hair flashed in her mind, silvery-quick like a fish. Her daughter, Cora, could see the magic worlds with stunning ease. And yet she had turned her back on her legacy, her gifts. Well, at least her granddaughter, Venus, had the sense to embrace the tradition and comfort of family, place, the old teachings. Kate smiled at the thought of Venus. She hadn't the natural gifts of her mother, Cora, but had her own unique sympathy with plants and animals. Venus was a good girl, not prone to the romantic whims that had grown unseen inside her solemn mother. At least not until Gerard Ventoux had exploded her and Venus' tranquil world. Kate had been happy for Venus, of course, finally in love, but from the beginning Kate had known that Gerard was trouble. Too slick by half, and too old as well. Venus had been drawn in; it was the music that had done it. Kate thought about the last few months of Venus' recovery from the treatment Gerard had given her. She felt a surge of anger and adrenaline, like a mother lion protecting her young. But now—now he was dead.

"Well, water's gone under the bridge for that one," she said, murmuring to the flowers at her feet. "And just as well." She turned and walked back up the garden to the house.

The kitchen was pleasant and cluttered. The door opened onto the garden. Kate put the basket on the worktable and bent to check the fire that burned in the old Rayburn stove. The aged stove heated the kitchen summer and winter. She had thought herself immune to the cold and wind of Orkney, but her old bones betrayed her, and she wore a lumpy bundle of jumpers over the cut-off man's trousers she preferred.

Kate poured boiling water into her teapot from the kettle and then refilled it, placing it back on the stove. The teapot was an old, chipped Limoges fancy, a gift from her dearest friend Anne, now dead and gone almost sixty years. She had died in France, too far away from home. Kate shook her head, impatient with her mind's turn to memory. She pulled two bags of Yorkshire Gold from a packet and, smelling them briefly, dropped them into the pot. She got two cups from the dresser and put them on the table with the sugar pot and a jug of fresh cream. The young English girl, Emily, was coming to tea. She had called that morning, rather early for manners, her voice pitched high and artificial.

"I know it might not be the best time," Emily had said, "but I need to talk with you."

"What about?" Kate answered curtly. "Venus has gone to work," she added.

"I need to continue my research. Things have become more urgent, with time and—and money." Emily's voice cracked. She cleared her throat.

"Well, I've no plan for the morning," Kate said, sensing the lies in Emily's voice. But what else could the girl want from her? "I think it's best if you come when Venus will be away. She's not up to social calls." Ridiculous. Venus had gone to work, after all. But Kate knew that Venus needed the solitary sanctuary of home to be just that, a sanctuary.

"I'll be up in an hour or two," Emily had said. "Thank you." The phone had clattered down, the girl's voice suddenly cut off.

Kate arranged the teapot on the table with the cups. "Now I guess she's not a *girl*," Kate said to herself, "near Venus' age I suppose. But they're all girls when you're my age." She nodded to the yellowed photograph that leaned from the wall. "Isn't that right, Hamish, love? We've seen some better days." She tapped the picture of her husband with a finger and went to the window to wait.

Kate soon saw Emily's Vauxhall sputter up the lane and pull into the grass verge. Emily got out and fumbled at the passenger side for a bag. She dropped the bag onto the ground and the contents scattered. Kate watched her shove the items back into the carryall. Emily wore a magenta fleece jacket that Kate thought was terribly ugly, though the color was becoming to Emily's fair skin and light hair. Her head was down as she trudged up the path to the house. Kate went to the back door and called her around.

"Come on this way. Don't bother with the front door."

Emily came along the side of the house and through a low garden gate to reach the kitchen door.

"Hello." Emily tried to smile as she wiped her feet on the mat and came inside.

"I've made us tea. It's a fine day but I expect you're still not used to the weather. And tea is suited to chat." Kate pulled a chair out for Emily.

Emily sat and set her bag on the floor. She freed her hair from its tie, scraping the blond strands back and re-securing it in a tight ponytail.

"You look tired." Kate settled herself and poured a cup for Emily. "Cream? Fresh this morning. I still milk my own cow," she boasted.

"Yes, you told me before. But no, I don't take it."

Kate frowned and pulled the jug toward her, adding a dose with her sugar before pouring the strong tea into her cup. "Suit yourself," she said. She sat back and squinted at Emily. The girl's hand shook as she lifted her cup to her lips.

Emily shuffled in her bag for her notebook and pen. She arranged her things on the table. Kate thought the girl was stalling. She barely knew Emily, had only talked with her a dozen or so times since the girl had arrived a few months before, on a research trip for a graduate project. Emily was especially keen on talking to the "old ones" as she called them, and Kate had found herself a target of interest as soon as Emily had arrived and got her bearings. Emily had begun her research in Stromness, but the local historian sent her to Blackstone because of its history of witchcraft and Selchie sightings. It was mostly old ones left in Blackstone, and Kate counted herself the oldest inhabitant of the village.

She had answered Emily's questions, happy to share her knowledge of Orcadian folklore and midwife wisdom. She felt sorry for the girl, despite her usual air of professional friendliness. Kate had seen enough life to know when someone had something to hide.

"What is it today, then?" Kate prompted.

Emily sighed and opened her notebook. "We left off last time with talking about the Fin-folk. How they were different from the Selchies."

"Oh, aye. There is a right difference between them. Fin-folk being more like mermaids and mermen—although the women of the deep prefer to take a human husband, because they turn terrible ugly if they marry a Fin man. They capture the lads off the fishing boats and haul them down to their kingdoms, teach them to live underwater." Kate chuckled. "But I told you that already."

"Yes, you did." Emily's voice was short and she kept her eyes trained on her notebook. She arranged the papers stuck just inside the notebook, stacking and restacking them.

"So—"

"What makes the Selchies different?"

"Well, Selchies are seal-folk. Grey seals that can become human. Usually it's the women you hear about, but the males can change too. Either way, anyone who lays eyes on them will fall in love. They come ashore not too often now, on Midsummer surely, though some say as it's every ninth night."

"They change completely, from seal to human?"

"Aye, they shed their seal skins and dance on the shore under the stars. Naked as the day they were born. Part of the attraction, I'd reckon." Kate laughed. "Now then, most often it's a woman as is caught dancing, and a man will steal her skin and hide it. That makes her fall in love with him, and often the marriage will be a happy one, with children and the like. But if she finds the skin, she'll be compelled to put it on again and return to the sea and her family there."

"Isn't there a story from around here?" Emily's voice was strained. "At Deernick or—"

"Deer*ness*," Kate replied. "It's an area over the southwest mainland. Very quiet there still, out of the way like." Kate took a sip of tea, ignoring Emily's obvious impatience. She didn't know what was bothering the girl, but something was wrong. Though Kate didn't find Emily's personality warm, she hadn't thought her rude on the other occasions they had talked. "There's a few Selchie stories I could tell you, but most not from this area here. What would you want to hear?"

"Oh, tell whichever you like." Emily's hands went up to smooth her ponytail, her glance a flicker of blue that settled on Kate's face and then back to her paper.

Kate looked at Emily a moment, her fingers tapping the table. "Well, the story takes place on Sanday. A fine island now for beaches and places where the seals haul out, especially the lighthouse there off Start Point or near Hacks Ness on the southwest side. There is an old settlement right there, worth seeing if you like the old things.

"So, a man who lived near there, name of Magnus—that's a common old name, after the saint, you know. He was gathering limpets out on the tip of the land. Quite a rocky shore along that bit of land, and as he walked he heard a strange sound coming from among the rocks. It sounded just like a person groaning with pain, then would grow louder and sound like a bellowing cow." Kate warmed to the story. "Magnus listened—a little worried, a little afraid—he didn't know who could be making such a noise in that deserted stretch of land. But he fancied that it sounded at times just like a woman giving birth; him with several fine young ones of his own, he knew the cries. But still, on his own, like, he didn't know what to do." Kate paused, and looked at Emily; the girl's face had paled. "Are you all right, Emily?"

"Yes, yes, please go on."

"Well, finally he was so moved by the pitiful sounds that he wanted to find and help whoever was making them. He could see nothing from where he was, but he spied a lone grey seal off the shore, quite near the rocks, looking at a small inlet not far away. Strange enough, the seal never dived or moved its position or its gaze. Though he wasn't over smart, Magnus reasoned that the noise must be coming from among those rocks, and it must be an awful scene to so distract a seal from his swimming and feeding. So, with a bit of fear in his heart, Magnus decided to walk to the inlet. When he rounded the corner to a small beach, what do you think he saw?" Kate paused again.

Emily wrote swiftly in her notebook. Her fingers were cramped around the pen, and Kate wondered as she had before why the girl didn't use a recorder.

"Should I talk slower?"

"No, please, just go on."

Kate looked out the window. Rain misted down. She poured herself another cup of tea. Emily's cup was still full. "Aye, well, he saw there a mother seal in the pain of calving, and it was her cries that he had heard. So, Magnus stood to watch the seal mother, with her mate still in the sea nearby. Magnus was not unkind, and was moved by her suffering. She finally birthed two fine calves, and Magnus—with a change of heart so typical of people—forgot all about his sympathy for her. He decided then and there that the skins of the babies would make a fine coat for himself. The peedie seals had begun to nurse right away, and Magnus jumped and grabbed them away from her dugs and began to walk away. The mother seal, as you'd imagine, was completely distraught and bellowed and beat herself with her flippers. Then she climbed further onto the beach and gazed into Magnus' face with a pleading look. The father seal was similarly affected, but stayed away in the sea."

"Oh," Emily said softly, her hand ceasing to write.

Kate nodded. "Aye, a selfish lout Magnus had turned out to be; but you must remember the seal is no friend of the fisherman here. There's many as would club them all as see them live the life Nature intended. Now, Hamish and I never would shoot the seals away from the nets, nor club them either. In our time there was the cull, and it was legal. A right slaughter. The environment people put a stop to it. We always left fish for the seals and they never bothered our nets. But my clan from North Ronaldsay do say as it's bad luck to kill a seal, because of the Selchie folk. If you do —"

"But is that the end? Was she left, were her babies taken away?"

"No, no. Finally the mother seal's pitiful wails moved Magnus to lay the babies down. The mama was full of joy. She grabbed the calves to her breast, just as a human mother would, and gave Magnus the happiest face he had ever seen. And it made his heart feel good." Kate rose to open a packet of biscuits.

"Is that the end?" Emily looked up from her writing.

"No, there's a bit more," Kate said, struggling with the waxed wrapper of ginger biscuits. "Magnus was young then, and many years later when his own children were grown, he was away fishing. He went to a good spot that was only accessible at a low tide. He crossed to the place and sat to wait; the fish wouldn't come until the tide turned and began to flood back in. The fishing was so good the man completely forgot where he was. When he turned to go, his creel filled, he saw with despair—because he couldn't swim, and there's many on the island that can't but take their life out onto the sea anyway—that the water in between him and the mainland was already deeper than he was tall. He cried out, but was too far for anyone to hear; though he yelled and called only the water came, covering his knees, then hips and shoulders. He was in a right state." Kate chuckled. She noticed Emily's notes, an incomprehensible collection of symbols and abbreviations. A personal shorthand, perhaps.

"Oh, aye. A right state," Kate continued. "The ripples were flowing into his mouth and Magnus had resigned himself to his death when something grabbed ahold of his collar and drug him through the water to a place where he could stand. He waded to dry land, and turned to see an old grey seal swimming toward him with his creel of fish. Magnus waded out again to get the creel, and as he took it from the seal, their eyes met, and he recognized that same mama seal that he had seen calving all those years before. If she could have spoken—well, her look said that one good turn deserved another. Magnus felt a wave of gratitude. The seal hadn't forgotten his kindness, and we should all remember to do the same. Never forget a kindness rendered, never forget to give to another creature in need."

Kate had spoken the last of her story to the blankness of the panes of the kitchen window. She looked back to Emily, scribbling in her notebook, a frown creasing her wide, smooth forehead. Kate shivered and pulled her cardigan closer to her.

Emily finished writing. "So was she a Selchie, the seal?"

"Well, some say as she was, and that's why she was so human like. But my mother, who told me the story, didn't say for sure."

"Does it have a name? Do you know what time period the story comes from?"

"*The Seal that Didn't Forget*, would be the most common. I think it must be, oh, two hundred years old or so. Hard to tell when the old stories originate." Kate wiped her mouth with a faded napkin. "That's one of Venus' favorite stories. She thinks that it shows the brutality of humans and the simple fairness of animals. The grey seals have long been a controversy here, as I told you. You're too young to remember when the Greenpeace ship was here, I reckon, to protest the seal culling. Now they're protected, but there is still a number killed every year. It's a waste. If the waters weren't overfished the seals wouldn't take from the fish farms. But then that's folks now. Always taking what they want and not giving in return." Kate looked at the picture of Hamish on the wall and felt a longing tug at her. "I've tried all my life to live in harmony with Nature. Before it was popular with young folks, when we lived rougher, times were harder. There's a law to things, my girl, and we oughtn't break it. A person's got to call the ones that do, call them to account."

"But how? How? Oh, it's too late." Emily looked up, pale blue eyes deep with tears, her clipped accent muddy with emotion. She shut her notebook and covered her eyes with a hand, biting her lip.

"Now, then, what's the matter?" Kate sat up and took Emily's other hand.

Emily's tears fell onto the table. "I—I'm just . . . tired. Last night. So sh-shocking." Her teeth chattered unnaturally in the heat of the kitchen.

"Have some more tea, there." Kate rose and went to Emily's side. She held the girl's hand as she brought the cup to her lips. Kate's heart beat a warning. "Aye, that's better, now. We've all had a right shock. Murder is a rare thing in a place like this."

Emily's shoulders shook.

"Did you know Gerard, Emily? Is it a loss for you?" Kate returned to her chair.

Emily dropped the tea cup with a clatter into the saucer. Her face was pale. "I? No, no. I didn't. Well, I'd met him before. But a long time ago. I didn't know he was here." The words tumbled in a rush as tears streamed from her eyes.

Kate put a hand to the back of her neck, feeling tension. She consciously relaxed her jaw. "Then of course you'll feel his death a blow." But she wondered. There must be something else; the death of a mere acquaintance would hardly elicit this reaction.

"I'm pregnant," Emily replied, as if reading Kate's thoughts.
Kate was surprised at the relief she felt. She realized that she had been expecting some worse confession. "Well, that's not too bad, is it? How far gone are you? Do you know?"

"I've done a home test. I'm three weeks late, so it can't be more than seven weeks. But it is bad, you don't understand." The tears flowed freely down her face. She wiped her nose on her sleeve.

"There's still plenty of time to make a choice. Now, do you know who the father is? Is it that young man of yours? Have you told him?"

Emily's face pinched into an odd expression. "Matthew. Yes, it's his. But I can't tell him. I can't."

"All right," Kate soothed, "that's your affair. You—"

"No, you don't understand, I'm frightened of him. I—I . . ." Emily's voice became a whisper. "We've been having trouble. He—he's not kind. Well, he's always been temperamental, and likes to drink. We've always had rows. But lately, it's been worse. He doesn't understand me, doesn't value my research, which is strange because he so loves the music and folklore of Ireland, but for some reason—" Emily stopped speaking and began to pick the already ragged cuticles of her left hand.

Kate sat up very straight. She felt her hackles rise. Her heart quickened in sadness. Such a familiar story; the excuses, the whispered fears, and then would come the bruises, the broken fingers, the shattered laughter.

"You'd better tell me, girl. Give me the whole story and it won't go a word beyond me. I want to help."

CHAPTER NINE

Venus and Sammy parted at the top of the track.

"I'll call round the café tomorrow to speak to you, Venus. That will be more pleasant for you than coming into Kirkwall."

"All right," she said, and squeezed his arm before he got into his car. She watched him reverse and turn to drive carefully up the track, past the cottage and barn and into the lane. She continued up herself, seeing an unfamiliar car in the drive. She went around the house to the north gate of the garden, intending to go in the back door to the kitchen. When she approached the half-open door, she heard voices inside. She halted, listening. Teke padded away into the garden. Venus eased forward to see who her Gran was talking to. She pulled her head back when she saw Emily's blond ponytail and pink fleece. Emily's voice, ragged with tears, stopped Venus from going inside.

What could Emily be doing crying in the kitchen with Gran? Obviously Emily had wormed her way into Kate's affections, since she was welcomed to cozy meetings in the kitchen. Resentment surged through her. What did Emily have to be upset about? How could Emily burden Gran with sorrows when *she* needed comfort? It was typical of the self-centeredness that Emily had shown since her arrival. Always probing, asking questions, displaying no sensitivity.

Venus retraced her steps around to the front of the house. She tugged open the little-used front door and stepped into the musty living room. She glanced at the wooden door that separated the room from the kitchen. It was slightly ajar.

Venus went on tiptoe to the door. Something in Emily's tone made her stop and listen. Venus pulled open the door a crack farther and held her breath.

"I don't know what to do. Our things are tied up together—the flat in London, car, credit cards . . ." Emily's voice ended in a sob.

"There's always something that can be done," Kate's voice soothed. "First you take care of yourself. A car and credit cards, even a house isn't worth what you think, not when it's your own safety and life at stake. But first you've got to decide about the baby, and fix what you want to do."

Venus sucked in a breath. Of course! That would explain the fight she'd observed between her and Matthew the night before. Venus' resentment for the girl ebbed, replaced by a mixture of disappointment and pity.

"But I can't have it! How would I manage? Matthew—" Emily cried.

"Women have gotten along since the beginning of time, and in far worse circumstances. Also far better but that doesn't matter. If you want it, there's a way to manage, and if you don't, there's a way to manage that too. You go on home and decide. Let me know and I'll help you either way."

Venus heard Emily's sobs resume, and Kate made the soft clucking noises that she used to call her hens to dinner. Venus stepped back from the door, wincing at the creak in the boards, and pulled the door silently closed. She went down the hall to her bedroom.

Venus took off her jumper and hung it on a hook inside the wardrobe that dominated the room. She flopped on her bed, the ancient single that had been her mother's. Why were women so stupid about getting pregnant? She couldn't understand it. She herself had been the product of a reckless union, and had been left by her mother and never known her father. She didn't feel the loss too much; her Gran had been a loving, careful mum. But she always had to bear the sly whisperings about her wayward mother and the charming Irishman that had danced through her life, impregnated her, and then vanished into the night. Before Venus and Mary had become best friends they were rancorous enemies, and Mary had teased that her mother made love to a Selchie, and that he had left her for the sea. Mary said that everyone really knew what had happened to Cora; she had sailed away in a boat to founder in the Eynhallow sound, calling for her seal lover to come back to her.

Venus could smile now at the thought of the bitter school-yard taunting. And now it was she who told fairy stories and folk tales to Mary's children. But the story could be true for all Venus knew. Her mother had left when she was only five, and Kate had refused to speak Cora's name again. She was gone for good, Gran always said, no help to her.

Venus began to slip into a hazy sleep. She remembered her thin and solemn mother. Cora's hair was dark brown and thick like Hamish's. Though Venus had never known her grandfather—he had died before her birth— Kate always said that Cora looked more like Hamish, but lacked his quick smile. Venus remembered many rows between her mother and grandmother. And the final night, Cora storming into the kitchen on the full moon as Gran sat with her, teaching her to scry with silver in a bowl of sea water. Her mother knocked the bowl away, spilling the water on the floor and breaking the pretty dish.

"I've told you not to teach her that rubbish. She's my child and I don't want her growing up simple and following your crazy ways!" Cora shouted.

"As soon as you act like she's your child, I'll give over raising her to you. But you've taken no notice of her since the day she was born. All you can do is mourn for that bastard. The only good thing he ever did was to bring us our Aoifa. You know he's never coming back, and who would blame him? There's no love in your heart!" Gran's voice was shrill.

Cora stood shaking in the kitchen and turned to stomp down the hall. While Gran soothed Venus in her lap, Cora had been packing the small leather suitcase with all she owned. They both heard the front door slam but never thought that it was Cora leaving, walking away for good.

Venus turned over, pulling the coverlet up under her arms. Soon after her mother left, the white streaks had started growing in Venus' otherwise black hair. She had looked up to the evening sky night after night, waiting for the first bright star to appear, so that she could wish her mother home. But in time she had forgotten to wish, and merely looked forward to the light of that star. It fascinated her, lonely but intrepid, the first adventurer in the sea of the night sky.

"It's not a star, but a planet, Aoifa," Gran had said. "That's the planet Venus, the planet of love."

When she turned six, and knew her mother was not coming back, Aoifa took for herself a new name, and in a solemn ceremony before her tearful Gran, claimed herself to be no longer Aoifa Cora McNeill, but Venus Kathleen, and gave to Kate her dedication as her daughter.

CHAPTER TEN

Finn turned his head in the wind, sticking up a hopeful thumb as he heard the sound of a car approach on the road. A lift would be nice for this, his second trip into the village today. It had been a long day, and a strange one. Hard to believe that less than twenty-four hours had passed since finding Gerard's body.

The truck sped by, two young men laughing in the front seat. One reached a hand out to fling a beer can in his direction. Finn returned the rudeness with a gesture and sighed. After his breakfast he had left Blackstone to walk over the tracks and lanes of Rendall parish, looking for comfort from the loneliness that had descended upon him. He had tried to reach his ma after returning to the cottage in the early afternoon, but no answer. And now, DI Douglas had asked him so politely not to leave. Not under suspicion, mind, but his cooperation was still needed in the early days of the investigation. So he would stay. He wasn't optimistic about the ability of the Kirkwall police to solve a murder case, but surely they wouldn't suspect him for long, if suspect him they did. And what else could he tell them but what he had found?

It was too bad that he had cocked up any chance he had now with Venus. He cringed at the memory of her face when he had told them about

Gerard. How had she gotten tangled up with the man? He had to be twenty years older than she at least. Gerard was good-looking, granted, Finn could see that. But from his interviews with him some months earlier, Finn had formed a cynical opinion about the Director of the Festival of Isles. Venus didn't seem the type to fall for a womanizing Frenchman. But they'd had a two-year relationship, a serious one at that from what Kate had said. Was she still in love with him? Finn was surprised to feel jealousy.

Fifteen minutes later he reached the village. The High street was deserted at tea-time. He made his way along the street to the pub. The wind blew as usual, and the loneliness that had dogged him that morning returned. They were all in at their tea, with friends and family, and he was alone. Finn hesitated outside the door to the pub. The mile walk had made him hungry and his thirst for a drink had only increased. But he waited, drew a hand up to his brow. He closed his eyes for a moment, before reaching for the worn brass door pull.

The interior was quiet, dim, and instantly a comfort. He crossed the scarred floor, past a table with two old men playing cribbage, over to the L-shaped bar. The barman leaned against the back counter, running his hand rhythmically through thinning brown hair. Finn saw Matthew sitting alone at the far side of the bar, near the wall, flipping through a newspaper. A cigarette smoldered in the ashtray in front of him. Finn took the captain's chair next to Matthew. It wasn't the first time the two had killed an afternoon drinking, sharing the *craic*.

"Hiya?" said the barman, and Finn smiled at the ubiquitous greeting of the Orcadians.

"Not bad. Yourself?"

"No' bad, no. Quiet day, like. What's your fancy?"

"Whisky, I think. Newcastle chaser." Finn turned to look at Matthew. "Can I get you another?"

"Ta." Matthew looked up at the barman. "Bushmill's again, double."

"And your choice, Mr. Ross? Will you give our single malt a chance, now?"

"No, no. Bushmill's for me too. I've the need for solidarity."

Finn sat quiet until his drinks were in front of him. The barman took Matthew's empty glass away and poured a stiff double into a clean tumbler.

"To the old country," Matthew lifted his glass with a wry smile. He folded the front page of the paper over to reveal the Belfast *Telegraph* masthead.

"Aye, to the green, green hills of home." Finn smiled in return. They drank, Finn finishing the whisky in one swallow. "Could you spare a fag, man?" He took the cigarette Matthew offered, and the lighter. "Do you always read the northern papers?" he mumbled, lighting the cigarette.

Matthew looked down at the newspaper. "No, but it was here. Don't usually find any Irish papers lying about. I don't read papers much, actually."

"Good for you." Finn took a deep, grateful drag on the cigarette. He looked cursorily at the front page, took a drink from his beer. The nuttiness washed away the burning of the smoke.

Matthew leaned back in his chair. He raised his glass again and finished the whisky. He set it down with a slight tremor. "Used to write for them, didn't you say?"

Finn looked sideways at Matthew through the haze of their smoke. The man was full, or well on the way. He reached for his pint and let the coolness of the ale pour over his throat. Getting drunk seemed like a good idea.

"Aye," he said. "Technically I still do. I'm on . . . sabbatical," he said finally. That word sounded better than leave of absence after leaving his senses. He laughed to himself.

Matthew looked at him with narrowed eyes. "Life's little problems getting the better of you, were they?" He inhaled and then blew perfect rings into the air. "This is a good place to get away, if a little boring." He smiled.

"I'll tell you the truth; I came up here to keep an eye on Emily. She's a little neurotic herself." Matthew nodded in Finn's direction.

"Och, aye, I'm well past neurotic, man. Well past. Or was, I should say. Had a right fucking meltdown when I got here." Finn tried to return Matthew's smile, but he felt a stab of annoyance. "Emily seems to be able to take care of herself. What—"

"She's a daft cow," Matthew stated, waving his hand to signal the barman who stood chatting with the two cribbage players at the table. "So what happened in Belfast? Politics finally get to you? Women?" Matthew showed his teeth again, even and square but yellow. He shoved the ashtray closer to Finn.

Finn nodded, warmed by the beer and whisky filling his belly. "Please," he said, to the barman's inquiring look. "Well, both," he replied to Matthew's question. He had not shared much of his personal life with Matthew; now loneliness lowered the barriers. "It's the usual story. Husband too wrapped up in work is cuckolded by bitter enemy, you know." He smiled again, and reached for the shot of Bushmill's as soon as the barman put it down.

Yes, the usual story, indeed. Finn well remembered the day it had all come crashing down, a day soon after Christmas, leaden sky spitting a mixture of snow and rain. He had been following up a story and found himself not far from his own neighborhood. A fateful, driving nervousness—his unerring reporter's instinct—had impelled him to go home, park a block away and sneak up the street, afraid, but already with some idea of what he'd find.

Nuala had been distant for ages, and her dark eyes would rarely meet his own. They hadn't made love in months; she always refused him with a shrug or icy stare. He spent his sexual frustration in the hollowness of masturbation—in the shower, in men's room stalls in a drunken haze at the pub. But he would never be unfaithful to her. Finn had no lust even for anyone else but her.

He had slipped through the unlocked front door. An unmarked police car was parked insolently in the drive. Maybe she had wanted him to find them. The house was quiet but full too, of the presence of people that is different from an empty house. Something stopped Finn calling out. He remembered creeping up the stairs, like some poor fuck in a film, holding his breath until he reached the door to their bedroom. Left ajar . . . he saw it all in the old mirror above her dresser, his wife's beautiful white body, the curve of her hips, the redness of her bum where their bodies had rubbed together. Saw a man's hands grabbing her waist as she sat astride him. His legs were bent with the effort of pushing himself up inside of her. They made hardly any noise, only their breathing.

Finn grasped the beer in front of him and drained half the pint in a swallow. "Aye, caught her right in the act. Walked right in on them, I did." He suddenly wanted to pour out the whole story, feel the sympathy from another man for the sorry state he had found his marriage—and his life.

Matthew winced and blew out a stream of smoke. "I wouldn't be able to take that. Sure, did you beat the fucker bloody senseless? That's what I'd do, then have a go at the wife."

"I couldn't face the confrontation or the futility of a crime of passion—running downstairs for the fireplace poker or kitchen knife." Finn gave a shout of humorless laughter. He remembered feeling, after the first humiliating half-erection of his penis, an equally mortifying need to shit. "Well, they didn't see me. I mean, I was outside the door, like. So after I saw them going at it—in the mirror, for fuck's sake—I just wanted to get out of it. I stepped back and hit my head on a wall sconce in the hall. I swore without thinking and they stopped. Nuala spoke something I couldn't understand." He finished his beer.

Matthew stood another round. He shook his head and lit another cigarette, offering the pack to Finn. "So was that it then? Did you not confront her?"

Finn felt the pain of the memory ease away with the first wave of alcoholic euphoria. It would return soon enough, but at the moment he could see the whole situation as an objective observer. At the sound of Nuala's whispered voice he had been struck by the jaded, blown-out bollocks of the whole thing, of their life, of his life. She groaned as her lover started again and he had made his way down the stair.

"I just went down the stairs, to the back garden to have a fag, sat on the bench my brother had made us years before. It was wet with rain and soaked my trousers, I remember. Smoked two; it was that long before I could think. I didn't know what to do. I didn't hurt yet, not then. It was shock, and then not really shock. I knew it, like you do. Sure I did." Finn paused to finish his cigarette.

Matthew nodded, his eyes narrowed in thought. The barman stood drying glasses from the washer, close enough to hear without appearing to be outright listening. But Finn didn't care. He'd had enough to drink now that everyone was a friend; he hadn't talked about that day to anyone since he left Belfast. And it had festered for four months. He took a long pull from the fresh pint that had appeared in front of him.

"The bastard left soon after. I heard the front door slam," Finn continued, replaying the scene again in his mind. "I went in and found Nuala in the kitchen in *my* old robe, smoking. She didn't look surprised to see me. I—" Finn stopped. Could he admit how much even in that moment he had wanted to fuck her himself? But then despair had started, killing desire.

"I asked her how long. Fucking RUC," Finn said with bitterness. The irony of Nuala betraying him with a Protestant policeman had been especially biting. "Couldn't stand not having it off with one of her own anymore. She smoked and didn't answer me. We had a drink and stood there looking at the mess on the counter, the shite laying about . . . a right fucking picture of Northern Ireland, Protestant and Catholic, women and men, betrayer and betrayed. Christ. 'Fuck you, Finn,' she finally said."

He stopped, remembering Nuala's ice-cold hatred, his desperate scramble to gather his things, his only thought to get to Una before Nuala took her away from him, as he was sure she would. Nuala had stood in the doorway of their bedroom, watching him pack. She hugged herself, her eyes were hard.

"Don't go near her." Her voice was dead.

Finn panicked and ran down the stairs, clothes falling out of his open carryall. He was at the front door when Nuala lunged for him, ripping his coat as she pulled herself close to him. He smelled the stink of sex and booze on her breath.

"She's mine. Don't go near her."

"She's mine, too, Nuala. She's my baby too. Whatever reason you have to hate me, don't keep her from me. Please."

Finn reached for Matthew's packet of cigarettes that lay on the bar and found it empty. Matthew's eyes had a far away, glazed look. Finn's face burned; a procession of emotions shuddered through him. He realized he was now halfway to drunk and Matthew even farther gone—he probably hadn't heard a word Finn had said in the last quarter hour, hadn't noticed the lapses of silence as Finn relived the memory. The barman had drifted away to serve an old man Finn recognized as Kate's friend Peter.

"I'd have fucking killed her, and your man in the bargain," Matthew stated clearly. "If Emily did that to me—" he shrugged and smiled, pulling a hand through his hair. "But she wouldn't. She knows better."

Finn looked at Matthew in surprise. He *had* been listening. But he was also taken aback by the venom in Matthew's tone. A shiver of dislike flashed through him, and Finn was aware of a sick heaviness forming in his belly.

Matthew pulled himself off the chair and onto his feet. He held the edge of the bar. "Sometimes, you know, I have a little side thing," Matthew whispered with a slurred voice. "All women are basically whores. But not in my own bed. No." He shook his head slowly and his eyes slitted blue and lucid. "What about our Venus, now? She seems harmless enough. And a challenge." He laughed. "You should have a go. Get your confidence back."

Finn tasted the sour burp of whisky in his throat. Any friendship he had felt toward Matthew vanished, and he was ashamed that he had told this man his story. Black anger pushed into him and he watched his hand rise to press into Matthew's chest. He saw the barman out of the corner of his eye, suddenly attentive.

Matthew raised his hands, placating. "Well, just a suggestion, man. If you won't have a try, I just might." And he maneuvered between Finn and the chair behind him, striding with surprising sureness across the floor. He turned and cocked a finger at Finn. "You owe me a pack of fags, my friend." With a slick smile he pushed open the door and stepped out into the bright, midsummer light.

CHAPTER ELEVEN

A rich lamb stew filled the kitchen with aromas of coziness and the memory of winter. Served with white beans and hot scones, it was her Gran's favorite comfort meal. Venus turned away from the kitchen window and the clouds whistling along the horizon. It was only six, and there were at least five hours of daylight left. She felt better after sleeping the majority of the afternoon. It would be good to spend the evening in the garden, perhaps walk down to Wickhouse wood with Teke. She sat at her place at the table, diagonal from Kate.

Kate's air was bemused, and Venus assumed she was preoccupied with thoughts of Emily's predicament. They said a brief grace in honor of the lamb and the abundance of the earth. Both women tucked into their meal, savoring the first heady flavors of the tender meat, beans, tomatoes and fresh herbs.

"I talked to Emily again today," Kate said. "She looked as if she'd had better nights. I told her the story about the *Seal Who Didn't Forget*."

Venus lay down her spoon. "She's keen on the old stories. But the way she does research seems a bit scattered. She talked to Gerard a few times too, about music, I guess."

Venus ate silently as memory surfaced. One of the worst arguments she and Gerard had ever had, and the last time she had seen him. Her jealous hysteria over finding him at dinner with Emily, even though their relationship was officially over. She hadn't known that Emily had cast her researcher's net so wide as to include Gerard. She had seen them in the cafe near the ferry terminal in Stromness, heads bent low over an intimate table. Venus cringed as she remembered waiting for them to leave, missing her bus, the cold. She had eventually gone to Gerard's flat, using the spare key to let herself in and wait for their arrival. He came home alone, and was incensed to find her waiting. It had been another case of her own paranoid behavior, actions that she looked back on now with shame.

Kate took a long drink of beer, which she often had at dinner. She ran her tongue over her teeth. "That girl's no smarter than any, for all her fancy education. You'd think that studying folk ways and the lives of simple people would teach her some common sense. No, it's all a play to her." Kate sighed. "I feel sorry for her. She tries hard, but there's a hollowness in her that will bring her trouble yet."

"She's been busy talking to everyone. I went to her flat a couple weeks ago for one of her interviews, and she told me that Lorraine McKay's son Mansie had given her his mother's old journals." Venus paused as she bit into the scone, let her mouth revel in the sweet lightness. "Lorraine was a friend of yours, wasn't she Gran? Though I don't remember her much."

Kate stirred her stew vigorously, heaping a spoonful atop the scone in her hand. "Huh," she said, and bit into it, tomato broth running down her chin. She grabbed her cloth napkin and wiped her mouth. "That can't be right. Mansie went through Lorraine's things years ago when she died. No respect he's got—threw a lot of things straight in the rubbish. But he gave all her songbooks and suchlike to the historical society, I thought. She was ever a great one for writing things down."

"Well, Emily said she had seen them. Maybe she meant at the History Center library. Anyway, I planned to tell you about it at the time. I suppose

I forgot." Venus thought of how irritated she'd been after the interview, and confused. "I guess Lorraine wrote down a lot about the old songs and stories, and her herbal knowledge. Emily said that the journals alluded to a 'circle of women' or something like that. Something suggesting secret meetings, where Lorraine and other women were present. She asked me about taking spiritual names—what it was about, if I had one, if *you* had one." Venus put her spoon down. "I just told her that using spiritual names is a way to create a sense of sacred space or ritual. But that we don't really do that anymore."

"Huh," Kate said again and took another pull at her beer. "Well, she didn't mention it today. Had other things on her mind, she did." Kate let out a healthy guffaw. "Secret meetings. For what, I ask? Dancing naked round the Ring of Brodgar? No."

Kate peered out the window. Her face took on a faraway look and the corners of her mouth turned down. It was an expression Venus couldn't fathom. Kate tapped her finger against the table.

"Gran?"

Kate looked down into her bowl and spooned up another bite. "Way back, before your mother was even born, Lorraine and I were friends. We had all been a pack at school—myself, Lorraine, Peter and his brother Gerald, Hamish—even though Lorraine left early to marry. She had two children right away . . ." Kate's voice grew soft, and her face took on again the strange, sad look. "Well, she was widowed early too, left with Mansie and Charlie both to bring up, when she was only twenty-five. She suffered enough, she did. Never remarried. And neither of those boys amounting to anything. She never had the luck, did Lorraine. She was a born victim, you might say. An innocent of a kind, head in the clouds. But a sweet girl." Kate suddenly focused on Venus with an intense look of pain. "She lacked common sense, but was gifted with plants and animals. And the most beautiful voice you'd ever heard. Knew all the old tunes; she played the whistle too."

Kate's voice trailed off. "You should have known her better, Venus. You were two alike in many ways. Aye, two alike." Kate looked into her lap.

Venus ate as Kate talked. She liked to hear stories from before she was born, even if they were increasingly tinged with bitterness or sadness.

"No," Kate said, as if to continue a line of reasoning in her head. "Lorraine didn't nearly deserve all the bad luck she got. We used to meet for tea and chat. People did then, didn't they? There weren't phones in every house and people valued human contact more. We were really like kin in some ways, being together; forming community was the important thing. Whether you liked a person or not almost seemed secondary." Kate looked out the window again. "Seems strange to your young ears, I know. Girls didn't keep their own company so much as you do, as you can now. Mind, the world was a safer place, but people did look askance on a girl that spent too much time by herself."

"I guess I would've been even a bigger misfit, then. Good thing I wasn't born 'til the seventies."

Kate reached for another scone. "You'd have been right enough. Now, Morag, Peter and Gerald's young sister, she was a one. Couldn't put two fair words together to save her life. We were all that surprised she ever found a man to marry her. But she used to come along too, to tea of an evening with Lorraine. I guess I was to her what Anne was to me. But Anne was gone by then, of course."

Venus knew Morag Leach. She was a thin, vigorous woman ten years younger than her Gran or thereabouts. Morag had lived in the village all her life like Kate, seldom venturing as far as the Scottish mainland. She had two children on the Mainland Island, and like so many women had been a widow for a long time. But Morag and her Gran rarely spoke; there seemed a strain between them that belied any friendship they might have had.

"I don't remember Anne," Venus said thoughtfully, searching her mind.

"No, you wouldn't. She was a friend of Hamish's brother Ferg. Was meant to marry him too—they were childhood mates all along just like

Hamish and I. She was seven years older than me." Kate's voice softened. She pushed her bowl away and sat with her hands in her lap. "Anne was like an older sister to me. I loved her like no one else, at the time. Or since. You know what I mean." Kate smiled, nodding.

"Aye," Venus said, encouraging Kate to go on. A bird sang in the garden; Venus could hear the bright repetitive chorus.

"Anne and Ferg were meant. Everybody just assumed it. But then the proverbial stranger came to town and swept her up. He was French, an archaeologist, come to study our ruins. Ha!" Kate suddenly cackled. "That was so early, nineteen . . . what was it? Nineteen twenty-seven, I think. So many things hadn't even been uncovered then. Well, Anne was only fifteen but very pretty and what we used to call gay. Anne's father was keen on all the ancient things and so offered the man a place to stay in their barn. It wasn't long before that Frenchman had taken a liking to Anne, and she to him. Poor Ferg was broken hearted."

"What was the stranger's name?" Venus said, thinking suddenly of Matthew.

"Pierre. Pierre Clermont. Of course he was handsome and very charming as the French almost always are—"

"Like Gerard."

Kate shrugged. "I'd agree with you there. As you mention it, Gerard looked a bit like Pierre did, about the nose. And Pierre was a lanky gentleman too. Huh." She toyed with the spoon in her bowl. "Well, where was I?"

"Pierre being handsome." Venus focused on Kate's words, pushing Gerard from her mind. She rose to start a pot of tea for herself, comforted by the familiar ritual.

"Oh, handsome he was, and he had Anne pregnant before the year was out."

"But she was so young!" Venus shook her head. It was always the same story. No wonder Kate was so accepting of Emily's plight—though Emily was old enough to know better. It had been the same with Venus' mother too.

"Fifteen wasn't young in those days, not really. Lorraine left school at sixteen to marry, myself at eighteen—and I was almost on the shelf." Kate cackled. "Poor Anne, she just couldn't resist him. He did the right thing; I think he loved her. He was twelve years older and very kind, really. They had a little girl and named her Clotilde."

"You must have been quite young then, Gran." Venus settled herself with a small teapot, cup and sugar.

"I was nine when Clotilde was born. Anne had been like an older sister since I was a peedie girl. I was the last of five, remember, all boys, with my youngest brother already ten and the oldest seventeen. My mother died when I was three. Her sisters and mother were still on North Ronaldsay—and they'd have had me back if my father could have borne to be parted from me." Kate smiled. "Sure, I had a need of a woman in my life. Anne and I just always took. I was as sad as Ferg when she left."

"Where did she go?"

Kate stood and took her dishes to the sink and began to wash them. "She went to France in the early thirties. Times were so hard here, and Pierre wanted to go back to his own country. She wrote often until the war, but then I lost track of her. She died, along with Pierre, in 1943."

"How did you find out about her death? And what happened to her daughter?" Venus sipped the strong black tea from her cup.

Kate's face closed. She replaced the lid on the soup pot and picked up Venus' dishes. "Clotilde told me."

"Did she write you? That was good she knew to contact you. I'll wash those, Gran." Venus half-rose.

"Don't bother. I can wash them, I'm sure. I've plenty of energy left." She soaped the bowl without speaking.

Venus waited. She felt that she had tread unknowingly on some forbidden territory. She poured a second cup of tea and watched her Gran, aware of a deep sadness that had crept into the room with the memories.

"Clotilde came up here a short while," Kate said, "right after the war. She was very young, only seventeen or so. She came back to get some help from Anne's family, since both Anne and Pierre had died." Kate's voice was tight.

"But she didn't stay? Did she go back to France?"

Kate didn't answer. Her hands were still, sponge and soapy dish forgotten in some long memory. Venus was surprised at the feeling of unease she felt, and the unusual awkwardness that rested between them. A sure, unwelcome weight lodged in her heart. For her to have never heard of Anne, of Clotilde, for this strangeness to have come over her Gran, some bad thing must have happened. Venus shuddered; she didn't want to know. She placed her hands on the table and breathed deeply.

"Do you like Emily? I mean, do you like talking to her, telling her the old stories?" Venus forced her voice to be bright.

"Hmmm . . . ?" Kate removed her coverall and took two ginger biscuits from a packet on the counter. She handed them to Venus and took two more for herself. "Oh, I don't mind. Like I said, I feel sorry for her. Let me top up that pot," she said, as she took the kettle from the stove. Kate poured more hot water over the tea leaves in Venus' pot.

Venus dropped her head and let her face bask in the steam rising from the hot water. With relief she realized the energy in the room had shifted. Her Gran had come back from the past with the mention of Emily.

"You know she said that she was afraid."

Venus' head came up sharply. "Afraid of who?"

"Now how would you know *who*, instead of *what*?"

"I don't know. I just thought—"

"It doesn't matter. You're right. She's afraid of that young man of hers." Kate looked shrewdly at Venus.

Venus shifted her gaze to the window.

"I know you've got a fancy for Matthew, and I don't blame you. He's a bonny young man. But he's not as he seems. You're a grown woman, Venus, but if the fact that he belongs to another woman won't keep you away, let the knowledge that he's a bastard do so. And I think you've had enough experience with that for one lifetime."

Venus stared at Kate. How could her Gran have seen what she wouldn't admit to herself? And how did he rate as a bastard? As far as Venus knew, Kate had never even spoken to him, except in passing.

"Don't give me that look." Kate wagged a finger at Venus. "I have my own way of knowing things." She poured herself a cup of tea.

Silence descended again as the two drank their tea. The bird outside had stopped its song, and the light was long in the garden. The scent of damp, fertile greenness washed in through the open door.

"What did you mean about Matthew?" Venus hugged her arms to her chest, pulling her sweater in around her.

"Just you stay away from him, girl. He's not a good one." Kate's eyes were piercing. "He's no one to mix with, and you believe it."

Two birds winged over the low stone wall behind the house. Venus stood and left the kitchen. She went to the bottom of the garden and looked out to Eynhallow. She fancied she heard a mournful singing, carried on the strong north wind.

CHAPTER TWELVE

Finn felt pricks of pain begin in the bottom of his stomach and regretted the chili sauce that had draped his omelet. *You know better, sure. When are you going to take better care of yourself, man?* He grimaced and watched the passerby on the street outside the Mourning Dove. His back to the comforting noise of the cafe, he found himself writing stories in his head about the girl outside with a pram, her high heeled shoes and cheap fringed top a sad attempt at fashion. She smoked self-consciously and looked about sixteen. Her friends popped gum. He let his eyes drift from them to two figures on the nearby beach. Morag Leach and Emily Haworth. An unlikely couple for socializing. Emily was writing on something that looked like an appointment calendar. Morag's expression was fierce. Finn glanced away to Rousay, sitting across the sound. He shook his head at the memory of the woman's sharp tongue. He'd had quite the run-in with Morag and her son, Neill, a few months back. In fact, it was in connection to his interview with Gerard that he had met Morag in the first place.

The business with Neill was strange: small town intrigue magnified by the proximity to relative fame. Neill had worked for and been sacked by Gerard, who was both an eminent musician in his own right and Director of the Festival of Isles. Finn met both because his editor at the Belfast *Tele-*

graph had asked him to write about Orkney's well-known music festival. Finn had argued was he not on sabbatical for chrissakes but he had needed something to distract him from the first terrible days on the island. He needed the money too and so he had interviewed Gerard, the man who had led the music festival from obscurity to Continental fame. He had interviewed members of the Festival committee as well, and stumbled upon a hushed-up scandal of operating money gone missing.

The story had not interested his editor but Finn had gathered an earful of abuse from Morag concerning Gerard Ventoux. Neill had been the financial officer of the Festival and dismissed in the confusion over the missing funds. A mother hen in full ire she'd been, when he'd gone round to ask Neill about the story. Morag had been there, and had not let Neill answer any of the questions himself. Well, this was months ago now and Finn had written his small cultural piece and had enjoyed a nice meal with Gerard. Finn rubbed his temples. *Strange enough too that your man Gerard was now dead.*

Finn had not heard what ever happened to Neill after the scandal and avoided his mother when he saw her in the town, or walking the paths that ranged over the fields between his cottage and her farm. He tried to imagine Morag's husband, whoever he'd been. Married life with her would have been none too pleasant. What had made her so bitter? So full of rage?

A plate crashed in the kitchen and jolted Finn into awareness. He heard Mary's voice from behind the pass-through and then Venus' answering laugh. That was a good sound. If only—

"Mr. Ross—Finn—could I join you a moment?"

Finn looked up into Emily's face. His eyes flicked to the window; Morag was gone. "Suit yourself." He pushed his empty plate aside and pulled the coffee cup toward him.

"So, I understand you were a reporter. Investigative. Politics."

"I *am* a reporter, aye. Why?"

"I—I need some advice." Her face turned a mottled crimson.

"I'm no man of virtue, sure. And not much of a success story either. Don't know how much help I'll be able to give you." He offered her a smile. But he was wary.

"I, well—" she stammered, finally looking up from her hands to meet his eye. "I need to know how to get into a crime scene."

"A crime scene? Why?"

She shrank in her chair. "Shhh . . . I—could you please not say anything to anyone about this? I need to get into Gerard's flat." Her hands pressed the table, her gaze desperate and fixed on him now.

He noted the use of the dead man's first name. Suggesting more than casual acquaintance, surely. "Did you know him?" Finn took a drink of his coffee. It was cold. He swiveled his head and caught Venus' eye. He motioned to the cup and she nodded.

"I . . . did know him. But only slightly. It's just that he has something of mine and I need it back." She paused. "You see, I may need to leave— sooner than I thought. And, well, it's mine. I need it back." She ended with a lowered voice and gaze.

"Mmmm . . . you could just talk to the police, right enough. If it's not pertinent to the investigation I'm sure they'd let you have it back. That would be smarter than breaking into a crime scene."

"I assume it *is*, the flat, I mean. Would they have a guard there, and the tape and all that?"

"I don't know about the tape. He wasn't killed there. I'm sure that the police have been through his things, though they won't be finished. But it will be secured. I won't tell you how to pick a lock. You're on your own there." He grinned.

But Emily's gaze remained intense. "Getting in is not a problem. I just wanted to know if you thought there would be a guard, or an unmarked car. I thought you might know about these things."

Finn smiled wryly. "Too fucking right. I've been in plenty of places I shouldn't have been. But Stromness is a small community, not too much manpower. I doubt they've got the flat under guard, unless they think the killer has left something to incriminate . . ." his words died as he realized what he was saying.

Emily's face blanched. "Oh, God, no. It's not like that, not what you're thinking. It's just that he has some of my research materials, some primary sources. I went to see him a few weeks ago and left them there by accident . . . I . . ." Her mouth worked and she looked at the wall.

"What did Gerard know about your research? I thought it was storytelling you were into. And you've waited a long time to get them back."

"He knew heaps of things about the songs and their relationship to local mythology. Gerard—"

Venus set Finn's coffee down with a clatter. Without thinking he reached for her arm, brushing it with his fingertips before she pulled away.

Emily waited for Venus to cross the cafe before she spoke again. Her voice was a whisper. "Do you think that I'll be able to get in, then? Without being noticed? I know where the—my things—are. He . . . told me on the phone. When he called to say I'd left them." Her words slid over each other.

Finn's journalistic instinct quivered. Something was going on with Gerard and Emily. Or rather, had been. He thought back to his conversation with Matthew in the pub, and hoped for Emily's sake she'd been discreet. He frowned. But Emily hadn't been on the island for long, six months at best—and he knew that much of that time she'd been away in Shetland. It was enough time to start something, possibly. At least a quick affair. And he now knew that Venus and Gerard's relationship had ended about the time that he himself had arrived in March. Emily had come on her own sometime in January; had Gerard wasted no time, then, in picking up another woman to admire him—or had the relationships overlapped? Emily seemed so slavishly devoted toward Matthew when they were together. Yet, if Matthew acted the bastard that Finn was sure he must, he wouldn't blame Emily for turning to another; fuck's sake, she should leave him all together.

"Have something going with the man, did you? It's no odds to me," Finn said, waving away her protest. "But I've no doubt the police would like to know. Or, if you've nothing to hide, then go straight to Sammy and tell him, ask to get your materials retrieved."

"Of course I have nothing to hide," Emily tried for a haughty tone, but it came out a harsh rasp. "Please, don't mention I asked you." Her voice softened to a plea. "Please." She rose from the table and left. He heard the silvery bells jingle on the door as she exited the cafe.

Well. That's something, then. Of course she *did* have something to hide, otherwise there'd be no need to talk to him or sneak into Gerard's flat. She had mentioned that getting into the place wouldn't be a problem—that must mean she had a key or knew of a spare. If she had been having a little fling, however innocently it may have started, then keeping it secret from Matthew would be a priority. And maybe it wasn't research materials Gerard had, but something more incriminating. Or more personal. Something that would prompt questions from the police. She was terrified, that was clear. But was it just Matthew she was afraid of?

Finn stirred sugar into his coffee and drank it down. Maybe Matthew had already had his suspicions. He was certainly strong enough to batter a man's head in. Emily was tall but slight; Finn doubted her ability to do so. And she had no motive that he knew of. But Matthew . . . yes, Matthew.

The bells stirred again over the door. Finn turned to see DI Sammy Douglas walk up to the counter.

"Mr. Douglas," Finn called. "Sammy—do you have a moment? I've got something I'd like to ask you."

CHAPTER THIRTEEN

"A man gets himself killed and all of a sudden it's 'Mr. Douglas' this or 'Inspector' that and folks are crossing the street to avoid me. Or else they're wantin' a chin wag. I'm no longer the simple man they know. Now I represent fear, or information." Sammy smiled wryly and sipped from a steaming paper cup. The two men had opted for a more private conversation outside. The wind blew the collar of Sammy's coat against his face. "Which is it you're after, Finn?"

"Life in the Plod, Sammy. You had to know what you were getting into." Finn smiled. He liked Sammy, and he realized that it wouldn't do to underestimate him. But still, he was a small town copper in over his head—and Sammy's haggard look and dark circles put paid to the fact. Finn pushed aside his sympathy. His journalist's impassive emotional screen fell into place. What he wanted was information. As long as he was confined to the island in his role of body finder and possible suspect, Finn felt he might as well have a go at finding out Gerard's killer. It was something he could do to feel useful. And it might help Venus see him in a new light—or see him at all.

Finn and Sammy crossed the High street and walked onto the beach. They were silent until Sammy stopped and selected a dry, seaweed-free patch of rock to sit on. He settled himself, legs apart, warming both hands on the coffee cup. Finn sat next to him and stared out to sea. It was a blowy day, promising rain.

"Did you work with police much in Belfast? Were you a crime reporter?"

"Me? Not by half. I'm on the wrong side of the Cross there, man. A Fenian through and through. Usually just trying to stay out of the way." He coughed and felt in his jacket pocket for his fags. He would not think of Nuala. "I've always covered international politics. Took me away a fair bit, war-torn countries, the lot. The police are usually the bastards making everything worse." He paused to light the cigarette. "But I've the opinion that politics are only good for those at the top, and the little folks end up suffering in the end."

"Christ, but you're a cynic." Sammy took another sip of coffee. "But would you have the country in anarchy, then? No laws? No control? Would you like the responsibility of bringing a killer to justice? And what would you do with him when you found him?"

Finn exhaled and shook his head. "I'm not saying there's no use to police. I just think there is a tendency toward the misuse of the power. But that's not what I wanted to talk to you about." He paused for another drag on the cigarette. "How is the investigation going? Got any suspects, aside from me, of course?" He shot Sammy another smile.

"A bit eager to be on the suspect list, aren't you?" Sammy's expression remained tired, his eyes staring into the tumbled grey of the sea, but his voice attempted lightness. "Fuck, no," he sighed. "I'm not getting far and that's a fact. But maybe you'd answer some questions for me, so I know how friendly to be the next time we meet." He looked at Finn, his brown eyes steady.

Finn resisted the pull of friendship that tugged on him. He had to remain objective. And for now, he wanted to keep what he knew about Emily and Matthew to himself. It wouldn't do to incriminate anyone unnecessarily. "Ask away."

"Where were you between eight and nine in the evening Thursday night? You said in your statement that it was gone eleven when you discovered the body. But you had no watch and had forgotten your mobile, so that's only your best guess gauged on when you left your cottage. You were at the pub by fifteen minutes to midnight, which fits with your run from the churchyard down toward town. Not an outstanding time for the mile, but—"

"I've the lungs of an old man, and I'll admit it. More's the pity." Finn laughed.

"But of course I've only your word that's the way it happened. Tell me again when you left your house that evening. You saw no one? And what were you doing earlier, between eight and nine?" Sammy had finished the coffee and pulled out a notebook.

"I've already gone over this with you and your man Crombie last night. D'you think I've left something out? It's my body that's rubbish, not my mind."

"I find it's helpful to keep reviewing the facts," Sammy bristled. "But if you'd rather, we can drive—"

"No, no, I don't mind. Well, as I told you, I left my cottage about ten or so. I thought Kate and Venus might come and have a drink with me in the pub, and I knew there was a session on—I had a text from Matthew at about 9:45. I wasn't sure if I should call so late at New Farm. It would be half ten at least before I arrived—it's over two mile away from my cottage, as you know. But I had to get out, get a bit of exercise."

"You went up the lane, and not around by the Wickhouse Wood?"

"Och, why would I walk so far out of my way? Though the wood is very fair. No, I was having trouble with my stomach too, so I went slow once I got to the road."

"Did you pass anyone? That track goes right the back of Knowehouse. Did you see Mrs. Leach about?"

"Aye, I did now, but only through her window. I doubt she saw me, and I never want to see her if I can help it. She's a right old crow. When I interviewed her son Neill about the Festival—here, now, I hadn't thought of it last night—but there's a connection to your man Gerard!" Finn grunted and moved to sit in the sand.

"A link between Mrs. Leach and Gerard, or Neill—her son?"

"Not the mother, no, although—" Finn paused for thought. "No, I wouldn't think so. But there was a bit of intrigue over some Festival funds."

"All right, let's take one thing at a time. First finish telling me about your own movements." Sammy stood, rubbing his bum. "Let's walk up to the bench there; we can be more comfortable."

Finn rose in acquiescence. They crossed the rock and climbed back up onto the high street. Finn hoped that Sammy didn't think he had been trying to distract him with the information about Neill. But it was something, and he didn't have an alibi for the time of Gerard's death. If the time in question was between eight and nine, he had been home in the cottage moping over a soggy bowl of rice and jar of curry sauce. A flurry of apprehension sifted through his body. Did Sammy suspect him or not? In the police's view, of course, he could have committed the crime. He could have planned to 'discover' the body later, feign shock and so on. What's more, if he had killed Gerard as early as eight, he would have had time to return to the cottage, change the inevitably bloodstained clothes and make his way back, perhaps hoping to have Kate or Venus along to provide witness to the discovery.

Oystercatchers screeched overhead. As the men began their climb toward the bench, teams of white and grey fulmars sailed in, impossibly fast and close to the edge of the cliff, joyriding on currents of air. Sammy was silent, apparently lost in thought.

Finn continued his own line of thinking. If he *had* been the killer, that would be over six miles of walking to be done in one evening—fuck's sake, he hadn't walked that far in years. Three miles to the churchyard, approximately, and then the same back; then to the churchyard again and a further mile down to the village, jogging over an uneven path, no less. And how to get Gerard in such a remote location? A woman might entice him there, but—

Finn stopped dead in his tracks. He did not want to believe where his thoughts were leading him. Who would Gerard meet late at night in a secluded churchyard? Emily? Or Venus?

"Finn? Finn?" Sammy had stopped with Finn, and was looking at him with interest. "What is it?"

"Oh. I—it's nothing, man. I was just thinking about the—my—wife. Ex-wife. Or may as well be." His voice rang false in his ears.

Sammy's glance was appraising. *Don't underestimate him. He's not your friend; he'll be watching you.* How might he clear himself, in Sammy's eyes, without pointing a finger toward Emily or Venus? He couldn't imagine that either had the strength or psychological capacity to batter a man's head in. But motivation was a powerful thing. Although Emily lacked any reason to kill Gerard as far as he knew, Venus, as much as he hated to admit it, had known the man best. Finn knew that murder victims most often knew their assailants. And who else could lure Gerard to that lonely churchyard, frequented by Venus alone?

They reached the bench and sat. Sammy uncapped his pen again and flipped to a page in his notebook half covered with an illegible scrawl.

"You reached New Farm at 10:45 or so, though this is only a guess as you didn't have any way to tell the time. It's only two miles from your place, maybe a bit more, yet it took you that long to get there. Why?"

"I *did* see the time on Kate's kitchen clock—10:42 if you're wanting to be exact. I had a look in the back to see if they were in, when they didn't answer at the front. I don't think it took me over long to get there; there are two hills and the track is uneven walking. Besides, I had to stop a bit on the lane, I told you. My stomach was acting up again. But anyway, can't you see that I'm not fit enough to have done in your man Gerard? I wouldn't leave my house at seven, walk for an hour, bash the man's head in, then walk back three miles, then turn around and come to the churchyard again and *then* run down to the pub. I'd not make it, sad as it is and as young as I am." His attempted smile stretched more like a grimace over his face.

"I'm not saying you did any such thing, Mr. Ross. I'm merely asking you to relate to me your movements on the night in question."

Finn winced at the use of his surname. They were both defensive, he could feel it, and it wasn't the tack he'd wanted to take. But foolish to think that he would just waltz into a conversation with the Inspector, garner the information he wanted and walk away. He was a *suspect* for Christ's sake. What percentage of murderers 'found' their own bodies? It was high, he was sure.

"Sure, they weren't at home, so I thought I may as well get on to the pub myself. I knew that track led down to the village, and I wouldn't have gone back the long way around. As I went by the churchyard, I stopped—"

"Why?"

"Because there was a bonny moon. Because . . . because . . ." Finn calculated the risk of telling Sammy of his infatuation with Venus. It was hardly motive for killing her old boyfriend and Sammy was sure to find out anyway, if he didn't already know. And maybe, because Mary and Venus were such good friends, it would calm Sammy down, make the man more sympathetic to him.

"You were saying? Because?"

Finn looked up the path from the bench. He couldn't see the church from where they sat, but knew it lay, haunted now, perhaps, over the top of the hill. "I've a wee fancy for Venus. I thought she might be hanging about there. I know she does sometimes. So I stopped and went inside. I didn't see her—or anyone. I walked around a few minutes and then looked over to the sycamore as I told you, and saw the shape there. It was dim under the tree, in the corner. I walked over and found him. After a moment I looked for his pulse, and then I left. It took me a minute to decide whether to come down to the village or walk back to New Farm and use their phone, since I didn't have my mobile. You know I ran down to the pub and that's what happened."

"But why did you choose to go to Kate and Venus first, and not come to my table?"

"I don't know, to be honest. I suppose I thought that the church was on their land—"

"It isn't—"

"I know that now, but I didn't then. So I wanted to tell them first. And I was in shock. As many bodies as I've seen, you don't get over the shock of it, especially when it is so unexpected, and someone you know. I wanted a little comfort, I suppose. And my first thought is never of the police," Finn finished in a low voice.

"So you've expressed," Sammy answered. "Let me understand. You were at home between eight and nine. No one saw you, you made no telephone calls, have no one to corroborate your story?"

"No. I talked with me ma on the mobile—there's no telephone at the cottage—but that was early on, seven or maybe before."

Sammy was silent. He pulled up the sleeve of his jacket and checked his watch. "What was it you wanted to ask me, Finn?"

"When your man died, how the investigation was going." Finn saw no point in being dishonest.

"It's early days, yet. Early days." Sammy stood. "I've got to keep an appointment. But I'd like to speak with you later, about Neill Leach. Will you be in Kirkwall at all this afternoon? Or could you come down tomorrow?"

"You'll not take Sunday off, Sammy? Do you plan to work round the clock—are there no other officers on the investigation?"

Sammy sighed. "I'll try to have a few hours off to sleep. But a killer is loose. Although I don't fear another murder, we can't let the case get cold. You of all people should know that. But Monday morning then, if that suits you better. I hadn't figured you for a religious man." Sammy turned to go.

"It's not that," Finn said, to Sammy's retreating form, "but there's no bus as runs on Sunday, and I don't fancy a fifteen mile cycle into the wind."

CHAPTER FOURTEEN

"You're lucky we're not busier today. It's cheeky of you, Sammy, to make us talk to you now, right in the middle of the day. A Saturday too." Mary's eyes had shifted to a strong, slate blue. But as soon as the words were spoken her face softened. She sighed and finished wiping the table where Sammy and Venus sat.

Venus crossed her arms over her chest and leaned back in the wooden chair. The Mourning Dove was temporarily quiet, although the bus due in from Kirkwall would soon empty its passengers, hungry after a morning's shopping, into the high street. From there it was a short walk to the cafe for afternoon lunch or early tea.

The day was almost over, at least her part. Mary would work until about four, serving Liv and Fergus, her children, their tea in the kitchen as she baked for the next day. She would putter in the cafe until Sammy made it home again from Kirkwall, then finally go upstairs to their flat for the evening. How did she keep her energy, her passion? The cafe was hard work and she essentially raised the kids alone. Venus liked Sammy, had known him for years, but his policeman's life was too erratic and exhausting despite the relatively low crime rate in Orkney. She tried not to judge him and usually failed.

83

Sammy returned his wife's gaze wordlessly. He turned to Venus. "All right. I'll try to make this as painless as possible. I know you weren't feeling too well yesterday."

Mary said, "I'll fetch us some tea." She walked to the back of the cafe.

Venus took the lid off the jam pot on the table. She toyed with the miniature spoon that sat inside of it. "Never mind, Sammy. Yesterday seems like a lifetime ago, already." She looked at him. Dark circles lay under his eyes. She knew her own face looked as haggard. "I'm ready to answer questions now."

"Good." Sammy was at once all efficiency, taking out the battered notebook. "Now you mentioned you had only seen Gerard once in the past few months. When was that?"

Venus watched jam drip off the spoon into the pot. She refilled the spoon and held it up again to repeat the process. The ruby mass, peppered with seeds, mesmerized her. "It was—I don't know—perhaps February."

"And? What did you talk about? How did he seem? Were there problems in his life?"

"We were barely on speaking terms. I don't know what this can have to do with anything."

Sammy let out a thin breath.

Venus felt her face go hot. "All right. We had a huge row, if you must know. It wasn't about anything other than . . . us. Our same stupid madness. But to answer the question, *he* seemed fine. All good cheer and—" her voice broke. She looked out the window, fixing her gaze on the beach.

"Did you meet him in Stromness? At his flat?" Sammy's voice was soft but persistent.

"Yes—no, well, I ran into him at the Harbor cafe. He was having dinner there with someone. I—" her voice lowered to a whisper. "I got upset. He was with a woman, and so naturally I thought, you know." She steeled herself to tell the rest. "I went back to his flat. I knew where he had an extra key. I stayed there and waited for him to come home. It was ridiculous. I know I had no right, but that was so soon after . . . I was still so upset with him." Venus raised her gaze to meet Sammy's eyes defiantly.

Sammy's face held nothing but the good nature she usually found there.

"Oh, I just felt so *fucking* stupid!" She let the tears escape.

Mary approached with a laden tea tray and gave her husband a quick glance. "Are you badgering her? I tell you, Venus has nothing to do with this—"

"Mary, would you let me do my job? Please, love." He reached for her hand. "Thanks for the tea. Sit down and join us."

Mary hesitated and sat down. "I wouldn't mind. I'm tired this week. What with Livvie's nightmares and Ferg *constantly* asking me—well. You know it well enough." She reached to pour out tea.

"Did you know the woman he was with?" Sammy asked.

"Is it important?" Venus responded, taking a mug of tea from Mary.

"I don't know. It might be. I take it you did know her?"

Venus took a sip of strong, sweet tea. She tried to think what harm could come if she revealed Emily's name. After all, it had been an innocent enough interview. Or so Gerard had insisted. But Venus remembered watching them through the window of the cafe. Emily had been animated in a way that Venus had never seen her with Matthew. Gerard had been all smiles, the charm radiating from him as always. She knew his flirtatious manner, saw Emily responding as most women did. But there had been something intimate about their conversation, though they hadn't touched. And she had known. Outside her own jealousy, her own fury at seeing herself so easily replaced, she had *known* that he and Emily had been together. The flush of anger and betrayal returned again.

"It was Emily." Venus set her mug down, letting her gaze return to the sea. Three fulmars slid easily through the sky, skimming the ocean.

"Emily Haworth?"

"Matthew's Emily?" Mary and Sammy's voices sounded in unison.

"They were just having dinner," Venus said.

"You don't sound convinced of that. Why didn't you tell me?" Mary demanded.

"Because I was humiliated. Besides, I have—had—no proof that they were *together*. Gerard told me she was interviewing him for research."

"But?" Sammy asked.

"But . . . well, I knew there was something else. I just did. And later, when I went to his flat, I—I listened to his answer phone."

"No!" Mary cried, with a laugh. "Oh, it's not funny, but—"

"I know." Venus shook her head. "He made me crazy. That's what it was like. The whole last year."

"But was there a message?" Sammy stuck doggedly to the point. "From Emily?"

"Yes," Venus blurted. "Yes, there was. It was only something about how she was looking forward to seeing him, and couldn't wait to hear what amazing thing he had discovered in some old book or other. It sounded like they had met before. She called him 'darling' in that toffee accent of hers. Ugh," Venus said, remembering how disgusted and sick she had felt.

"So the message implied that they had previous meetings, but it didn't confirm any intimacy on their part?" Sammy looked up at the ceiling, tapping his cheek with a finger. He added to the notes in the notebook. "Well, it's good gossip material, but it might not mean much. It does establish a connection between them. I'll have to ask her about it."

"No! Sammy you can't! Oh, I shouldn't have told you."

"I have to talk to everyone that knew him, especially those that might have been closely connected. What should it matter? She knows you saw them, doesn't she? Didn't you say you saw them *in* the cafe?"

"I don't know. I mean, no, I never went into the cafe. I just watched them for a while through the window and went back to his flat. So I don't know if she saw me."

"Well," he persisted, "I can't not talk to her just because you don't want me to. I don't have to tell her how I know of their association. It probably *is* innocent. After all, she seems pretty devoted to her own Matthew."

"But women know, Sammy. Women know." Mary nodded. "And Matthew wasn't here in February, remember. He's only been here five or six weeks—he came after Emily returned from her time away in Shetland, and that was mid-May some time. If Emily is—was—having a thing on the side, that would account for her strange behavior around Matthew. I mean, you only have to watch them five minutes to see they don't get along. She alternates cringing and crooning all over him. I think she's scared he knows."

"Wait a minute." Sammy held up a hand. "There's no evidence of anything. Don't go spinning out theories. Let's get this back on track." He turned to Venus. "So that argument was the last you saw or talked to him?"

"Yes."

"Why do you think he was up in the churchyard Thursday night?"

"I don't know."

"Did you ever go there with him?"

Venus let out a sigh. "Of course we did. But not often. He didn't see the point." She was aware of the loud hum of the cold case behind the counter. They sat silently a moment.

"Then why do you think he would go there alone at night?"

"I don't know! To meet someone, maybe. To leave me something. I don't know!" The residue of pain began its slow ebb around her heart. "He did sometimes," she said, in answer to Sammy's questioning gaze. "He left me little gifts, or a bunch of flowers. Or a song." She squeezed her eyes shut.

"Recently? Always at the churchyard?"

"No. It's been a month at least. And the last time was in our garden."

"You mean he would come to your house from *Stromness* and leave you flowers in your garden?" Mary's voice was incredulous. "You never told me any of this."

Venus didn't answer. She knew that Mary would have been furious, would have made her confront Gerard, make him stop. Her thoughts spun. She'd hated and liked the attention at once. There had never been a note, but she'd known the gifts were from him.

"What did Kate have to say about all this?" Mary's voice was fierce.

"Nothing. She didn't know. And I don't want her to. Please, Mary. It was meaningless, and now it's over."

"So perhaps he was there to leave you something, or in the hope that he might meet you there," Sammy said. "And encountered someone else instead. That is—" Sammy stopped himself abruptly. "Where were you, Venus, between eight and nine o'clock Thursday night?"

Chapter Fifteen

Venus plodded up the track toward the churchyard and home. Sammy had assured her that she could visit the place now and she was both eager and reticent to be in her special spot. What would it be like to stand in the place where the man she had loved more than any other had been killed? The thought twisted her stomach. But she had to go there, face it, cleanse it from the blackness of evil. Her Gran had taught her many things, including that there was really no such thing as evil in the world, only positive and negative. Kate had been very serious when she told Venus to never make a judgment about someone's evil. Create the positive, acknowledge the negative. Light and shadow, she had said.

But murder was different. Venus didn't think that Kate would argue that point. Venus couldn't stand the thought of her safe and peaceful sanctuary violated with the stench of unnatural death. She must undo what had been done, rid the churchyard of the fear and hatred that must have precipitated Gerard's death. Kate had shown her how to clear the energy of a place too, but it would require ritual and concentration. Venus knew the best time to banish was during the waning moon, but she wouldn't wait. She must do it soon.

Wind raked the tall grass and flowers to either side of the path. It was so familiar, this walk over the hills and along the sea. She could see the island of Rousay, the farms scattered between low hills and the main road, the Tingwall ferry plowing away from the small ro-ro pier. Over the hill, her home, New Farm, nestled. All the houses in Orkney were named, sometimes for the original family, or for some feature of landscape, or, in the case of newer houses, a romantic notion of the owner. New Farm was so called because it was, simply, the newer portion of the original land holding. The main house was small and made of stone, dating from the mid 1800's. It had a basic rectangular shape and a chimney rising up from either end. The garden was to the back, framed by a low stone wall, and a narrow lane led away from the house, past a stone barn for the cow. It had always seemed safe, not far from neighboring farms. The landscape was a well-loved friend. As were the ruins that scattered their land—the old farm with its beehive dovecote and decaying barn, the tiny, original house where her Grandpapa's family had lived.

As she gained the top of the hill she stopped. The crumbling wall of the churchyard lay silent; the stone mellow in the sunlight, but emanating cold. She shivered and looked over the field to the east. Venus could just see her Grandpapa's fishing boat bobbing in the waves in the little cove cradled by their land. Kate had kept Hamish's boat even after his death, kept it running and, for the last thirty-odd years, had loaned the boat to a collection of boys or men needing a vessel for small fishing. Peter was the only one who used it now.

Peter . . . yes, he was around so much, so much a part of her Gran's life. Thursday night, in the pub, it had come so clear to her. He was sweet on Gran, she was sure. Perhaps he had always been. Venus felt she had been unobservant, self-absorbed.

She lifted her arms and felt the wind buffet her body. Her long hair flew loosely around her face. She longed to wash free the weight that fell heavy on her heart and mind.

After telling Sammy of her last encounter with Gerard, the conversation had turned to what she felt had been a relentless and repetitive questioning of where she had been, who she and Gerard had known, what he had done, his past. The first two questions had been easily answered. At eight p.m. on Thursday she had been at the bingo with Gran at St. Magnus parish hall until their decision to leave around nine for the pub. This was their usual routine, a comforting weekly ritual that rarely varied. The music session had been a spontaneous addition to what was typically a quiet and fairly early night.

As to who she and Gerard held as intimates, there hadn't been much to say. They had consumed each other, or at least she'd thought. Venus didn't know now what had been real. But beyond the choir they had few relationships in common, no mutual friends or couples to share time with. Even Mary and Sammy had been outside the circle of her world with Gerard.

Venus hadn't been able to answer most of Sammy's other questions. It had obviously bothered him how little she had actually known about Gerard. But he had been closed about his past, even though he had accepted the job in Orkney because he had been born there. Raised in a convent orphanage in southern France, the one thing that Gerard had learned from the nuns about his mother was that she had been an Orcadian woman. He had few memories of her; he had been only four when she died. His father he had never known. When he had left the orphanage at sixteen, the nuns had given him a thin folio with a faded picture and a yellowed note. The picture had been of himself as an infant and presumably his mother. Her head had been turned away from the camera. The back of the photo bore only the name Gerard. The note was brief, a request for a 'Mme. Brosnard' to take Gerard to the convent in the event of his mother's death. Venus had given Sammy these details and he had duly noted them down. How far Gerard had progressed in identifying his mother she did not know. They hadn't spoken of it more than once or twice.

Sammy had also asked her if she had heard anything of trouble with the Festival's finances, or of a problem with Morag's son Neill, who had been the Financial Officer of the organization. But she had not. At the end of the interview she left, empty and stretched, feeling like she had never known Gerard at all.

Venus watched the top of the sycamore lash over the stones in the wind. She must go in. She walked to the rusted iron gate. The grass still bore the mark of tires and was strewn with cigarette butts. The wrapper of a Mars bar fluttered, caught in a crack of the wall. Deep sadness enveloped her. She longed to have some final word with Gerard. Despite the pain he had caused her, she had now only a wish to forgive him, and tell him so. And a final kiss on his cheek, always so brown and smooth, to send him to the unknown land of death. Venus laid her hand on the cold iron of the gate. She closed her eyes, wishing for the vision that sometimes came to her, wishing to see Gerard, to feel his presence. All around her birds cried in the wind, their familiar sounds contrast to the loneliness she felt. Opening her eyes, she glanced at the sea. A seal bobbed in the water, rising with the swell of the tide.

Venus pulled the gate open without a sound and stood within the churchyard, letting the stones and markers imprint themselves on her again. She closed her eyes, letting each of her senses be filled. The taste of salt, drying her lips; damp freshness of moss and wildflower; the susurration of the wind blowing over the grass. The branches of the sycamore creaked rhythmically. A rushing shadow clouded her mind's eye and her body prickled with goose flesh. She opened her eyes, heart drumming in her chest.

She saw a figure twenty feet away, standing in the shadow of the crumbling sanctuary wall. A strain of whistled song reached her, the pure, plain notes of a Scottish air. It was a song she and Gerard had often sung together. Blood pounded in her ears. Her vision clouded. In the shadow the figure seemed black, ethereal, and then was gone as it moved behind the wall. Venus began to walk, winding her way through the stones toward the remains of the sanctuary.

The wind carried the whistled melody toward her. She hesitated and then continued. Her mind was blank; she was aware only of her skin and breath. Venus stopped again as she reached the wall. She saw the nettles growing rich and reached a hand to brush the leaves. Her skin flamed with the burning sting. She stepped around the side of the wall.

It was Matthew. He turned as he heard her surprised intake of breath. His eyes were sharp, the color of the horizon in winter. They didn't speak. Venus was aware of part of her mind posing rational questions. What was he doing there? What was he playing at, in this silly game of hide and seek? He must have seen her come in. But the thoughts were far below. Her breath. Her skin. She was freezing cold. Venus took her gaze to her hands, clenched and white-blue at her sides, the nettle sting an angry red blotch.

"Well," Matthew broke the silence. "What brings you here, my Venus? Such a lonely, and apparently dangerous, place." He gave her a wolfish smile.

"I thought—" she began, but he was swiftly behind her, one hand on her neck, one bringing her left arm painfully behind her back. His breath was sweet with whisky, his tongue warm where it met her ear.

"Venus," he whispered. "This isn't a safe place. You oughtn't be here." He kissed her cheek and her neck, pushing her face against the rough stone, pressing himself against her, his body imprisoning her arm.

The world was slow. Pain throbbed in her wrist and shoulder and she felt herself sinking into the dim acquiescence that had allowed her to continue loving Gerard even through the abuse. Was it always this way? Passion fluttered on the edge of the pain, but as she felt a trickle of blood upon her cheek where her face had rubbed the stone, the desire died. In its place, suddenly, was a grey and numbing fear. This was not Gerard. She did not belong here, not now, not like this. She squeezed her eyes shut as she felt Matthew rub against her. He was speaking but the words were formless.

His hand groped around her waist, unfastening the button of her loose trousers. She heard his sigh as his hand found the warmth between her legs. A cry rose in her throat.

"Do you want me then, Venus? Will you make it so very easy?" His voice was an engaging whisper, a quiet laugh. "I thought you might give me more of a challenge. But then you *innocent* girls are all the same." Matthew's Dublin accent became thick and slurred. His hand was rougher in its touch.

"No!" Her cry was muffled, eaten by the stone pressed against her mouth. "Stop!" It was the futile plea of a victim; she knew Matthew, like Gerard, would not stop until the blackness inside of him was satiated, his own sense of power briefly restored.

"It's past time for that," Matthew answered, his voice low. One hand pulled her trousers and panties down, while the other, gripping her neck, pinned her against the stone.

Venus began to struggle, the wind a shocking cold against her stomach and thighs. Was it this easy, then, to lose control of your own life, of what happened to you? Had Gerard felt this powerless at the moment of his death? Had he struggled against paralyzing fear, limbs and voice unresponsive, mind drifting in dazed disassociation?

"No!" she cried again, and turned her head painfully against the stone. She saw Teke before Matthew did, saw in slow motion the dog launch his tawny body toward Matthew's shoulder. In a second Matthew fell back, Teke's jaws closed upon his shoulder.

"Teke!" Venus called, tugging up her trousers. The dog pulled away, his face an angry snarl. A bass note of warning growled from his throat.

"Jesus Christ!" Matthew rolled away instinctively. He pushed himself to standing. "Cunt! What are you playing at? Keep that fucking animal off me or I'll kill him!" Matthew's eyes were slits.

Venus felt a serpent of anger uncoil itself at last, deep in her belly. "Get away from me. Leave this place. Leave *my* place. Or I'll let him tear you to pieces." Her voice was thick grey ice, melting underneath with flame.

Matthew's shoulder bled. His jumper was torn. He took a step toward her and Teke lunged, his hackles high, mouth drawn back in grotesque anger.

Matthew backed away. "I wouldn't have it be this way, Venus. I thought you fancied me," his voice sank to a whisper. "You know you do." He stepped back, hand behind him to guide his way around the stones. "I'll see you again, *love*. You'll beg me next time." He turned and strode away.

Teke followed, a low growl in his throat. Venus sank to her knees against the sanctuary wall. The nettles grew thick. She gathered the waving plants in her hands, and sunk her face into the leaves. She felt the welcome sting as she rubbed the leaves against her face, let the burning warmth fill her nose, cover her lips and neck and throat.

The leaves of the sycamore twisted gray and green in the climbing wind.

CHAPTER SIXTEEN

The wind sped across the sky. Kate saw the clouds billowing and rising, tumbling over each other on the north horizon. Her vision blurred and she blinked; the clouds were like the flying horses of Odin's Valkyries, speeding in with dark bellies toward the Mainland. Kate blinked again and looked down into the sink. Her hand held a soapy scrub pad and the plate she had just used. She shook her head and finished washing the plate, setting it on the drain board to dry. She picked up her teacup. Something was niggling in her mind, an unhappy pinprick of memory.

"What is it now, what is it?" she crooned to herself. She needed to re-member. Seeing the Wild Hunt on the horizon was an omen of trouble. "*One, two, three, four, let me find the open door. Down memory's lane let me walk, hear time's stones of ages talk.*" Kate chanted the rhyme to jog her memory. There was something that her visit with Emily two days before had triggered. More than the apprehension for Emily's own situation, but... or was it something Venus had said, last night?

Kate cried out as the thin china cup in her hand shattered to pieces. Blood ran over her fingers. She turned the cold tap on full strength and let it run. But the pain was secondary to the dread in her heart.

Quickly she bandaged her hand in a tea towel, leaving the broken cup in the sink. She muttered, pacing the length of the kitchen. She had to see Morag. A telephone call wouldn't do. She must go to Morag's farm. Kate rummaged in a small basket on the counter for the keys to her ancient Morris. Her hand shook as she withdrew the keys, and they dropped to the floor. Kate's breath came fast as she stooped to pick up the keys, and as she rose dizziness overcame her. She set the keys on the counter, steadying herself with her good hand.

"I'm better to walk. I'll go by way of the doocot," she whispered. "Yes, that will be much better. But first I've got to see to this hand." A quick rummage in her rag bag produced a piece of flannel and a strip of muslin to bind it with.

Kate grabbed her shawl from over the kitchen door, and walked away from the house, wind whipping the fringe of the wrap against her face. She would take the long way round to Morag's, and thus avoid meeting anyone on the lane, unlikely as that was. On the way she could stop for a few quiet moments in the comforting shadow of the old beehive-like building that sat on her land. The structure dated from centuries past, and it had been her own sanctuary for fasting and worship for more years than she could remember.

Kate's bones cracked as she scrabbled up the path. The hill was steep enough to hide the old buildings on the other side, and it winded her. Soon she came to the top and began down the other side, her eyes trained on the dovecote. She tripped and almost lost her balance. Kate admonished herself to slow down. She stopped for a moment and closed her eyes, holding fingertips to her forehead.

"Now, Kate, now, just think, think things through," she muttered. She drew in two deep breaths, steadying herself. She opened her eyes and made her way down the path to her sanctuary. The dovecote had been fitted with a new door, but otherwise was as it had been built hundreds of years before. Her regular presence there discouraged doves from nesting, but the inner dome still held the alcoves meant for the doves. Kate entered and stood inside the dim chamber, lit only by the central hole in the room that now allowed out the smoke of her full moon fires rather than flying birds. She had a pallet for resting and meditation—and if she were honest, more sleeping than meditating took place there now—and a table with her collection of objects that helped her personal rituals take shape. She hadn't shown Emily this place, despite the girl's interest in what she called "witchcraft."

"Huh," Kate said to herself as she breathed in the familiar smells of old stone and the frankincense she burned. "A romantic notion!" The idea of witches seemed absurd to Kate, who had never thought of honoring the lunar cycle, using plants, and delivering babies as something out of the way, unnatural. Of course some of the village women, friends since they were able to walk, formed deep alliances. And there were times, of course, when life called for special wisdom, ritual, or prayer. Like a birth. Or a death. Kate swayed a little in the dim light. But she had never thought of herself, of the others, as definable as *witches*. It was the natural ways they honored, not some hocus pocus of spells or sacrifices or bubbling cauldrons. Kate heard a little moan escape her throat. She felt disembodied and distant from herself.

"Here, now, Katherine. You get ahold of yourself and get on your way. There'll be no nonsense now. Do what needs to be done." She exited the dovecote and walked with slow but steady steps down the path toward Wickhouse Wood and the tracks beyond that led to Morag's farm.

CHAPTER SEVENTEEN

Venus was unaware of how long she knelt with the nettles. The sting of the leaves, at first so fiery, became comforting, a welcome distraction from the pain in her heart. Why did she call these men to her? What place did brutality have in her life? Was she so weak? She thought that after Gerard, she would never allow another man to touch her in any way, least of all with violence. But it had happened again. Had she asked for it? She *had* fancied Matthew; obviously he had sensed her attraction and decided to make the most of it. Why hadn't she seen him for what he was? She knew in her heart that his and Emily's relationship wasn't good—she had recognized herself in Emily's cringing manner and   eagerness to please. And what was it about her own personality that invited men to dominate her?

Venus hugged her knees, tucking her head into her chest like a child. She was repulsed, angry, ashamed. She could feel her face swollen with the nettle sting—it would last for hours; how would she explain herself to Kate? Her Gran had warned her away from Matthew. She had been right. How could he act so? Did he have no regard for Emily at all? For any woman? Venus felt a stab of pity for Emily. Pregnant with a child she didn't want, by a man who didn't love her. Venus forgot her anger and jealousy toward Emily, shuddered as tears worked their way to the surface again.

Life seemed incredibly complicated. She longed, for perhaps the first time, to be in a place where no one knew her, where she owed no explanations. But a dull ache spread through her chest at the same time, wishing for someone who wouldn't judge or admonish her that she could tell this story to. For she must not let Kate find out, nor Mary. Through the wrath of either, the entire village would know of Matthew's attack on her. And she couldn't stand everyone knowing, everyone with the question—did she ask for it? Was it her fault?

Teke, in position nearby, came to his feet with a low growl. Venus heard again the strains of whistled song and felt cold sweat dampen her back. She shrank against the wall of the sanctuary. Teke began to bark. Venus could not see the gate from where she sat, and knew that she was also unseen. Teke continued to bark; she wished he would stop and let her hide from whoever it was. But it had to be Matthew again, because who else would be here? Teke wouldn't bark at Kate, and no one   else—unless, the police? Oh, how would she explain herself to Sammy or Sergeant Crombie?

"There's a dog, now, what's the matter? Where's your mistress?" Finn's voice came friendly toward her. Teke ceased his barking but stood at attention at the corner of the crumbling wall, between her and Finn's approach. Venus wiped her eyes, thought about standing but leaned back against the wall instead, pulling her hair around her shoulders and neck.

"Venus? Are you here? Where's your mistress, Teke?" Finn's voice came closer, and then he was there, his shadow falling across the grass. "Venus, are you well?" He squatted down. "You look a sight. Are you all right?" His voice was soft and honest. She looked into his eyes.

A vision came to her, a swift, unfolding picture of a child in training pants, her skin white and fragile as the blue of her eyes. She sat alone on an unkempt linoleum floor that was cluttered with plastic toys. The vision was gone quick as it came, and Venus blinked away from Finn's warm, brown gaze.

"I—I'm not. No, I'm not well. I—" her voice was dry and stopped in her throat.

Finn sat down slowly, crossing his legs with a grimace. He did not come close to her, letting Teke settle warily between them. He pulled his jumper away from his neck.

When he didn't speak, Venus closed her eyes. Here was a stranger, almost, and she felt an overpowering desire to disclose what had happened. She didn't care what Finn thought, and in her heart she knew somehow that he held a similar pain to her own. "I . . .someone . . . I've just been . . . attacked. Oh, God." She held her stomach as it twisted.

"What?"

She opened her eyes at Finn's voice and sharp intake of breath.

"What do you mean? Fuck's sake, woman. Are you all right? Shall I get the police? Take you to hospital? What—" He was on his feet extending a hand toward her. Teke growled.

"No, no. Please," she gestured weakly, suddenly tired of everything, all the illusions of life. "Sit—would you sit with me?"

Finn stared at her a moment. She saw kindness there, and, yes, pain. She looked past him to the sycamore, felt a bitter taste rise in her throat. Finn sat down, rubbing his face.

"Aye, I'll do whatever you like. Whatever helps. *Can* I help you?"

Venus pressed her hands to her face, feeling the puffiness of the nettle sting. At the same time, Finn asked, "What's happened to your face?"

"It's the nettles," she answered. "I rubbed my face in them."

"But why—" he began, and stopped. He picked up a small stone from the ground and began to tap it against another larger rock embedded in the grass. Teke watched him, still sitting up between them.

Venus welcomed the silence, surprised at how comfortable she felt in Finn's presence. She knew clearly in that instant that he would never hurt her or anyone, despite his jaded manner or casual talk about all the violence he'd seen in his life.

She watched the clouds move across the sky. She remembered her and Kate's conversation the night before, her Gran's reference to Lorraine. A born victim, Kate had said. And her face, as she had described Lorraine to Venus, realizing how similar the two were. Did Kate see *her* then, as a victim? What in Lorraine's past caused Kate to think of her as such? Had Lorraine's husband been brutal in the short time they had been married? Venus had seen sadness in Kate's face, as if she somehow had, in that moment, resigned herself to her granddaughter's own lack of strength. Anger rose like a spike in her belly. She placed her palms on the ground, feeling the cold stability of the earth.

"Matthew," she said, breaking the silence. "Matthew was here and he tried to—he attacked me." Her voice was flat, stone under deep water.

"Fuck me," Finn whispered, and his face colored immediately the words were out of his mouth. "Jesus Christ," he amended. "Fuck. Did he—are you—that fucking bastard!" Finn covered his face with a hand.

"He didn't . . . Teke stopped him. I think he was drunk."

"But what was he doing here? Did he surprise you, or—"

"He was here," she said, patting the ground, "when I came in. I heard him whistling. But I thought . . . I thought . . ." she couldn't finish, couldn't tell Finn that it was somehow Gerard she had been expecting to see. "I came in," she said, struggling for calm, "to find out, to see what I felt. To see what it felt like *here*. Because this is a sacred place to me." How could she explain?

Finn was still rubbing his forehead with a hand. Venus saw his nails were clipped and neat, the fingers blocky but smooth.

"I never thought," Finn said to himself. "I just never thought." He looked up at Venus. "I'm sorry, Venus. God, the bastard." He stopped speaking and Venus watched his face. He was struggling to say something.

"I should have warned you," he said, voice low. Finn looked away from her. "I just didn't think it was anything, just talk, you know? But Friday I was in the pub with him and he said, well, he said that he fancied you. But I didn't think—"

"You aren't responsible," Venus said.

"But I should have known. He was on about women being whores and how he'd beat Emily senseless if she—anyway, he was full of his own and how he'd know if any woman was going behind his back . . . what a laugh! And Emily at it with Gerard the whole time. And now this, it makes me think—" Finn stopped speaking, his face burning bright crimson.

Venus stared at him. Her mind worked to take in what he had said. Of course she knew that Emily had something with Gerard. Of course she did. She had just told Sammy about it after all. But to have Finn confirm it! How did he know? Had he seen them? Had one of them confided in him?

"What do you mean?" Venus asked, her voice a ragged croak.

"Oh, fuck. Fuck. I'm sorry. Jesus. I just don't think, sometimes, of what I'm saying."

"Well, you've said it. Tell me what you mean. I knew anyway," she added.

Finn winced as he met her eye then looked away. "She just said something to me, is all. She didn't say for sure, but I put it together. I might be wrong. Anyway, I don't think Matthew knows. He's full of shite."

"No," Venus said clearly, "no, Emily and Gerard knew each other. I saw them together. And I knew then. But it was after . . . after us." It was pathetic, this need to save her now nonexistent pride. She began to wish for Finn to leave. "She's pregnant," Venus blurted out. "And she's afraid of Matthew. So he might know. Maybe that's why . . ." She looked away from Finn, lifting her hand to stroke Teke's silky fur. The sycamore was still in a sudden cessation of the wind. The sun felt hot and she smelled the strong, green odor of the nettles.

"Is she, right enough? Is she?" Finn was quiet. After a moment he put his hand to his eyes again. "Did you know that Matthew had cancer when he was a wee boy?"

"No. How do you know that?"

"He told me one night when we were talking. A week or so ago. I saw him in the pub. I was telling him about me brother's kid, for some reason, that he'd had cancer but they'd treated it and he was fine. Oh—the hospital in Dublin, that's how it came up. Matthew worked there. Anyway," Finn waved a hand, "that doesn't matter. He said that he'd been there too, as a boy, for a cancer in his stomach. He said he'd had radiation and the whole mess. But that it was fine."

Venus looked at Finn blankly. She couldn't understand the digression of the conversation. She felt far away, absurd. Why were they talking about Finn's nephew in Dublin?

"It's nothing," Finn said in response to her quizzical stare. "I had just wondered about it running in families, and—because of my Una—and, fuck, never mind. It isn't important." But Finn's face wore a look of unease. "Listen, do you want to talk to Sammy? Shall I walk you up to your house?"

"No. I don't want to talk to anyone—yet. I'm not sure it would do any good."

"But it does! Don't you see that the fact he's been, that he—well, don't you see that it shows he's capable of violence? Venus, in my books he's a prime suspect for Gerard's death. You've got to tell Sammy what's happened, because it proves that Matthew is violent and unpredictable. And he's got motive. *I* can vouch for that. I wasn't ready to say anything, but, Christ, he's fucking crazy and a drunk besides. Now that I know about Emily's pregnancy, well, I've got to tell Sammy what I know. Can't you see that even if we can't charge him with any wrong done to you—and I'm not saying we can't—at least the motive for killing Gerard will be clear."

Venus cringed at the words. She didn't understand what Finn was saying. "I don't want to say anything. It's *my* affair. I don't want the entire village knowing. Or Gran. Because she—"

"Venus, I'm sorry, but it doesn't matter what you want. If Matthew killed Gerard—and who else would have?—don't you want him convicted? Do you want him free to kill or—or attack you—again? My God—"

"But I don't understand," she said, thrusting her chin out. "Why are you so convinced that he's killed Gerard? Because he attacked me?"

"No, not alone that, but don't you see? A man who's had radiation as a child is often sterile. *Matthew can't make anybody pregnant.* He told me himself. It's what the doctors told him."

Venus thought of her Gran and Emily's conversation that she'd overheard. Emily's distress. But could it be possible? Could Emily be carrying *Gerard's* child? Venus squeezed her eyes shut as a new, bright pain tore at her belly and chest. "Oh." In among the sharpness of this new grief, the serpent stirred, a gleam of anger. "All right. All right. I'll tell Sammy."

Finn let out a breath. Silence stood between them. Venus heard the low drone of the ferry. A fat, lumbering bee paused on the petals of a ragged robin growing high on the wall near her face. Gerard had hurt her; Matthew had hurt her. And maybe he had killed Gerard. Fine. Let it be done. The serpent inside of her rose, edging away trauma and grief. Let Gerard be dead, let his killer be found, let her move on, away from the dark pool that threatened to drown her.

Venus turned her face to Finn. His look was distant, gaze trained over the far west wall to the sea. Venus' mind was filled again with the image of the pale, blue-eyed child. The girl was in a dining room, beyond her a glass door led outside. She sat inside on the floor with a stuffed lamb. Her face was crumpled with tears, eyes afraid. There was a woman, with black hair . . . she was smoking in a large public garden. Venus squinted at Finn. She realized that she knew him not at all.

"Your little girl is alone, Finn. She's alone and she's crying."

CHAPTER EIGHTEEN

Kate stood at the door to Knowehouse. It was painted a dark green, a fresh coat by the looks of it, too. The doorknob was in the middle of the door, in the old tradition. Kate knocked for the second time, louder. She waited. No sound came from inside. She made her way around the house. Morag stood in the back, axe flying to split a weathered board in two. The ground around her was littered with fragments of wood, and nearby a stack of haphazardly split planks attested to a morning's work. Morag didn't stop when Kate approached, merely served her an unfriendly glance.

Kate stopped when she reached the stack of lumber. She reached out a hand to feel the smoothness of the old, time-sanded wood.

"What's this, then?" Kate asked.

"None of your affair," Morag replied, and stood straight, axe resting lightly in her hand.

"Looks like a bit of flooring. Renovating, are you?" Kate glanced toward the house. "It's lovely old wood, can't see why you wouldn't stick with it, your time of life."

"It's my property. I'll do what I like."

Kate saw beads of sweat line the pale fuzz of Morag's upper lip. "You ought to have that strong lad of yours in to do this for you."

Morag considered Kate a moment and resumed splitting the boards.

"Well?" Morag said after a time. "What's brought you here, Kate?

"I have some cause for worry," Kate said slowly. "I think that Emily Haworth might have information about something that concerns us both. I think you'd better listen."

"You always did think you could tell me how to act, what to do. Why should I listen to you? I did once too often and it was the ruin of my life. I've nothing to say or hear from you. Leave me be."

Twists of gray brown hair fell from Morag's braid. Her forearms were brown and leathery under rolled up shirtsleeves. Morag, like her brother Peter, had aged remarkably well. As had she herself, Kate thought. There was a lot of life left for all of them. Future, not the past. Kate felt powerful energy pumping in her veins. Morag *would* listen to her.

"Lilith," Kate said softly, using the spiritual name she had given Morag long ago. "It concerns the circle. We're the only two left now. I think old evil is calling, and it is time to set it right."

"Don't you call me that," Morag hissed. "You lost that right sixty years ago when you took *my* life into your hands." She plunged the axe into the tree stump that she had split the boards upon.

"Once we are bonded in sisterhood, that is never broken. You know that. No matter what we feel for each other now, we are bound to protect each other." Kate began to drift toward the back door of the house, moving slowly by Morag's fire pit in which she burned yard debris and trash. It was empty, swept clean. She looked behind her and was startled by the intense anger that flew to her in Morag's gaze. But she shouldn't be. The women had been enemies longer than they had ever been friends. Morag rolled her shirtsleeves down with an angry gesture. She muttered under her breath and followed Kate into the house.

Kate took a seat at the kitchen table. The floor of the kitchen was a new, cheap lino, still gleaming with its factory sheen. Morag stood a moment and then sat down opposite. Kate held up her hand, palm flat. Morag looked at her wordlessly, fire blazing in her eyes. Kate waited, would wait all afternoon if she had to.

Morag's hands remained still on the table, but her entire being pulsated with visible rage.

The two women sat in silence a while longer. Kate felt no fear at Morag's hostility, only sadness. After so many years, had Morag still not come to terms with the past? Had she learned nothing? No acceptance? No forgiveness?

"We did what we felt right at the time," Kate said, as if to answer an unspoken question.

Morag said nothing.

"Emily told my Venus something. She told Venus that she had seen Lorraine's old journals. And that there had been references to the circle." Kate paused. "Well. You know what she was for writing things down. In that time of trouble she was having, I've no doubt she recorded it all in her diaries. Never thinking, I'm sure, that they'd find their way into strangers' hands. Strangers who would read them and take an interest." Kate watched Morag's face. It remained perfectly blank. "Do you understand what I'm saying?"

"I was a fool once, and young," Morag replied. "But I'm neither now. I don't know what you think Emily knows about anything. I'm surprised you care. But perhaps *you* still feel the shadows of the past?" Morag's voice was sharp, stinging.

"I'll never be free of what's been done. But I've learned from it and I believe that the gods have given my penance. Hamish, Cora . . ." Kate spoke the names softly and looked at her gnarled hands. What was she doing, stirring up the past, swimming in this current of old sorrows? "But my life is beyond saving. Whatever judgment is coming, I'll see it soon enough. I've done what I can with Venus, to raise her not to judge. But—"

Morag let out a humorless bark of laughter. "You're a fool, Kate, and you've raised Venus to be one as well. Do you think it *matters*, what you think or how you try? What we *do*, that's what counts. Actions. It is only what is *done* that matters. And what's done is done." Morag's hand balled into a fist. "You may believe that the good you've done erases the evil, but that isn't true. Your ignorance—no, your *denial* of that fact influenced and damaged the lives of three women, not to mention Thierry—"

"Enough!" Kate commanded. "We all agreed! We—"

"No! *You* decided and we followed. Two girls not old enough to know better and Lorraine, well, she was in no state to deny your wishes. I won't take responsibility for your actions, Kate. If Emily comes to my door with secrets she thinks she's found, I'll send her straight to you."

"I'll not have Venus suffer more because of me. We took our oaths of loyalty and silence. It must stay that way and end with us."

"Do you know how you sound? An old woman living in the past. Some pathetic notion of loyalty! Oaths! We were playing, Kate, playing at the "old ways", playing at magic. But it was a game. It was never real. I owe you nothing. As you said, we're the only two who know. My word against your own. I'll not bow to you again. *You* bear the weight. Now get out of my house." Morag stood.

Kate rose. Her hands shook and she felt the dampness of sweat under her arms. Morag turned and strode out of the kitchen. Kate watched her walk into the rear yard. "But Lorraine knew," Kate whispered. "And I know she wrote—and thereby speaks—the truth." Kate shook her head. She wiped her face with the soft end of her shawl. It came away wet and Kate was surprised at the tears that bathed her face. Quietly she left the kitchen, walking through the stale orderliness of Morag's sad rooms to let herself out the front door. She looked west and saw Rousay rising large behind New Farm. She felt a surge of love for Venus, a fierce animal warmth rising inside of her. She would not let Venus down, would not allow her grand-daughter's fragile belief in good to be shattered. Kate set her lips as she let herself out of Morag's gate. No. A bargain must be struck with Emily. Kate nodded with satisfaction. She knew exactly what to do.

CHAPTER NINETEEN

Finn lowered himself onto the sand. He lay flat, letting his head fall back onto the grainy warmth. The wind couldn't reach him here, positioned as he was between the northwestern headland and a large outcrop of rock that marked the end of the beach. It was a cozy spot, and fairly hidden; only ten feet or so lay between the rock and the slight overhang created by the headland. Above him was the embankment of the high street, which dead-ended in a dirt pile at the base of the headland. From there the footpath took off leading to the McNeill's farm. Halfway up the path there was the rough wooden bench where he had sat with Sammy yesterday. Tomorrow he would ride the blue bus into Kirkwall, tell Sammy what he knew about Neill Leach. And what he knew about Matthew.

Finn kept his eyes shut against wayward grains of sand. Against the red-black backdrop of his eyelids, he drifted into abstract visions of shifting shapes and colors, a kaleidoscope of meaningless forms. The clouds moved swiftly across the sun, alternately placing him in light or shadow. His thoughts were fuzzy. What should he say about Emily wanting to get into Gerard's flat? He didn't like the idea of giving that information to Sammy, though he barely knew Emily and certainly owed her nothing. But he felt sorry for her; recognized in her all the women he had known who let their husbands or boyfriends abuse them. His own ma—well, he knew now that she had taken the blows to keep his da away from him and his siblings. Why were things this way? He had never in his life hit a woman, never even been tempted to, even when he was really on the drink. And he had always partnered himself with strong women. Women who would never stand for a man's violence against them. Perhaps that had been the attraction to Nuala. She was from a wealthy Protestant family in Belfast, educated in London, beautiful. Everything he wasn't, in fact. Growing up in the Catholic slums . . . then shuffled off to his aunts in Eniskillen when his da finally put his ma in hospital. Belfast had called him back, for University and his career. He loved the city, felt an ache in his heart for the troubled streets and familiar buildings. The noise, the buzz, the feeling of something happening.

Finn smoothed his hands over the sand, moving his arms to make angel's wings. He was neither warm nor cold. He felt the support of the earth beneath him, strong but impartial. *Well, something's happening, now, sure, and you're right in the middle of it.* He must think what to do about Emily. Would it be enough to tell Sammy about Matthew's violent assertions—both in word and action—and corroborate Venus' story? Or should he tell Sammy that he knew Emily must be carrying Gerard's child? Of course, he didn't *know* that for sure, it was an assumption both he and Venus had made. But it seemed unlikely she would be having more than one casual affair while her boyfriend was on the island. From what little he knew of her, Emily hadn't seemed the type to have casual affairs at all. Appearances deceived, however, how well he knew that. Nuala—but no, he must force his thoughts away from her and from Una. The best thing he could do would be to tell Sammy all he knew; the sooner he was free of the investigation the sooner he could leave and pick up the pieces of his life. What would—

"Whore!"

An angry voice shot through the spiral of Finn's thoughts. He sat up quickly, head spinning. He squinted against the morning light.

"You're wrong. You don't know what's been happening, what I've been through. You never know. You never give a fuck!" A female voice, mottled with sobs.

Finn looked around. He looked up; there was no one on the headland, but he realized that he couldn't see the bench from where he lay. He thought the voices came from there. Either the arguers couldn't see him either or they didn't care. Finn was embarrassed for them, but the reporter in him raised its curious head. The voices were familiar but he couldn't quite place them.

"Ouch! Stop it, leave off! Matthew!" The woman's voice came shrill.

Of course. A mental picture of the voices' owners clicked in his mind. Emily and Matthew. He half rose. It sounded as though they were having a proper row.

"You fucking whore!"

There was a muffled scream of protest. Then Matthew's voice came again.

"You're no better than shite. Shite! How many other old buggers have you spread yourself for? Lying whore! "

Jesus! Will you fucking leave off, ya bastard? Finn's face was red with fury and shame for Emily. He was still on his knees. He felt he must rise now and let them know he was there, but he wanted to spare Emily the humiliation she would feel knowing someone had overheard their argument. Maybe she would think he couldn't hear them, and he could just walk away. As he started to stand he heard the sickening thud of a body taking a punch.

"Christ!" he shouted, lowering himself instinctively, then jumping to his feet. He expected to see either Emily—or Matthew—crumpled on the ground. But what he saw shocked him: the sight of a couple in a passionate embrace. Matthew and Emily's mouths were fastened hungrily on each

115

other. Matthew hands were buried in Emily's hair, and Finn could see Emily gyrating against him. Finn stood openmouthed. Had he not just heard the most bitter of arguments? As Matthew moved his hand away to her breast, Finn could see Emily's left cheek was red and beginning to puff. Finn watched, fascinated, as Matthew turned Emily in his arms, fumbling with his trouser zip and rucking up Emily's long cotton skirt as she leaned forward against the back of the wooden bench. A wave of voyeuristic desire passed through him, and he struggled a moment to tear his gaze away. Disgust and shame replaced desire as Finn dropped to the ground.

Jesus, Jesus, man. Finn crawled to the steep side of the headland. He pulled himself up against the rough, cold stone and pressed his face against it. Shadowing the vision of what he had just seen, Nuala's naked back and hips, sitting astride her lover, flashed into his mind. He heard Emily's cries from above, a mix of despair and passion. His own voice echoed in his memory, begging Nuala for lovemaking after their vicious arguments, sadness mixed with satisfaction when she'd let him take her in the kitchen or against the bathroom wall. Pain tore at his gut. Too close to home, too like home . . . this wasn't someone else's culture, someone else's problem. Not violence on a scale he could distance himself from. Finn's lips formed the words of a well-worn prayer, a talisman against human cruelty.

CHAPTER TWENTY

Venus reclined in the shabby, upholstered rocker, cheek leaning against the delicate arch of Liv's foot. She blew on the pink toes, and the girl squealed with laughter.

"Hold still," Venus smiled, "if you move, you lose, and I'll get your sticky buns."

"Or *you'll* lose, getting a kick in the jaw for your trouble." Sammy laughed from his position on the sofa. "She's too old to sit on your lap now anyway."

Liv ignored her father. She was tiny and compact like him, with dark curly hair and an elfin sense of humor. Venus blew again on the girl's toes and felt her quiver with suppressed giggles. She grabbed Liv's ankles and pulled her feet away from her face, looking down at the girl balanced on her lap.

"Your da's right, Livvie. I don't think you'll fit on my lap much longer." Venus rolled the girl gently onto the floor.

Liv sprang up and ran into the kitchen where Mary was making breakfast. Her brother, Ferg, looked up from his comic book, headphones cloaking him from the tiresome world of his little sister and the adults. Venus rocked in the recliner. The sun was losing ground against scurrying clouds; the light from the windows flickered over the room like a dance.

"Mary, won't you let me help?" Sammy called laconically into the kitchen.

"Keep away, you," Mary called back. "I like to cook, remember? If you come in, then I have to leave. It's crowded now with just me and Liv." Her voice was happy and light.

Sammy shook his head. "That woman," he muttered fondly.

Venus took in the room. It was small but clean, crowded with the things of family life; toys, books, bills, keys. An upright piano sat against one wall, a bunch of dried flowers tossed across the top. Sammy had inherited the instrument from his mother. Though none of them played, Venus knew he kept it because of his mum. And there was hope that Liv might start, Fergus having disregarded music for rugby and fishing.

"No crime solving today, then, Sammy?" Venus rolled her head over the back of the chair to look in his direction. The woolly fabric rubbed her neck. She breathed slowly, through the churning in her stomach. She had gladly come, at Mary's invitation, to share a lazy Sunday breakfast. It was her and Sammy and the kids' only day off together; how could she ruin Mary's happy mood and Sammy's first chance to relax in three days with her story about Matthew? But she had promised Finn, promised herself.

"I've got the lads poring over every inch of Gerard's life. There's been a forensic team up from Inverness to go over his car and conduct a fingertip search of his flat in Stromness, and we're still waiting for results from that. Crombie will call if anything turns up today."

"You found his car?" Venus' voice was small.

"Aye, we did, right away, at Wickhouse Wood. He'd made no attempt to hide it." Sammy ran a hand over his short hair. "I'm speaking to Finn tomorrow about a possible connection to Neill Leach, but we've already interviewed everyone Gerard currently worked with. Shining example of a man according to all his staff. No, we've really no strong suspects. *You* have an alibi," he smiled, "and honestly, Venus, you are the one with the most obvious motive to kill him."

"Sammy!" Mary warned from the kitchen.

Venus pulled at the long ends of her hair, squeezing her throat against coming tears.

"I'm sorry, but it's true." Sammy's tired voice held a defensive note. "Look," he said, raising himself up on the sofa, "almost all murder victims are killed by people who know them. Gerard's was definitely not a random killing, so out of the way, like. No, he went to that churchyard to meet someone. He came up from Stromness, parked his car at the gravel verge at Wickhouse Wood, and *walked* up to the spot. Two miles. Crossing *your* farm. Which implies that he was meeting someone he knew, that he—"

"If we're going to talk about this," Mary said from the kitchen door, throwing Sammy a meaningful look, "I think it's best if the kids go watch telly in our room."

Ferg looked up from his spot on the floor, suddenly hearing past the headphones blaring music into his ears. He sat up as Liv darted out of the kitchen.

"*Little Mermaid*," she shrieked. "I'll get there first!" She thumped down the hall and Ferg followed, racing to beat her for his own choice of film.

Sammy rose with a sigh from the sofa and picked up the small TV/VCR combination from its stand in the corner of the living room. He carried it down the hall, admonishing that *he* would choose the movie.

Mary stood in the doorway, a wooden spoon in hand. The sweet, yeasty smell of baking drifted in and surrounded Venus with an odd feeling of comfort, despite her apprehension.

"Are you up to this, V? It's meant to be a day off for us all. I guess Sammy just wants to process a little. He often does, you know. That's why I know more than I ever wanted to about everyone and their vices here." She tried a smile.

"I don't know," Venus answered. She still didn't want to talk to Mary about what had happened with Matthew. But Sammy would probably tell her anyway; it was better, perhaps, to just get it out.

Mary retreated to the kitchen and then brought out oversize mugs of coffee for herself and Venus. She sat on one end of the sofa. Her face looked drawn and tired too. Venus realized again what a strain Mary's life had become, though she believed that Mary enjoyed herself most of the time. Gerard's murder had touched everyone's life, perhaps, not just her own.

Sammy returned from the bedroom and fetched himself a cup of coffee. He sat by Mary, reaching one arm around to rest on the back of the sofa.

"As I say, I think he had a rendezvous with someone he knew, and didn't want his car to be seen close to the spot. Anyway, there's nowhere to park closer except your farm, or to drive down the track itself—which he wouldn't have done with his flash car. I've never seriously regarded you as a suspect; if he was coming to see you, then why not just come up the drive?"

Venus wondered at the times Gerard had left her the 'anonymous' gifts. How had he managed to come to the churchyard or her garden without someone seeing? She shuddered, suddenly finding the thought of him sneaking around in the night frightening, obsessive.

"No," Sammy continued, after a sip of coffee, "I can't figure who he would have met, unless it was Emily. And her Matthew has kindly provided her with an alibi for the time. I don't know, though. They were both nervous when I questioned them—especially Emily. My gut told me they were lying, but I can't prove it. What I can't figure is why he'd protect her if he knew she was having a fling. He seems the jealous type to me."

Venus looked at her hands, clenched and cold in her lap. She heard the rhythmic tick of the timer in the kitchen, the strains of cartoon voices drifting down the hall.

"Then maybe it's Matthew you should suspect," Mary said. "Maybe he found out about their affair—"

"*If* they had one, which I can't prove either, and she denies," Sammy pointed out.

"Well, he may have known anyway. He could have somehow lured Gerard to the churchyard with a note, pretending to be Emily."

Sammy looked at his wife with a small smile. "You watch too much telly, Mary. It's never usually that complicated in real life." He paused and ran his hand over his hair again, and laughed to himself. "But then again, this is my first murder, so how would I know? All right, let's consider Matthew. He's a damn sight more likely to bash a man's head in—"

A small sound escaped Venus' throat. She closed her eyes.

"Jesus, I'm sorry," Sammy's voice held a mixture of contrition and impatience. "But—"

"No, it's all right. It's the truth. Someone beat his head in. It sickens me, but it's a fact, and I can't avoid the truth of that," Venus said, her voice low. She must say something now about Matthew. And what of her knowledge about Emily's pregnancy and connection to Gerard? She felt the words sticking like wood in her throat. Her hand went to the scrape on her face. She held her stomach.

"Well, it's more a man's crime," Sammy continued. "We found what looked like rust flakes in his—his—" Sammy glanced at Venus. "The postmortem results confirmed that, so we're looking for a tool—like a sledgehammer, spanner, or pipe. It takes a lot of strength to make a killing blow. But he was—there were multiple blows." Sammy finished uncomfortably.

"Are you all right, Venus?" Mary asked.

"I've got something to tell you, Sammy." Venus fingered the cut on her face. "It—it concerns Matthew." The name barely slid from her mouth. "He . . ." she took a deep breath. It was all right, she was among friends. "He attacked me yesterday."

There was a moment of stunned silence as Sammy and Mary stared at her, openmouthed. Then they were speaking together.

"*What?* When did this happen?" Sammy's voice was sharp.

"Venus. Oh, Venus, are you all right? What happened? Does Kate know?" Mary asked, her eyes full of shock and compassion.

Venus gulped in air. It was this she wanted to avoid, the well-meant concern, pity creeping into her friends' eyes. She leaned her head back on the scratchy wool of the chair. She narrowed her eyes, keeping tears in, and focused on the cracking plaster of the ceiling.

"Venus—can you talk about it? Do you need—?" Mary had risen and knelt now at her side. She placed her hand gently on Venus' arm.

"I don't want to talk about it," Venus said, surprised at the strength in her own voice, "but I will. Because I think Matthew, well, *Finn* thinks that Matthew may be Gerard's killer. So I need to tell you."

"Finn? When did you—how does he know about this? You told *him*?" Mary stared up at her.

"He came along right after it happened," Venus said, answering Mary's question. "I needed to tell someone. And it felt better to tell someone I didn't know, somehow."

Mary glanced at Sammy. "But isn't Finn a suspect, still? You told me he had no alibi for the time in question."

"Aye, and he doesn't. Finding the body doesn't make him the killer, although it involves him, sure. I haven't ruled either way on him, but he's no motive that I can find. The word from Belfast is that he's clean, no recent involvement with the police, no recent arrests."

"Implying arrests at some time, though?" Mary asked.

"Well, it's Northern Ireland. Almost every able-bodied man has some kind of troubles there. He's an IRA sympathizer, to be sure, but his record shows no actual illegal activity. He's on a watch list, Crombie said, because of his reporting background—revolutions and the like, I guess. But he's got a wife and kid, big family—"

"As if that makes a difference. You only have to watch the news and see how many terrorists and killers have families," Mary said, sitting back on her heels.

Venus let the conversation flow around her, glad for the chance to not speak.

"But Finn doesn't matter. Christ! Venus, please tell us what happened." Sammy leaned forward, elbows on his knees. "You said he attacked you. Did he hit you? Try to—was it sexual?"

Venus bit back laughter. It bubbled inside her. She knew that it was the shock, the darkness . . . if she started she would never stop. "Teke saved me. He jumped on Matthew and bit him."

"Good!" Sammy cried. "He'll have the dog bite, then. No denying it."

"I was in the churchyard. I went there to see how things were. I wanted to . . . Well, I walked in and I didn't see him until I got round the sanctuary wall, and there he was. He was whistling. I surprised him, I think. And it was—it just—" tears began rolling down her cheeks. "He grabbed me and pushed me against the wall. He smelled of whisky. He was whispering in my ear, and . . ." Venus struggled. Her face burned crimson.

"It's all right, love." Mary stroked her arm. "Take it slow. No one blames you. You're all right."

Venus grabbed Mary's hand in her own. She focused her gaze on the piano. Someone had written the names of the notes in marker on the ends of the keys. C, D, E. She was aware of Sammy writing, heard the scratch of his pen against paper.

"He bent my arm. I couldn't move. Then he . . . he pulled my trousers down and touched me . . ." She heaved a shuddering sob. The memory of Matthew's slippery voice, his hand moving against her contrasted horribly with the distant sounds of Liv's voice, bossing her brother in the bedroom.

Mary jumped as the timer from the stove went off. She hesitated, giving Venus' hand a squeeze, before rising to turn off the oven and the insistent timer.

"Then what happened?" Sammy asked.

"I was struggling, and I cut my face on the rock as I turned my head. I saw Teke and then he jumped. Matthew fell down and I—I got very angry.

Matthew yelled at me and I called Teke off. But I told Matthew to leave. He did, but he said, 'Next time you'll beg me,' or something like that."

"Bastard. I'm so sorry. Christ, but I'm glad he didn't—well, I'm glad you're all right."

Venus nodded, closing her eyes and giving in to tears. She heard Mary walk through and murmur to Sammy that she would just settle the kids with their buns and milk. She returned after a few moments and sat quietly on the sofa.

"Venus, I'm so, so, sorry. Did you tell Kate? Surely you didn't just go home and not say anything? What about your cheek?"

"I didn't tell Gran. I don't want her to know. I'm fine. I told her I slipped while I was swimming. She doesn't need to worry about me. She's been odd lately. Preoccupied, talking about the past a lot. I'm worried about *her*, actually." Venus paused. "No, I only told Finn, as I said, because he came along soon after."

"And what did he say? Why does he suspect Matthew of killing Gerard?" Sammy's voice was keen.

Venus felt heavy with all the knowledge she had. She wished there was a way to tell about Emily and her pregnancy and Matthew without speaking. She wasn't sure what she should reveal about Emily. She only knew about the pregnancy from overhearing a conversation she shouldn't have listened to. But now Finn knew, too. Venus didn't want to destroy Emily's life, didn't want to endanger her. She knew that Emily hadn't killed Gerard; no woman carrying a child could commit murder. Unless her life were threatened. Unless . . .

"Sammy, I know something about Emily that I shouldn't. I mean, I don't know it from *her*. But I told Finn, and because of that he thinks that Matthew—maybe I should let him tell you."

"No. Venus, this isn't a game. This is very, very serious. You've been attacked. A man's been killed. It's no time now to worry about gossip. Whatever you know, tell me. It's my job to follow it up and find out if it's true or not."

"That day, was it only Friday? The day I saw you at the churchyard. When I got home, Gran had a visitor in. It was Emily. And I heard them talking about Emily being pregnant."

"Is it Matthew's?" Mary asked. "Oh, God. Poor woman. No wonder she's looking half-dead and terrified lately."

Venus cringed. "Well, that's what I thought, and what she told Gran. But when I told Finn about it—and I don't know why I told him. I was angry, upset . . . So, when I told him, he said that it couldn't be Matthew's. Because Matthew had radiation for cancer when he was little and it made him sterile. I'm sure Emily knows that; obviously Matthew knows it."

"So is the child—who is the father?" Mary asked, her eyes betraying that she knew the answer already.

"I think it's Gerard's," Venus whispered. "I know they were having an affair, though as you say, Sammy, there is no real proof. Finn believes that they had a connection too. I don't know why," she added thoughtfully.

"So if Matthew knew about the baby, and somehow suspected the affair with Gerard, that is a powerful motive for killing him. Yes," Sammy said, tapping his notebook with a pencil. "And now Matthew has attacked *you*, which proves that he's capable of violence, aggression."

"Sammy," Mary shifted to the edge of the couch. "Is it possible that Emily is in danger? If he knows, and killed Gerard because of it, then what's to stop him from killing Emily?"

"Well, it depends on how his mind is working. If he loves Emily . . . I don't know." Sammy shook his head. "Maybe it was an accident—"

"Accident! No—" Venus sat up sharply.

"I mean, perhaps he had got Gerard to the churchyard somehow, and he was drunk. Maybe he was going to try and get some money out of him and things got out of hand. He killed him. Maybe he and Emily were in it to-gether. Perhaps Emily confessed to Matthew and they decided together to extort a little cash in exchange for saying nothing. Gerard was surprisingly well off. That would explain why I felt they were lying about their whereabouts Thursday night."

"Sammy, I don't believe they could kill a man—especially if Emily was in love with him—and then saunter down to the pub and play music all night. I saw Emily's face when she learned what had happened. She looked shocked," Mary protested.

"She was crying and arguing with Matthew out on the beach, after you left." Venus shook her head. "I don't think Emily had anything to do with it either. Anyway, I think she planned to abort the child. That's why she really came up to see Gran on Friday."

"Did she? *Did she?*" Sammy's voice was faraway. He stood and went in the kitchen.

Mary met Venus' gaze. Her eyes were full of sympathy and love. Venus felt a rush of gratitude. She had good friends and her Gran. She was loved, she was not alone—but Emily was. Venus surprised herself with the lack of rancor she felt. Emily was far from home, alone, and she had no one to comfort her. And, Venus felt sure, she was very much in danger.

CHAPTER TWENTY-ONE

Finn stepped off the snorting blue bus, nodding to the grizzled and gen-ial driver. He followed the pack of kids who also used Orkney's public transport to get to school across the street and watched them disperse to-ward the Safeway and the High street. He had listened to a group of four friends talking about the summer work they had with their family farms, shearing sheep, inoculating them, building fence to keep them in. There had been a friendly rivalry about who could shear the most in an hour. It sounded strange to him, city boy that he was, and he felt homesick for the buskers and shoppers and drunks of Belfast's busy streets. The lanes of Kirkwall were deserted by comparison to home, and he made his way to the police station without speaking to anyone.

Finn checked in with the Desk Sergeant and stood in the waiting area gazing at announcements for missing children on a notice board. He paced in the stale room. Suddenly it seemed imperative for him to get shut of this place, this island, the people here and their small, pathetic lives. He was indifferent to Gerard's death; the important thing was to return to *his* life, return to Una. Venus' words of two days before flashed in his mind. She said she had seen her, a red haired little girl. He hadn't believed it at fir-st—how could she know such things? But Venus had described Una, his kitchen, the fact that she was alone. He'd since been unable to contact Nuala; his ma hadn't seen her or Una. The knowledge that he did not belong on Orkney rose huge before him. Anxiety for Una that he had been pushing down deep roared into his gut. He took a deep breath and sat down, leaning forward with his head in his hands. After a moment he fished his mobile from his pocket and checked for any calls. Nothing.

"Mr. Ross, if you'll come along?" Sergeant Crombie stood at the check-in desk.

Finn rose and followed him down the now-familiar corridor to the interview room. The Sergeant showed him in and invited him to sit on one side of a scarred table. Finn settled into the only slightly more comfortable chair than the one he had just vacated in the waiting area. He was tired, his gut hurt, and he wanted a cigarette. His fingers picked at the dingy cuff of his Aran sweater. Crombie left; Sammy entered a few moments later. He placed a tape into the recorder on the table and stated the date, time, and the persons present. Finn felt a cold sweat begin under his arms.

"All right, Finn. Thank you for coming in. Let's get straight to it. I know you've been concealing some information about Emily Haworth, and I know that you have information about Matthew as well. I'm sure you understand that withholding information can be, in itself, a crime. Obstruction—"

"I've been holding nothing back. I had no information that I was sure of." *Keep your head, now. Keep it cool.* It wouldn't do to get on Sammy's bad side, not when all he wanted was to get off the island. "I'm happy to tell you everything I know about anyone, for any good it will do you."

"Fine, then. Let's start with Matthew."

Finn was glad to get the whole story out. He told Sammy about his conversation with Matthew in the pub, then Emily's desperate plea for help in the cafe. Finn also mentioned the fight between Matthew and Emily, and he described Venus' story as she had related it to him. He explained what Matthew had told him about the radiation treatments making him sterile.

"We'll get the doc here to confirm that, check his medical records in Dublin," Sammy said. "Venus is convinced that Emily must be carrying Gerard's baby. Do you agree? Did Emily say anything to you that would point to that?"

"Other than her need to get into his flat? No. I didn't know she was pregnant at the time. But it makes me wonder what she was really after. She told me, as I said, that he had some primary research materials of hers—"

"And what would that be?"

"Primary materials are those that are firsthand information. Like, oh, diaries, letters, original maps, a ship's log. You get the idea."

"Aye," Sammy said. "I wonder too. I'll need to ask her, you realize?"

"Right enough. She'll have to understand." Finn's words came out easily, but he felt a twinge of conscience at betraying Emily. She hadn't killed Gerard. She couldn't have. He just didn't think her capable.

Sammy settled back in his chair. He still looked tired, despite the fact that he said he had taken Sunday off. He wasn't saying much, and Finn wondered again how the investigation was progressing. Police work was slow, he knew that.

"What do you have to tell me about Neill Leach?"

"The *Telegraph* called and asked me to do a series," Finn began. "They wanted a few pieces for the cultural section. My articles ended up part of a group about music festivals in Britain. Not my usual line of work. But I was here, and I needed the money."

"So, you spoke to Neill first?"

"No, actually I talked with Gerard. As the Director of the Festival he was the logical source of information. Very smooth and professional, he was. He had been on the island just over two years. Before that he came from a teaching stint at London University, I think it was."

"Yes, we have that information. But go on."

"Aye, well. He's a very educated man, and a fine musician, which I expect you know. He taught in a folklore program, and music. Ethnomusicology was the word he used. The connection between music, stories, and how that tells about a culture. Very interesting, like."

"Similar to what Emily is working on, I think."

"Maybe. I don't know much about her studies. Just that she's hanging about asking questions all the time of the old folks." Finn paused to think. "Anyway, Gerard and I talked a few times. He's originally from France, but he told me he was born here. That was part of the reason he accepted the position to direct the Festival. Plus he had an eye for the chance, saw an opportunity to make more of a name for himself. That's what I think." Finn smiled.

Sammy's gaze remained serious. "Did he ever mention a connection between himself and Emily?"

"I've been racking my brains to remember that. I don't think so. I mean, he wouldn't have, would he? He was all business until our last interview, when he told me some of the personal details of his life. That was it."

"So he didn't refer you to Neill?"

"No. That's where the story gets interesting. I wanted to learn about the financial part, write a bit about how folks might organize their own festivals, on a smaller scale. I asked Gerard if I could speak to the Financial Officer. Gerard said they didn't have one, that he'd just been sacked. Wouldn't say another word about it or tell me who it was. I found out easily enough from the secretary and I rang him up. I went out to his house one Sunday, in Stromness. His mother was there—Morag."

"And . . .?" Sammy prompted.

"I started asking questions. Neill was uncomfortable, that was clear. Finally he told me that he'd been fired over some forged checks. Checks he swore he didn't write but Gerard produced with both their signatures; Gerard accused Neill of forging *his* signature. It was a case of the boss' word against the employee's, so Neill was let go."

"Neill spilled this information to you, just like that? Seems like an odd thing to tell a total stranger. And a reporter to boot. No one on the Festival staff that we interviewed had a word to say about this."

Finn shrugged. "Murder makes people nervous, they close the ranks, mind their own. As for Neill, well . . . his ma helped with the 'confession.' She sat down right in the middle of the conversation, eyes blazing, and told Neill to tell me what was really going on. What a crook Gerard was, and a liar. He squirmed a fair bit, but he's obviously under her thumb. Funny—he's a big man and all too. She was *mad*, I'll tell you." Finn smiled at the memory.

"She knew all about his troubles, then? Why would she call Gerard a liar?"

"Aye, seems that Neill had been pouring his heart out to her. To make a short story of it, Neill began to notice checks coming through for contract employees—that would be performers or guest teachers, for example—that he didn't remember. He overlooked it a while, since that area of the Festival wasn't his, and there were two signatures on every check, in this case Gerard's and the Event Manager's. Then there was the problem of some grant money being spent that was earmarked for operating costs. It was a lot of money, and Neill noticed large chunks were being spent and attributed to building expense. They were working on the new Festival Center—still are—and so he wasn't immediately suspicious. But he decided to double check some invoices for work done, and found that some were either missing, or there were two alike, that kind of thing."

Sammy sighed and rubbed his eyes. His face had a gray tinge. "Would you like a coffee? God knows I need another." His voice seemed friendly for the first time.

Finn shook his head. "I'd take tea if you had it."

Sammy called through the intercom for someone to bring in tea. He leaned back in his chair. "Neill must not have been the one processing the daily accounting, otherwise I'd think he would have noticed sooner."

"Aye, that's what I asked him. He had an assistant to do all that while he worked on the budgets, financial planning, and fundraising. He asked her about it, careful not to get the rumor mills going, and the checks were all in order, two signatures on every one. What finally tipped him off was when he saw checks with his own signature that he didn't remember signing. Neill swore that he reviewed every purchase before he signed for it. I don't believe that necessarily, but he's going to cover his own back."

"How long did he figure this had been going on?"

"I don't know. He was vague about that—I think that whether or not he is innocent of forgery and embezzlement, he's guilty of not paying attention. It was happening under his nose."

Sammy looked skeptical. "What are we talking, five hundred quid or thousands?" His glance moved to the door as Crombie came in with a tea tray. The Sergeant set down two chipped mugs, steel pot of hot water, and haphazard arrangement of biscuits, teabags, and instant coffee sachets on a plate, and ambled out of the room.

Finn helped himself to tea. "I gathered from his ma that it was thousands. Significant bits going out to all kinds of people or for all kinds of services, a lot of them from mainland Scotland or even London." Finn nodded at Sammy's raised eyebrows. "Very clever."

"Yes." Sammy's voice was thoughtful. He poured instant coffee and hot water into a mug. "When did Neill confront Gerard?"

"December. Gerard was cool as can be, I gathered. They went through the checks together, but when Neill produced the ones that he and Gerard had both signed—the ones that *Neill* didn't remember—Gerard claimed the same thing. Essentially he fired Neill for embezzlement. Told him that if he made a fuss he'd bring a lawsuit."

"So our boy Neill is professionally ruined and goes on the dole for his trouble." Sammy sipped his coffee with a grimace and grabbed a sugar packet. "A fine motive for murder, I'd say. But why wait six months to do it? Why not bring his own lawsuit for wrongful termination? Well, I'll go round and have a chat with him myself. Find out where he was Thursday last."

After a few more questions about his own background that he had already answered when he had found the body, Sammy stopped the tape and thanked Finn for his time. The interview was an odd mix of cold professional and tired friendliness, and Finn thought again that Sammy was out of his depth. And he still had no word on when he could leave the island.

Finn stepped out into the quiet street that bordered the police station. He thought for a moment about lunch, as it was getting on for noon. The interview had taken a long time. In the end he opted for a stop at the Safeway opposite the bus station, grabbing fags, a sausage roll, and bottle of iced tea. He ate absently in the bus parking area, sitting on a low concrete wall. Finn felt scoured inside, unhealthy, and vaguely sad. He smoked two cigarettes before the bus came.

Finn had his pick of seats, and he chose the back. He looked out the window, past the shadowy reflection of himself to the hardware store and Safeway. It was midday; buses going to other parts of the island, to South Ronaldsay, pulled into line. His own bus driver talked with another driver out the window. Two older ladies boarded the bus. The driver greeted them as old friends. A few moments later, the bus pulled away.

Finn settled in for the long ride. Though he was going fifteen miles at most, this bus ran along all the B roads. In an hour he would be home, forty-five minutes if he was lucky. The bus was quiet. The two ladies had pulled out their knitting and murmured to each other. Finn leaned his head against the window and surrendered to sleep.

He awoke as the bus lurched to a standstill in front of the small grocery in Blackstone. Finn swore; he had missed his road and now was a mile's walk away from home. He swung down from the bus. *Might as well have something to eat, since you've missed the fucking stop.* He looked down the High street. The hill beyond rose up, green with waving grass, cut by the path that he had run down only a few nights ago. The bench part way up was empty. He saw Emily and Matthew in his mind, the terrible scene from yesterday morning. Was Emily all right? How could she let a man fuck her like that, especially when she was carrying a child? It was beyond him. He felt sorry for her, felt sorry for Neill Leach. People who were weak, let others take advantage of them. He snorted. He was one to talk. But he hoped Emily was all right. Finn glanced at his watch. Half-past one. Perhaps he'd just go round and see her, invite her to tea. He had an idea that she might need someone to talk to.

CHAPTER TWENTY-TWO

Shyness swept over Finn, mixed with anxiety. The feeling of waiting on the doorstep on a first date. Only he wasn't waiting for a woman he loved, or was even sweet on. He was waiting for a woman whom he felt that he had betrayed. The street shone with rain. Matthew and Emily's rented flat was near the top of the town, in an old but freshly whitewashed building. He raised his hand to knock again, but the door opened a crack. Emily's grey blue eyes peered out. She registered surprise to see him.

"What do you want?" Her voice was flat.

"I'd like to talk to you. I've—we've got some things to discuss." Finn ducked his head, pulled his collar against the wind. He could see the ocean peeking between buildings two blocks down. He was about to speak again when she closed the door and unhooked the chain latch, letting him in.

They walked silently down a short hall into the sitting room. The air was stale. A bunch of flowers stood rotting in brackish water. Finn could hear a radio from another apartment, the thumping familiarity of BBC 1. They stood awkwardly a moment. Finn looked at Emily. Her face wore an ugly bruise, and her eyes were red and puffy.

"I fell," she said, before he could ask. "I fell on the rocks. At Evie beach. The seaweed was slippery."

It was a rehearsed speech and wouldn't have fooled him even if he hadn't heard her take the punch. "Matthew about?"

Emily hesitated and swallowed. "No."

"Good. Let's sit down." He pulled a packet of cigarettes and a lighter from his pocket. "Mind?"

She shook her head and sat on the edge of the sofa, hands folded in her lap.

Finn breathed in the smoke gratefully. He wouldn't mind a drink—he was sure there would be a bottle somewhere—but now didn't seem the time to ask. "All right," he said, almost to himself. "All right." He leaned back in the flowered chair, pulled a saucer half-full of stale ashes across the side table toward him.

Emily's eyes were wide. She looked sick. Finn fought the urge to stand up and leave, run from this pathetic girl and her situation. *Best cut to the chase, man. Get on with it.* "Emily, I've been talking to the police." "I've had to tell Sammy about your . . . interest in Gerard's flat. Now, don't fuss," he said, as she sank back against the sofa cushions, hand over her eyes. "Nobody thinks you've killed Gerard. But the police were bound to find out the connection. I had to tell them what I knew. In light of—" What should he tell her of Matthew's attack on Venus? "Listen, Emily, you need to get away from Matthew. He's dangerous."

A rough bark of laughter escaped her throat. She shook her head back and forth. "What do you know about it?" she finally asked. Her eyes were downcast. One hand patted her cheek, the other rested on her belly.

"Emily, I know you told the police that you and Matthew were together Thursday night, before you went to the pub. That's not true, is it? Why are you lying for him?" Finn leaned forward in the chair, stubbing his cigarette in the saucer.

"Because he asked me to," she said simply. She started to cry. "That's what you do for people you love. You do what they ask."

Finn expelled a breath. *Jesus.* But how different was this from his own situation? How much of his own life had he been living for himself? And how much for Nuala? And for what, and the end of the day? Not loyalty, not love in return, not his daughter, not any fucking thing. He shrank back into the chair.

Finn forced himself to focus on Emily's face. "Listen, I'm sorry for your troubles, but I've got my own heap of shite to deal with and I've a need to get off this island. Only I can't until Gerard's death is cleared up. *You* know something. You're covering up for Matthew, and you know something about Gerard, perhaps the thing that led to his death. It's time to find some guts, girl. If not for yourself, then for the wee one you're carrying."

Emily met Finn's eyes. She held his gaze; her eyes were clear. In them he read resignation, and perhaps, relief. Satisfaction surged within him; he recognized her need for confession.

"Matthew has gone to Stromness. But he'll be back soon, he promised me. I've got an interview later. He's coming with me." Emily looked vaguely about the room, as if Matthew might emerge from a cupboard or from behind a closed door. She took a deep breath, as if preparing to go underwater. "He was in Stromness last Thursday, too. He's been working with a woodworker there, making a guitar. He said he left at six and decided to stop at the Ring of Brodgar on his way home. He likes the standing stones. He didn't arrive home until around twenty minutes of nine. He said time got away from him. We left for the pub soon after; there were already plans for the session to start around ten. When we heard Gerard had been killed, he said we should give each other an alibi, just so the police wouldn't hassle us. So we wouldn't have to be involved." Emily gave another thin laugh. "Of course he didn't realize that we—that I—was already *involved.*" She fell silent.

Finn waited for her to start again. He knew she might tell him everything; it was clear that she needed someone to talk to. He just had to be patient. He let his breath come slowly, in rhythm, exhaling past the twisting discomfort of his stomach. The radio in the next flat fell silent. He looked not at her, but at the coffee table in front of him, stacked with notebooks and papers, evidence of Emily's ongoing work. He was aware of the wind pushing round the corner of the building and the distant screech of gulls.

"I've known Gerard for years. I met him in London, at the University. He was a professor for one of my classes. It was just social at first. Groups of us meeting, talking about our studies, hearing music. He was the one who encouraged me to do advanced study." Emily smiled sadly, eyes directed toward that other time. "We became lovers. It was discreet; it had to be. Then he went away, to France, on sabbatical. I thought we would keep on, but he didn't ever contact me. I didn't know where he was . . ." Her face contorted with the memory. She closed her eyes.

"I met Matthew while he was gone. In a pub. He was playing music. It was like a train smash, the two of us meeting. We—he—we got together that first night. I thought I could forget Gerard. I did, for a while. But he came back," she whispered, opening her eyes to stare past Finn. "He came back and found me. It was so easy. I was teaching as a graduate student. Our offices were on the same floor. We would meet . . . well, Matthew never knew. Neither one could get enough of me." She smiled.

Finn lit another cigarette. Emily was lost in the memories; he knew that for her he had disappeared. In a way she was talking to herself, working out what had happened. He felt a shiver of anxiety—but no, she wouldn't have killed Gerard. She wasn't going to tell him that.

"He left London again, this time to come here. He just sailed out of my life. Didn't even ask what *I* wanted. Things were getting difficult with Matthew. I knew he had other women, but I didn't care. *I'm* the one he loves . . . and it made things even, you know? I decided to redirect my thesis work, so I could come here. I had to *show* Gerard that he couldn't just leave me. I knew he was the one I wanted to be with. It took me almost two years but I came. I found him. I had been following his career, of course. I was so happy to see him again. He was surprised when I telephoned, but it was easy to make him see he needed me. Venus and he . . ." her voice faltered, "she didn't understand him. Didn't understand his needs." Emily's hand made smooth circles over her still-flat belly.

Finn wondered if she had gotten pregnant on purpose. He thought it likely. Her words held the ring of delusion; obviously she had made herself available for Gerard's easy use and didn't even see herself for what she was. Had Gerard loved her? Finn doubted that; it was more likely he enjoyed playing with her, liked the power he had over her. Matthew was the same. Finn shook his head as he exhaled a stream of smoke. He felt a crawling embarrassment for himself and Emily. He could see himself in the mirror she held up, see how they were the same. But he was angry now, at Nuala. Emily had never gotten angry with Gerard—or had she?

"Emily," his voice was soft, "who do you think killed Gerard?"

"I don't know," she replied. "I have an idea. Gerard had found something about his past—he was born here—something about who he was or—I don't know." Her voice was suddenly tired. She closed her eyes again. "He had these diaries that belonged to an old woman named Lorraine. She had been a friend of Venus' grandmother, and of Morag Leach. He was very excited about them. I have them now. He told me they contained a lot of information about stories, and songs. For my work. So I have them now." Emily fastened her gaze on Finn.

Finn squinted at Emily. He was unsure what she was saying. The diaries must be the 'primary materials' that she had told him were her own. "What else did you take from the flat? They had a search of it, Sammy said. I'm surprised they didn't take what you were looking for, if it showed a connection to you, to Kate, Morag."

Emily's gaze fluttered away. "He had a storage closet in the basement of the building, maybe the police didn't know about that. He kept important things there. But he told me about it, because I'm important too." She smiled to herself. "There were only the diaries. And, just . . . letters."

Emily sat on the edge of the sofa. Finn understood that she had said all she would, for now, anyway. But he was no closer to knowing why Gerard might have been killed. He felt uneasy. Emily had said nothing about her baby. Nothing about being afraid of Matthew.

"You should be going, Finn," Emily broke into his thoughts, her voice suddenly urgent. "Matthew will be here—and I have to get ready for my interview." She scanned the table. "My mobile . . . what is the time?"

Finn took his phone from his pocket. "Ten of three."

"Fuck. I'm late. And Matthew was supposed to be here —would you come with me, to Morag Leach's? I've got to go and interview her. I made an appointment. She'll never agree to talk to me again if I don't go."

"I don't think I'm the best person to take along. Why can't you go by yourself?"

"I just can't. I'm a little afraid of her, I guess." Emily's face colored again. "Please? Matthew said he would but of course he's not here."

"Why are you so interested in talking to her? It seems, Emily, that you've got more pressing things to think about than your dissertation."

Emily looked at him blankly a moment. "Because . . ." She looked down at the floor, a frown creasing her face. "She knows something about Gerard's death. I know she does."

"What? Why do you think that?"

Emily's mouth pressed into a thin line. She seemed to be considering how much to tell him. Finn's mind raced. It had to be the connection with Neill, if Morag did indeed know anything. But was she likely to speak of that to Emily? And in what context? Was the interview about folklore just an opening—did Emily hope to lead the topic to other things?

"I found some notes, among his personal things. He mentioned Morag's name. He had gone to see her a few times."

"What about?"

"I don't know. That's what I want to find out."

"You should just tell the police," Finn said. "You—"

"No." Emily's voice was obstinate. "I loved Gerard. I want to know. For the baby."

Finn watched Emily's face. Her expression was closed, and his instinct told him that she wasn't revealing everything. She had some other motive for talking to Morag, she must have. He felt she was being naive. If Morag was protecting Neill, she wasn't about to spill information to Emily. He sighed. He had no wish for another dose of Morag's temper. But he might learn something.

"All right. But I think you'd get more out of her if you went alone."

CHAPTER TWENTY-THREE

The drive to Morag's tiny farm took place in silence. Finn kept his eyes trained on the road ahead, and didn't offer conversation. He felt uncomfortable accompanying Emily on her errand. He wondered what had happened to Neill since their talk, months ago. Finn had never seen anything in the local paper about a lawsuit, or, for that matter, a new Finance Officer for the Festival being hired. He wondered how Morag would react to him showing up on her doorstep.

Emily was silent too. She seemed lost in her own thoughts, and Finn wondered about her desire to keep the appointment with Morag despite her bruised face and obvious anxiety.

They approached the ill-maintained track leading to the farmhouse. A few sheep grazed in pasture on either side. The sun shone through a ragged mass of clouds, and the wind kept up its unrelenting pace. Emily pulled into the yard next to an aging Mini and decrepit tractor. They got out of the car and went to the door, Emily striding ahead of him with notebooks in hand. She answered the door before Finn had even reached it, but he caught Morag's sharp glance as she let Emily into the house.

"How are you, Mrs. Leach?" Finn inquired, feeling suddenly six years old and out for Sunday tea.

Morag looked at him suspiciously. "What are you doing here?" As an apparent afterthought, she added, "As if Kate coming round yesterday wasn't enough."

Finn didn't know what to say. Emily was silent. He spoke, "Oh . . . why?"

"I expect you know." Morag directed her gaze at Emily, as if *she* had asked the question.

Emily looked away from Morag. She went into the front room, and began examining the photographs that lined the rough fireplace mantle in a jumble. Finn followed, his skin itchy under his wool jumper.

"Well, then." Morag stood with them in the center of the room.

It was an oddly staged play. Finn felt compelled to sit, to take himself out of the drama that he felt sure was about to unfold. The air was charged, and Morag's eyes burned very bright, two flushed spots of color showing on her cheeks. She looked as though she'd just had an argument, and Finn sighed inwardly. *Is there no peace anywhere?* Emily seemed to carry trouble with her, or to bring out the worst in people. He sat on the edge of a rocking chair close to the fire and stared at the door.

"I'm sorry I'm—we're—late," Emily said primly. "I had some . . . I wasn't well this morning . . ." her voice became a whisper as she unconsciously fingered the bruise on her cheek. She flushed violently. "Um," she said, recovering herself, "I wanted to ask you some questions about your involvement with a secret women's circle, some years ago. I've uncovered some information in these journals," she gestured with the notebooks held in her hands, "of a local woman that suggests that such a group existed, at least in the late forties and beyond. What I've read mentions you specifically, and records a ritual where you received a new name. Could you tell me about that?" Emily paused, her gaze fixed on the shabby carpet. It was as if she were reciting a speech.

Finn felt his jaw hanging open, and forced it closed. He didn't want to look at Morag. He felt embarrassed for Emily. For all her supposed experience interviewing people, her directness surprised him. Emily had plowed into private questions without any prelude or finesse. Hadn't she learned by now the best way to get information was to gain trust and sympathy with the informant?

Morag was silent, her face even more ablaze, yet Finn thought he saw the gleam of triumph or satisfaction in the woman's eyes.

"The journals are rather specific as to rituals and . . . and events. I'm very interested in the history of witchcraft, Mrs. Leach, and—"

Morag's derisive snort cut off Emily's speech.

Emily backpedalled. "Of course, witchcraft is a loose term, because—"

"You listen," Morag said, pointing a bony finger in Emily's face. The two women were still standing. "A girl with your fancy education, I'd expect more of you than to go raking through ashes looking for shite. If you think you have trouble now, my girl, you'll have more than you ever bargained for hunting for 'witches' from sixty years ago."

The venom in Morag's tone intrigued Finn. Her eyes snapped, and her tight, dry skin strained over the bones of her face. A wisp of fine grey-brown hair fell over her brow.

"I have primary source material that alleges to—"

"You've got nothing." Morag spat the words out. Her hand snaked forward, tearing the journals from Emily's grasp.

Emily's face drained of color. "You can't—those are mine!" she cried, and lunged toward Morag. The old woman stepped back nimbly, avoiding Emily's reach.

"Yours!" Morag's voice rang in the stale room. "You take a care with what you lay claim to! These stories don't belong to you. Lorraine is in her grave and they should lie there with her. Get out!"

Finn rose, not knowing what to do. His stomach began its familiar churning, signaling that the acid pain that plagued him wasn't far behind. He was reminded of the violent scenes between his ma and da, the anger that cracked through the air like electricity.

Tears began to run in a steady stream down Emily's face. "You've no right," she stammered. "Those were given to me. Gerard—"

Morag froze. Finn sensed her tensile strength, like a lion, about to spring. "Oh, my girl, you've no idea the sorrow you're bringing on yourself. And you don't even have the sense to keep away from a man that beats and humiliates you. That's right, I saw you, and I'm not the only one. You're pathetic!"

"Emily," Finn began, "come away, now. Let's leave Mrs. Leach in peace." He was sure that Morag was referring to the scene on the hillside that he himself had witnessed. He had a suffocating need to be out of the low-ceilinged sitting room.

"I know what you did!" Emily shrieked. "I know! You—and *Kate*." She uttered the name with particular venom. "I *know*." Tears ran down her face. "*Bitch*! I *know*." Emily whispered the last word, and rushed for the front door, pushing past Finn.

Morag watched her go, eyes alive. She clutched the journals with a white hand. Emily stopped outside by her car, leaning on the door and sobbing. Finn retreated to the kitchen, Morag's words ringing behind him.

"Stay away from me, girl. You ask Kate McNeill about your *witches*. But *I* won't have you spreading lies and digging up a past that's dead and gone." Morag slammed the door on Emily's anguished cry.

Finn remained in the kitchen as Morag turned away from the quivering door. She began to pace in the front room. Morag was still a fit, thin, woman for all her seventy-odd years, and the energy of her anger was palpable. Finn, pursued by a strange panic, let himself out the kitchen door. He rubbed his forehead as he descended two steps into the rear yard. He looked up and came face to face with Neill, apparently on his way into the house. Finn's eyes flicked past him, taking in piles of boards stacked by a stone-lined, circular pit. Neill didn't speak, and Finn's tongue stuck in his throat, the scene he'd witnessed still filling his mind.

Morag flew out of the back door. Neill started backward and Finn whirled to face her.

"What are you doing?" she hissed at Neill. "Don't talk to him. Get back to your work."

Neill scowled but turned immediately.

"And you," Morag pointed a bony finger at him, "tell Kate that I've told her. Tell her." Morag looked fiercely at Finn. "Tell Kate that I won't be responsible, not now." Their eyes met. "Well, go and tell her, man! What you waiting for?"

Finn nodded, mute. He had no idea what she meant, but he'd take her command as an opportunity to extricate himself from the situation. He turned into the biting wind, intent on catching up with Emily before she drove away. But as he rounded the house, Emily's car rumbled down the track with speed. Finn sighed and retraced his steps to cross the yard, making his way to the footpath that ranged over Morag's field, towards home. He turned as he climbed over the stile to the neighboring pasture. Morag stood near Neill, lashing him with words. Neill was too far away for Finn to read any expression in his eyes, but there was no mistaking the tension in his body. Neill was afraid.

CHAPTER TWENTY-FOUR

Sweet greenness blew in on a freshening breeze. Venus' face was flushed with the work she had been doing in the garden. Now she stood in the kitchen, glass of water in hand, looking out at her Gran still meandering among the plants. The weather was fine. Despite the breeze they had been hot in the garden. Venus drank the water down and set the glass on the counter. She felt peace for the first time in almost a week. Hard to believe that it hadn't even been that long since Gerard had died. Venus realized with a start that the full moon was tonight. It was unusual for her to lose track of where the moon was; but the last week had passed in a haze. It didn't matter—she would mark the full moon, as always, with a solitary meditation. She would send her thoughts to Gerard's spirit, to comfort him if she could. Venus did not believe that he could depart until the mystery of his death was solved; she was impatient that Sammy and the police moved so slowly. That she herself could not divine Gerard's killer.

Venus began washing up the few dishes in the sink. Outside, Kate kneeled in the tattie patch, pulling a few weeds and talking to the young plants. Venus smiled as she watched Kate's lips moving. Her Gran had taught her to talk to the plants too, and to all the elementals that lived in the wind and sea, earth and animals. And she, Venus, had the special sight as well, the sight that her mother had. Though Kate never spoke of Cora now, Venus could just remember the three of them sitting together, Cora's eyes closed as she described a place or event she was seeing in her mind. These memories were rare, because most often Cora had rejected her abilities, and grew angry with Kate for teaching Venus the old ways.

Venus adjusted the water from the tap, making it hotter for rinsing the soapy dishes. She herself had little control over the visions that came to her, and often she didn't know what they meant. She had been surprised at her vision of Finn's little girl—she had known exactly what she was seeing. She hoped that he had called home, found the child all right. He was a strange man. She found him unexpectedly kind. She sensed that he had much confusion and pain in his heart. Now his life had been complicated by finding Gerard, becoming involved with so many lives that had nothing to do with him. Venus shuddered as she placed the last of the rinsed dishes on the draining rack. She was very, very glad that she had not been the one to find him. After all, it could have been her; she was the most likely to visit the churchyard.

Kate stepped into the kitchen, placing her basket of cut herbs from the greenhouse on the table. "A fine day. I do love the long light. We've pulled almost enough docken up for the Midsummer bonfire." Kate laughed. "Full moon tonight," she said softly.

"Yes," Venus replied as she stretched her arms over her head. "I'll go down to the beach, I think. Not—not the church. Not yet." Venus had not returned to the churchyard since Matthew's attack. She desperately wanted to cleanse her sacred space of the atmosphere of fear and violence that had settled there, but she wasn't ready to go alone, at night.

"Aye, that's best, I think. Or you can join me in the doocot."

"No, thank you, Gran. I'll be better on my own."

"As you please." Kate smiled at her. "I must be getting some docken root down there, so I can have my fire. Now, who's that, then?" A frown creased Kate's face as she stepped out the door to peer over the garden gate.

Venus joined her, heart jumping as she heard the noise of a car coming down the lane. Would it be Sammy?

"It's Peter," Kate said. "That's fine. We'll have some tea. Is there any bannock left?" Kate bustled back into the kitchen.

Venus waved as Peter's old car rambled into the drive. His brown, knobbled hand shot out the window in reply. She smiled and felt a surge of happiness. Love was always here, even in the midst of sorrow, death, the enmities of life. She waited for him to park his car and come round to the gate.

"Hiya, Peter?"

"No' bad, yourself?" He put his hand on her head briefly as he walked through the gate. They went into the kitchen together.

Kate smiled and clasped Peter's hand. "Come in, young thing. I'll just get the tea on." She had already placed a plate of bannock and cheese on the table. Three mugs sat, along with the fancy old teapot, awaiting the boiling kettle.

"Where's your violet cup?" Venus asked.

"I broke it the other day. I was sad—it was my mother's. I dropped it right there in the basin. Cut my finger, too, I did," Kate said, waggling a bandaged finger at Venus.

"Gran! I didn't even notice. I'm sorry. I—" Tears suddenly threatened to come again. Her fleeting mood of happiness slipped away, replaced by the tightness in her throat as she held emotion back. She hated her tears, always poised near the surface, ready to fall at any moment. She wished that a year had passed, that her trouble with Matthew and Gerard's death were part of history, instead of the emotional nightmares of her daily life. So far Kate did not know of Matthew's attempt to rape her. Sammy had promised that he wouldn't tell her or make the attempt public knowledge until or unless they arrested him. He had urged her to bring charges, so that they would have a reason to hold him on suspicion. She had not been able to, though both Mary and Finn had encouraged her to do so as well. But she was afraid of how angry Matthew would be, what he would do to her when he was released. Sammy didn't have enough information to hold him long. Emily had given Matthew an alibi for the time of Gerard's death; no other evidence that she knew of pointed to Matthew's involvement.

"Venus?" Kate's voice pushed into her thoughts.

"What? I'm sorry, Gran. I'm just so tired, yet, I think." She was; her energy had dissipated and now her eyes were heavy. "I'll just go have a lie down." She smiled at Peter. "You two have a chat without me."

"Don't worry about an old man," Peter waved her away.

Venus took a mug of tea that Kate had poured and went to her bedroom. She opened a window to let in the light, blue air. She sighed as she lay down on the bed, focusing her attention on the blossom-laden branch of the climbing rose that crossed her window. The petals were pale pink, the color of a baby's toes; the fragrance was innocence and peace. Venus drifted into sleep.

CHAPTER TWENTY-FIVE

"Aye, I reckon that you know as much as I do about it," Kate said, in response to Peter's question about how the police investigation was progressing. "I feel sure it's Matthew, but Venus tells me that his girlfriend, Emily, says they were together. Finn told her that. Don't know how *he* found out. Talking to the police himself, I guess. That Emily is a right piece of work. Creates no end of trouble wherever she goes, I'd wager." Kate shook her head and poured fresh tea into their mugs.

"It's a bad thing, this killing," Peter said. "It puts me in mind of other times." He leaned back in his chair, long legs extended. His workman's coveralls were a bright blue.

Peter did not look at Kate as he spoke. She watched his face. The creases and lines were familiar to her after so much time, more familiar than Hamish's face had been. Her eyes flicked to her husband's picture, leaning friendly, as if to speak, from the wall. Peter sipped his tea.

"Morag's been round," he offered.

"Has she? Has she, indeed?" Kate wet her finger and picked up the bannock crumbs from her plate. Morag and Peter weren't close.

"Aye. Neill's in a bit of trouble. Well," Peter cleared his throat and sat up at the table, "he has been, hasn't he? Been out of work some months now. That trouble with Gerard. Did you know about it?"

"No." Kate tried to mask the excitement in her voice.

"Neill and Gerard worked together, for the Festival of Isles."

"Aye, so they did! I had forgotten that. Did Neill get sacked?"

"Well, Neill confronted Gerard about some kind of forgery, or embezzlement. I don't pretend to understand it."

Kate felt heat in her face. "Was Neill skimming off the top, or was it Gerard?"

"Well, it's one word against the other, isn't it? Gerard claimed that he knew nothing about it. Told Neill to pack it in, quiet like, or he'd have a lawsuit against *him*. Neill's never had much fight in him, I didn't think. Took it lying down, I guess."

"So Morag came round to tell you this? When? And why?" Kate was surprised that Morag would wait until months after the fact to tell Peter. Unless, of course, Neill's job loss had led to something else: Gerard's death.

"She wants me to buy Knowehouse."

"*What?*" Kate was incredulous. "Why would Morag sell her farm?"

"Needs the money, she says. She wants to help Neill get off the island. Give him a start in Scotland." Peter's face wore a wry expression.

"But he's a big lad, good education. What does he need her money for? And what about Laura? Does she know about all this?" Kate's mind ran through all she knew about Neill. He was a weak boy, for all his size. A mother's boy. Always done as Morag wanted. Laura had gotten away, married early. But Kate didn't know about Morag's relationship with her daughter.

"That's all I know. Morag came round yesterday, in a proper fettle. She was unhappy, too, about your Emily who had been round to see her."

"My Emily! Huh." Kate snorted. "What did Emily want with your sister?" Kate felt a flutter in her stomach. Oh, she knew very well.

Peter's gaze met her own. "You know, Kate. Morag told me the two of you had spoken."

"Aye, that's no secret I'll keep from you, Peter. I did go see her. Emily's got Lorraine's old songbooks and diaries somehow. Or she's read them. Venus mentioned that to me." Kate paused. The tap dripped, a small noise against the hum of the fire in the Rayburn, the sighing of the kettle.

"I wouldn't want you hurt, Kate, not after all this time. Nor Morag. We've drifted apart, but she's my sister." He looked into his cup. "I know she's never forgiven you," he said after a moment, "but I never blamed you. I never did. Something had to be done—"

Kate quieted Peter with a hand. "Venus—she's not to know. That's my concern, now. Not myself. But we shouldn't speak of—who's that now? I hear a car in the lane." Kate rose. It might be Sammy again, to talk to Venus. She hoped it wouldn't be Morag. She stepped out of the kitchen into the garden. The fresh air slid over her; she received it gratefully. Kate relaxed her shoulders as she stepped up to the gate. A car sped down the lane toward the house. She recognized Emily's Vauxhall. Kate's heart jumped. The car stopped abruptly and Kate watched Emily fling open the door. The girl was obviously upset. Kate ducked back into the kitchen.

"Peter, go into the sitting room. It's Emily, and she looks in a temper. Just stay. I won't let on you're here. I don't know what she wants." Kate began clearing the tea things.

"All right," Peter said, his voice slow with worry. He rose and pushed open the door to the front room.

"And if Venus wakes, keep her out there with you." Kate smoothed her hand over her jumper. Impulsively she reached up and cradled Peter's face in her hand. "I'll take care of it, whatever it is." She smiled, and Peter turned and left the room.

CHAPTER TWENTY-SIX

Emily had been near hysterics, blundering into the kitchen with a bruised face, swollen fingers, eyes bleary with tears. She was calmer now; Kate had brewed more tea and had checked her fingers for broken bones. One bruise on Emily's face was a dull red, older; the other was a fresh, violent purple. Kate found that she was not surprised. Since the girl had told her about Matthew she had been expecting it. Although Kate was disgusted to see Emily in such a state, she was aware that it could have been much, much worse.

"Now, then, you're safe here. Talk to me, girl. Tell me what happened." Emily's sobs were stilled and she wiped her face with a faded blue bandana.

"He found the letters. I had them stuck inside my bag of notes and files. I didn't think he'd look there; he doesn't care about my work. But he knew anyway," Emily said, fingering the bruise on her cheek. "He did this when he found my diaphragm." Emily's face flushed a deep crimson.

"I don't understand," Kate said.

"Don't you see?" Emily's voice rose to a wail. "Matthew can't have children. We both know that. We never used birth control. After he read the letters he realized I was pregnant. Of course he knew it couldn't be his!"

Kate was stunned into silence. Hadn't Emily told her before that Matthew was the father of her child? She knew nothing of what Emily spoke but felt fear sparkle in her belly. "Tell me the whole story, then. What letters? Do you know who the father is? Does he?" She made her tone soothing, hoping urgency would not show in her voice.

Emily rubbed her face with her hands and sighed, as if weary of telling an oft-told tale. "Matthew is sterile because he's had cancer treatments. The baby is Gerard's." Her voice broke. "I wasn't going to tell Matthew, but he found out. When he found my diaphragm, he knew there was someone else, and we had this terrible row." Her face colored deeply again. "And then I had letters, that I had written Gerard. I kept them inside these old journals. I didn't think he'd look there. But I took them out when I went to see Morag, stuffed them in my bag. And now Morag has the journals . . ." Emily buried her face in her hands.

Kate struggled with the details of Emily's story. Her head spun. *Gerard* the father of Emily's child? How had the two of them—or when? And what journals? Her thoughts tumbled over each other. A flame of anger rose inside of her.

"I left to go to the shops, to get something for our tea," Emily continued, "and when I came back Matthew was sitting there . . . he was just sitting, with the letters. And this look on his face." Emily's voice dropped to a whisper. "He was so angry. He was white. I was so afraid. I thought he would kill me."

"What happened?"

"He—he struck me across the face, and then in the belly. I was so scared, the baby . . . then he grabbed my hand and bent my fingers back." Emily's sobs began again. She wiped tears and snot from her face with the bandana.

"I want to understand you, Emily. I want to help you. But you must start at the beginning. How did you have letters that you wrote to Gerard? Had he given them back to you? And—" Kate stopped as she realized that the journals Emily referred to must be those of her dead friend Lorraine. "What happened to the journals?" The question hissed from her lips before she could stop it.

Emily looked up, startled. "I told you. Morag has them! She took them from me—oh, god, I should never have brought them with me. But I wanted to know—about the names!" Her voice became calm. Her eyes fixed on the door behind Kate. "All these *bloody* secrets." Emily's voice trailed off to a giggle.

Kate resisted the urge to look behind her. Emily was in shock, if not truly on the verge of breaking down. "Emily, why did you go and see Morag Leach? What was in the journals that made you do that?" Kate held her breath, felt her heart leap in her chest.

"Because she knew about Gerard's family. He told me as much—that he had finally found his mother and father. That a terrible injustice had been done and he meant to set it right. I found his notes, the file he kept on his family. I have that too." Emily's face creased into deep anger. "But she wouldn't tell me anything. She threatened me." Her face crumpled again into sorrow. "It's all I have left of him, it's all I have left for the baby. I need to know!" She looked up at Kate, and her expression became sly. "Maybe you can tell me . . .?"

"Emily, what happened after he struck you?" A shiver of unease ran over Kate's body. She felt, at this moment, that Emily was completely insane. Underneath her dismay ran a current of sorrow, for Emily was replaying a tragedy from so many years ago. The circumstances, so similar, that had been Lorraine's. "Did he force himself on you?"

Emily's laugh was bitter. "Not this time. No. He left. *He left*. He was so enraged, but it was like he just switched off." Emily shuddered. "But he'll come back, and then—and then . . . Oh, you must help me, Kate! I'm really afraid of him now! I think he killed Gerard; I think he's known all along."

"All right, all right. You must get off the island. Is there no one you can call? Have you no credit card, no way to book a flight or even a ferry?" Kate would not let her go back to her flat in Blackstone. Matthew was obviously dangerous; he was probably out drinking himself into a proper rage at the moment. She realized that Emily would not choose an abortion. Kate was glad, in any case, to not go through that with the girl. She doubted that Emily's nerves would handle it. In fact, Kate wondered if Emily were stable enough to even travel off the island alone. But she did not want her in the house, not if a crazed Matthew were to come calling. She thought about contacting Sammy. But no, much of this matter was not for the police. She looked out of the window. The midsummer sun sat low in the sky.

"You'll stay tonight in my doocot," Kate said briskly. "It's clean and it's comfortable. And Matthew won't be able to find you there. Tomorrow we'll call your family, or a friend. Find someone to meet a plane for you in . . . London? Wherever."

"Doocot?" Emily's voice was strained.

"The dove house. Over the hill, down at our old farm. I meditate in there all the time, spend at least one night a month in there. No birds live there now, and I've a nice pallet of blankets and space for a fire. You'll be cozy and safe. Don't argue. Now, drink a cup of tea and I'll just get you some herbs to calm you and help you sleep."

Kate poured Emily a cup of tea, wincing at the dark color. Well, the girl could use the strength. She slipped out to the sitting room. "Peter," she whispered. He was sitting on the faded sofa, hands dangling between his knees. He looked up as she approached. "Would you go down the hall and fetch a packet of herbs for me. They're all there in the baskets. You know them apart as well as I do. Get something to help her sleep. Melissa, or lavender—or both."

Kate pushed open the door of the kitchen. She half expected Emily to have vanished, but the girl was still there, staring blankly out of the window. She was quiet enough now, though she had made quite a racket. It was a wonder Venus was still asleep. "Drink your tea, there. I'll be just a tic."

She went back into the hall as Peter emerged from her room, a fabric wrapped packet of herbs in hand.

"I took the Melissa and put in some wormwood too, to protect her." He grinned, blushing.

"You're a love, Peter. You always had a way with the plants. A pity you've wasted yourself on sheep and fish all your life. I'm going to get her settled—can you wait a peedie while longer?"

"I can wait as long as you need me, Kate."

"Thank you." She put her hand on his arm before returning to the kitchen. "All right, then, Emily. Let me get you down to the doocot. I've got some herbs here to help you sleep. Once we get you settled I'll move your car into the barn so Matthew won't know you're here. You mustn't leave the doocot. You mustn't be frightened. He'll not find you and everything will look better in the morning."

Emily looked at Kate with her pale eyes. "The Lord deliver me," she said, her voice flat.

Kate reached for the chair back. She smelled the strong, acrid smell of Emily's sweat.

"As you wish, my girl. Perhaps He will."

CHAPTER TWENTY-SEVEN

Finn shifted in the wooden rocker. He crossed his legs one way and then another, finally settling with his chin in his hands, elbows resting on his knees. A coal fire burned in the miniature tiled fireplace and the room was unbearably hot. But it had been windy earlier, and the cottage had seemed damp. He still wasn't used to the Orkney weather and didn't see much difference between June and February, except the wind wasn't quite as fierce.

Finn stood and went to the window. He wanted a pint, an evening with his friends in the pub. He sighed and paced back to the rocker. Finn glanced at his mobile laying silent on the end table. *How did life get so fucking complicated? Christ on his cross but you're a mess, man.*

Finn realized he had been ripe for a mid-life crisis, even if he was only 38. He smoked too much, drank more than he should, was away from home too much, ate an unhealthy lot of crisps, and finally had discovered Nuala's long standing affair. And her unnerving mental decline.

And in no less a decline of your own. Finn laughed bitterly and ran his hands over his hair. His mobile rang, a tinny rendition of a popular techno song. He reached for it, banging his knee on the rocker. "Fuck," he whispered and pressed the call button. The number was his mother's.

"Ma. I've been waiting to hear from you."

"I'm sorry. I didn't want to call until I knew for sure. Until I had something to tell you."

"What? What's happened?" He knew the tone in his mother's voice too well. "Is Una all right?"

His mother hesitated. Finn held his breath. He knew it would be bad news, it must be.

"Ma!"

"Una and Nuala—well, it seems they're missing. I mean," she amended hastily, "no one has seen them in Belfast."

"Missing?"

"They could just be away, on holiday, like. I've been round to the daycare and been round to your house but no one has seen them in two days—"

"*Two days?* And you're just calling me now? Ma, what the hell is going on there? Have you rung the police?"

"That's the problem. It's not a matter for the police, they say. Nuala is an adult and Una is her child. They've a right to go off together. I had your sister ring her office. The voicemail message said she would be out of town until Friday."

"So they're not missing," Finn said. "Just away, then. Jesus, Ma, why get me all flustered?" But his heart beat rapidly in his chest. Where would she go away to? Was Una all right? He cursed Venus in that moment for making him worry about Una, with her crazy visions. Cursed his ma for her weakness, her inability to do anything for him. And himself for his cowardice, for running away in the first place.

He realized his mother was speaking again, her voice high and agitated.

"You see, the door to the house was just unlocked. I walked in, I thought it strange, if she was away—and there were things everywhere. It's a right tip, Finn, and the back glass door was wide open. It felt strange, like something had happened."

Finn felt pain begin to seep into his stomach. "Fuck. Ma—you need to get onto the police. Nuala wouldn't just leave the house standing open. Listen, listen to me. I can't leave Orkney. There's—I'm involved with a murder investigation here, and I can't leave just yet. But as soon as it's cleared up, I'm away."

"Murder?" His mother's voice dropped to a whisper.

"I found a body. It's nothing to do with me, don't worry. Now, get onto the police. Something's not right. And call me as soon as you talk to them."

Finn rang off and flung his phone into the chair. The fire shed a false cheer. He crossed the room to unlatch the window, leaning over the sofa to do so. He smelled dust, and the faint sourness of mildew. He pushed the window open wide, inhaling the smells of the sea. As Finn looked over the drive and grassy patch that made the front of the cottage, he was struck by the loneliness of the island, its essential unfamiliarity. A stranger might compare it to Ireland, but the likeness was superficial, if that. Finn felt the pull of his old life, the ties and tangles, in a way he hadn't before. But as he had told his mother, he couldn't leave.

"Fuck it!" He struck the cushion of the couch with his fist, and coughed. He ached for a fag and a pint. Finn strode into the bathroom, wrenched open the door to check his store of perishable food kept there, as the cottage had no refrigerator. The plastic bin held a soggy packet of chips from the pub, days old, a pot of mustard, a half-eaten packet of sausages. He closed the door in frustration. Finn turned and went to the small bedroom. His coat and clothes lay on a chair in a jumble, falling onto the floor. He frisked the pockets of his coat and threw it aside.

"Where are you now?" he murmured, digging through the pile of clothes. He seized the flask when he found it, lodged halfway between the cushion and arm of the chair. In a moment he had it to his lips, but he was disappointed. Finn tossed the flask back to the chair and sat on the bed, raking his hands through his hair. He shook his head; he didn't like to want so much for a drink. If he didn't get out of the stifling cottage he'd go crazy. Ten minutes before eleven and the light was still in the sky, though the sun had lowered into the sea. He grabbed his coat and left the cottage, slamming the door behind him.

As soon as he was out the door, the air greeted him, fresh and clean with salt and the stink of seaweed. He inhaled and immediately felt better. The pain in his belly eased. Nuala must have gone off to her ma's holiday cottage in Donegal. In her state it wouldn't actually surprise him if she left the house wide open. Perhaps someone had broken into the place; it was a posh enough neighborhood to attract thieves. At any rate there was nothing he could do from here. The best thing would be to get this crime solved, get himself out of it and away.

Finn reflected on the strange afternoon he'd shared with Morag and Emily yesterday. He hadn't yet delivered Morag's oblique message to Kate. Now was the time perhaps, to visit her and Venus, share what he knew and compare ideas. One thing he knew for sure: Sammy was in over his head and they'd be waiting a long time for him to solve the puzzle of Gerard's murder. If it was ever solved at all.

Finn felt a sense of anticipation as he took to the path and fields. He was ready to start working, ready to try and face his crumbled life back in Belfast. He would get custody of Una. He would find a way.

The evening was fine. Gulls swept low over the fields, rising up and down like waves in the air. His ears filled with the now familiar sounds of oystercatchers and lapwings, mewling in the grass or in the sky above him. Finn remembered the scene he had witnessed two days before, between Matthew and Emily. After his initial shock and desire to help, his cynical sense of non-involvement had taken over. He'd seen enough women beaten—men and children too—over the course of growing up in his own country, let alone his forays abroad. Emily's problems were none of his business; there was nothing he could do. He was ashamed to admit that as much as seeing Matthew and Emily had sickened him, it had titillated as well. He always struggled with the meaner, baser part of himself, the part that liked violence and the ragged edge of life. Perhaps his ma was right—he should have been a soldier.

Finn tried to imagine life in the military. He'd heard spine-chilling stories of life in the various special, secret forces of the British government. A life constantly tinged with danger. He shook his head. Maybe before Una . . . but Finn wouldn't allow his mind to fasten on thoughts of his daughter. He brought his eyes to the sea and forced himself to wonder where, over the pale blue-gold expanse, lay Iceland, the Faroes? And what beyond? And in the other direction, where Shetland, and Norway?

Finn paused as he reached the outer pasture of Knowehouse. Should he call on Venus and her grandmother at this late hour? Well, why not? The worst Venus could do was rebuff him, and anyway the granny liked him. He felt he should tell Kate about the scene with Morag, and in any case, he'd like to check on Venus. He hadn't seen her since the day in the churchyard, when Matthew had attacked her.

Finn set off across the next pasture. The ground was muddy from recent rain, and after slipping and nearly falling once, he slowed his steps. He forced himself to enjoy the beauty of the evening. There was no hurry. He let his breath come full and even, calming the lingering pain in his stomach.

Finn walked along a fence, past companionable clumps of ewes with their lambs. They watched him warily, the lambs bounding away if he came too close. He smelled sweet damp hay and vegetation. He came to a stile and began over it. A board cracked sharply and his foot caved through a step. Finn flailed, one leg sunk to the knee, scraped by the ragged edge of board, the other leg bent deeply now and poised on the step above. He felt a straining in his groin. Finn grabbed the top of the stile and pulled himself up. He sat, panting and rubbing his leg. Finn could see across the pasture to Morag's farm just beyond. A light burned in the window and he saw smoke rising.

Finn climbed down and headed off again, sliding in the mud and sheep dung mired under his feet. The path ran along the fence, angling up slightly beyond the line of the house. He could see behind Morag's cottage now, still a ways off, and saw the source of the smoke: a bonfire blazing in the back. Finn increased his speed, slipping as he did so. What could she be burning? The house didn't appear to be on fire, and the flames were well away from the small, shabby cluster of outbuildings. A rubbish heap, then? Was this the pile of wood he had seen earlier? Finn realized his heart was beating fast.

Hard up for excitement, sure, when seeing an old lady burn her rubbish gets the blood goin'.

Still, it seemed strange to be burning such a fire so late at night. At least she'd be up so he could tell her about the stile. Soon he approached another fence. He climbed carefully over the stile there and into the pasture in which the house sat. Finn increased his pace to reach the cottage.

"Hello? Hello the house?"

There was no reply. Finn walked to the bonfire. It burned safely inside a shallow pit of stone. Finn could still see the constructed pyramid of boards crackling in the center of the blaze. And paper. Pages and pages of paper, filled with a loose writing, lay scattered at the edge of the fire, and flames sucked greedily at thick bundles of pages. Small flecks of charred ash swirled in the air around him. Finn swiped at the drifting ash, blinking in the smoke of the fire. He stepped away. What could she be burning—the journals she had stolen from Emily?

"Hello?" he called again.

It was clear no one was outside, at least, and he wasn't so concerned about the stile to go to the door. Automatically he looked at his mobile. Ten past eleven. Finn shrugged and moved away from the cottage, catching the footpath that led from Morag's yard across the field. He strode away from the house, wanting suddenly to distance himself from the eerie bonfire burning in the twilight. He began to whistle the brightest song he knew.

Finn continued along the fence, watching his feet on the slippery ground, to the next stile. He peered at the boards; they seemed sturdy enough. Finn was up and going down the other side when he came face to face with Morag.

"Jesus God!" Finn yelped and stopped. He felt the bite of the bottom step against his achilles. His heart beat in his ears. Morag stood facing him, dressed in stiff trousers and wellington boots. Her hair was loose and flying; Finn realized it was quite beautiful in its length, though drab in color. Her face wore an expression of fever and astonishment.

She let out a small sound. "What're you doing out?" she demanded.

"I was just walking. You've left your fire burning. Inadvisable, even in this wet. By the way—"

She pushed past him and climbed over the stile. "Stay away from my place. What I do is my own business."

"—the stile on the far pasture is broken," he called. *And where have you been you old crow?* Finn watched her walk on a moment, before continuing on himself. He was determined to get to the McNeill's in time to catch them up.

The track soon intersected with the lane leading to New Farm, and he hesitated. It would be shorter to walk down the road to the house, but something called him toward the Wickhouse Wood. He knew Gerard's car had been found here, and Finn found himself wanting to traverse the path the man must have taken on his way to the churchyard. He hurried forward and soon was walking into the only standing forest on Orkney. The air was humid, and darkness hung in the branches. It occurred to him that he should be afraid of Gerard's killer, still at large. But he wasn't fearful, not for himself. As he swung along through the trees he thought of Venus and Emily, both beguiled by Gerard, both vulnerable. And Emily, seemingly enslaved to Matthew. She reminded him of his mother, who always stayed on with his da.

Finn was startled by the light still in the sky as he cleared the tiny wood. It was less than a mile now up to the farm. The track swept along the fences, rising slightly with the swell of a hill. It dipped down again into a small draw, before leading up and around to New Farm. Finn was glad to see the draw, and the old dovecote and milking barn that sat there as part of the 'old farm.' He was only minutes away from Venus now. He looked at his mobile again. It was twenty of midnight, very late for a call. As he passed the dovecote he slowed, eyes lingering over the beehive shape. It would be a perfect place for teenage lovers to meet—what few there were in Blackstone. He thought of Venus, leading her down the little track, into the musty building. Had she and Gerard met there? He stopped; the air was charged, electric with a pulsing energy. Finn felt the hair on the back of his neck rise. His hands clenched into fists, answering the sudden rush of adrenaline through his body.

Fuck it. Get ahold of yourself, man.

Finn shrugged off the eerie feeling and, surprised at his own fascination, walked to the door of the dovecote.

It was a newer door, newer than the original building. It fit snug and had a regular brass knob with a keyhole in it. Kate had probably added it to keep trespassers out. It wouldn't be open; still, he tried the knob, and it turned. He pulled the damp-swollen door open and stepped inside.

Candles burned, throwing shadows on the masonry wall. Finn stepped back, banging his head against stone. He barely stifled a curse, feeling instinctively that he should be silent. The room was perfectly round. He could make out unused nesting alcoves in the sloping walls. Finn was aware of a strong odor of burning leaves, reminiscent of marijuana. In the center of the room was a pallet and blankets, and alongside of that, a low table on which sat a jumble of candles, bottles and what looked like statues. Finn squinted in the gloom. He heard no sound but the wind and guttering of candles and the throb of his pulse roaring in his ears. He moved one step quietly, eyes fixed on the glowing altar. What could it be? Was there a tryst or a ritual of some kind going on? Kids smoking pot under the full moon? He stopped abruptly. Someone must be inside, here, with him . . .

Finn looked at the pallet that lay before the table. Yes, there was definitely something underneath the thick blankets. He edged forward again. Someone sleeping, perhaps? Was it Venus? The thought came to him quickly and he felt a string of tension pull in his groin. He reached the blankets, sucking in his breath.

Finn's belly dropped. Before him lay Emily Haworth, her hair long and tangled. Her face was whitish-blue. Her mouth was open, head to the side. Her light blond hair lay matted in vomit. On either side of her, well-used copper dishes held the smoldering ash of some material; it was this that he smelled. Finn blinked, feeling slightly dizzy. He brought his hand over his mouth and nose.

Emily lay in a twisted position. Her arms were flung back and the blankets bunched between her curled legs. Finn saw the light tufts of her underarm hair and found himself surprised that she didn't shave. She seemed a person to be concerned with these things. He looked away from her body, squinting at the table that held the burning candles. Finn saw rocks and shells laid out in pattern, a knife and other objects he couldn't quite make out. He recognized a St. Brigit's cross, woven from grass, and what looked like a crude doll. Beyond the altar he saw the foundation of a fire, a careful pyramid of yard debris underlain by crumpled paper. Morag's blazing balefire flashed through his mind.

But now, Emily. Finn squatted carefully by her side, reaching to feel her neck. A wrenching cramp ripped through his gut. With a cry he fell forward over Emily's body, his hand striking one of the copper dishes by her side. It was very hot and he jerked his hand away, rolling ignominiously over Emily's inert form. Finn scrabbled to his feet, his head spinning. The stench in the air was strong and burned his lungs. His glance flickered upward, through a thick haze of smoke that hung beneath the top entrance hole to the emerging stars beyond. He couldn't understand why the room was full of smoke. Claustrophobia gripped him and Finn ran from the building, gasping as he stooped to exit the door. With a hand pressed to his side, he slipped up the hill toward New Farm and Venus.

CHAPTER TWENTY-EIGHT

Venus sat on the damp sand facing the sea. Overhead seabirds called. Her eyes were closed, her ears attuned to all the sounds of a summer evening. The sun had set, and the lingering twilight drew itself out across the sky in muted blues and pinks. Venus sat within a circle of shells and one white candle burning in a hurricane lamp. Teke panted nearby. The flame of the candle danced despite the glass chimney that sheltered it; the wind was gusty even in the semi-protected cove. Venus' hair was wrapped in a bun and pierced with beaded hairsticks. She wore a thick black and white marled turtleneck and long linen skirt with leggings underneath. Her feet were bare and she felt the bite of the sand with pleasure. Before her sat a bowl with sea water and a silver coin.

She sat to honor the full moon and to receive the visions that she hoped would come to her and guide her. Venus felt especially grateful for the time to be alone and reflect. The week had been a stretched out gamut of shock, disassociation, and grief. Gerard, Matthew—thoughts of both ran through her mind. She wondered at her own ability to be so weak; before her relationship with Gerard she had felt strong, in touch with herself and with nature. Venus reached to pull the neck of her sweater up tighter. She willed herself to focus. She breathed slowly, recognizing each sensory perception:

wind, salt, cold, the cries of birds, the soft lap of the waves as they rushed onto the sand. In a brief cessation of wind she heard the slap of water against her Gran's boat, which sat at anchor in the cove.

Venus thought about Emily, sleeping, hiding, down in the doocot. She had woken from a dream-sloshed sleep to hear Kate and Peter murmuring in the hall outside her door. The light had fluttered in her eyes like moth's wings. She hadn't heard what they were saying. When she had pushed herself groggily to her feet and left her bed, Peter was sitting quiet in the front room. His face was strange and closed, but he smiled when he saw her. He put his finger to his lips and she came to sit beside him, a frown of confusion on her face.

"Is someone here?" Venus asked.

"Aye. It's that Emily. She's got the wind up about something and come to bother your Gran'ma with it." He shook his head. "Sounds like to me she doesn't know when to let well alone."

"What's the matter with her?" Was it something besides the pregnancy? Why couldn't Emily leave Orkney, leave them all to their own lives?

"She's got a problem with that man of hers, for one. He's beaten her proper. You know, I reckon, that she's pregnant?" Peter's brown hands whispered over each other.

"Yes." Venus was thoughtful. "Where is he?" She asked the question with rising alarm; suppose he would follow Emily here?

"Emily doesn't know where he is." Peter shook his head. "I heard their whole conversation from here—surprised it didn't wake you, she was goin' on so. Seems like they had a row over her catting around—I'm guessing you know the story." His voice dropped.

"I know that the child is Gerard's." Venus barely squeezed the words past her lips. Her mouth was dry, bitter. She longed for a glass of water. It was bad that Matthew knew about Emily's pregnancy. "Are they in the kitchen?"

"Aye. Kate's just getting her organized. She'll stay in the doocot tonight, as it's nowhere Matthew would look for her. We'll put her car in the barn. Tomorrow Kate's going to take her to the ferry. They should be calling her people in England somewhere, so someone can meet her in Aberdeen, drive along home with her. Kate doesn't think she's fit to drive all the way by herself." Peter rose. "I'll be seeing to the car, I suppose." He paused to listen. No sound came from the kitchen. "They must be on their way down." Peter opened the door to the kitchen. "Aye, they're away. Left the flask of tea, though. I'll take it on down, then I'll see to the car." He tried to smile. "I'm sure your Gran will tell you the whole story when she gets back." He had picked up the flask and walked out of the back door, into the bright summer evening.

Venus shuddered as a strong gust of wind blew over her, dislodging some of her fine hair from its twist. She felt a sprinkle of rain. She opened her eyes with a sigh. She had been lost in thought for longer than she realized. Her mind would not quiet tonight. Venus knew it would be useless to try and scry in the bowl of sea water. She raised her gaze to the sky. The moon rose full behind a thin, scrolling screen of clouds. She felt as though everything was obscured.

Venus hunched her shoulders and stretched her arms out and up. She opened her mouth wide, as if to drink in the light of the moon. There were ways to protect herself. She must regain her own power. As she reconnected her gaze to the sea, she saw the sleek head of a seal, bobbing just near the boat. By instinct she raised her voice in a soft, lilting song. The seal dove and resurfaced closer. In the twilight their eyes met, seal and woman, and Venus was filled with a rush of happiness and love. She finished out the song, holding her breath as the seal drifted closer.

A wail of sirens reached her ears. The seal disappeared in one quicksilver movement. Teke raised his head, alert. The sound grew closer. A panda car, or ambulance, neither of which was heard often in Blackstone. The sound drifted toward her. She raised the glass of her candle and let the wind snuff the flame. Venus rose to her feet and collected her things, slipped on her shoes. The moon rose above the clouds, as the last of daylight seeped away. Venus shivered in the wind's growing force. The sirens seemed closer. She turned and saw the bright lights flashing along the lane to their cottage. Venus lifted her long skirt to run awkwardly toward the house, her heart filled with dread.

CHAPTER TWENTY-NINE

Venus half-jogged toward the house, slipping in the loose sand. Teke panted behind her. Shreds of clouds hung loose in the sky, following the winds east. Venus was afraid, knowing that something had happened. It was her Gran, she was sure. Had she fallen on her way to check on Emily? Had Matthew arrived, drunk or angry? Venus waded through the thick grass that grew in the pasture separating her from home. Her skirt caught on thistle and she pulled it up roughly above her knees. She could see the farmhouse beyond, blazing with light. An ambulance sat silent in the drive, the lights flashing mute warning. Next to it was a panda car, and, she recognized with a start, Sammy and Mary's new car. She saw three men walking up the hill away from the house, on the path that led to the old farm.

Venus froze, watching the men ascend. Teke whined and she placed a hand on his head. He shook it off, eager to be away.

"Stay," she whispered, "wait." In her mind's eye she suddenly saw Kate making tea, hands shaking over the pot. And Finn beside her, taking the pot from her hand, guiding her toward a chair. Breath slipped through Venus' lips in a stream of relief and heat. She opened her eyes; the men were almost to the top of the hill. Venus waited until they had disappeared down the other side before she began to run, holding up folds of her hindering skirt in clenched hands.

Venus came in the far gate and walked through the garden along the length of the house. She paused by the window and peeped in quickly, half expecting to see Emily seated at the table. But it was Finn she saw, and her Gran, having tea. She saw his back, standing near the sink, heard the voices coming from the open kitchen door. Venus took a breath and went inside.

"—as soon as you can give me a brief description of what you found." Sammy looked up from his notebook as she entered.

Venus stopped. She hadn't seen Sammy from the window.

Kate rose, but Sammy placed a hand on her shoulder.

"There," he whispered, and Kate sat again.

"Venus," Finn said. His voice was full.

Venus looked at the three in turn. They were solemn. Her Gran's eyes leaked at the corners and her mouth turned down into the deep creases of her face. Finn's eyes drank her up. She remembered her Gran's words, 'he fancies you . . .' She turned her gaze to Sammy. He was grave, the policeman, not her best friend's husband now or Livvie's dad, but a man doing business, restraining, questioning. Venus put a hand on the worktop. Her belly was tight, falling in on itself. She felt skeletal, insubstantial. But her Gran was all right.

"Gran? Gran, what's happened? Sammy?"

"Venus, would you sit down?" Sammy left Kate's side and pulled out another chair from the table, standing like an attendant behind, waiting for her to sit. She went to the table uncertainly.

"Kate, if I may, the sitting room?" Sammy's voice held polite authority.

"Yes," Kate rose, "please, let me just see . . ." her words faded as Sammy placed his hand again on her shoulder.

"Don't trouble yourself. Mr. Ross and I just need a moment and then I'll be off down to the scene." Sammy nodded at Finn, and the two left the kitchen.

"Gran," Venus asked again, "what's happened? Why are the police here? And Finn?"

Kate sat and placed her palms in her lap. "It's that girl. That silly, sad girl. She's gone and gotten herself killed." Kate sighed and a tear rolled down the side of her face, disappearing into the collar of her shirt.

"What?" It was the standard answer of television drama, of novels. But Venus could think of no other word. "What, Gran?"

"Emily. She's dead. Down in the doocot." Kate's tone was now flat, and her expression of sadness fled, leaving a blank stare.

"Emily," Venus repeated, hating the fog of her own disbelief, ignorance. "Emily is dead. But what—"

"Finn found her. He was on his way here to see you," Kate looked up with a sad smile. "He went in the doocot and found her."

"But why . . . and weren't you . . .?" Questions piled over themselves in Venus' mind. She breathed, closing her eyes, willing herself to focus. Venus pulled on the collar of her sweater, itchy and warm around her neck. Hours ago Emily had been alive. Now she was dead, on their farm. Kate's spiritual retreat now tarnished by the stain of death. Venus felt warm waves of anger at Emily's incomprehensible selfishness.

"All right, Mr. Ross, I'll need you—" Sammy reentered the kitchen.

"Finn. For the love of God, man, we're not strangers." Finn followed Sammy, ducking his head under the lintel.

"—to come to Kirkwall tomorrow and make an official statement," Sammy continued smoothly. "Venus, will you be at work in the morning? I know it's a shock, but I'll need to talk with you as well. And Kate, if you'd stay home in the morning, I'll be round as soon as I can." Sammy pushed through the mire of silence in the kitchen. "Right, I'm off to the scene." He strode out of the kitchen and through the open gate, flicking on his torch as he gained the path.

"It's been Finn these last few days, right enough, and now it's Mr. Ross. All business again, isn't he." Finn's voice was tired. He sat and leaned in the chair. "I'm not likely to leave soon now. As often as it is a murderer finds his own body—wouldn't finding two be a little hard to believe?" He put his head down on the table, cursing softly.

"Murder?" Venus gasped. "What do you mean, someone's *killed* her? Not—suicide?" But it must be suicide: the baby, Matthew's violence, Gerard's death.

"That's the usual definition of murder." Finn tilted back in his chair, fingertips drumming the table. "I hadn't thought of suicide, actually," he said.

Venus saw Kate glance sharply at Finn. He didn't notice, staring at the table.

"Well, you don't know anything about it," Kate said. "All you saw was a dead girl under blankets. Of course she killed herself, or it was some kind of accident. Who would murder her?"

Finn and Kate exchanged a long look. "Well." He turned suddenly to Venus. "Are you all right?"

Venus felt bewildered. The room shook slightly, now rocking, now swaying and blurring at the edges.

"But what are you doing here?" Venus asked at last. "Why are you *here*?"

"Let me tell you. I was walking. I—I thought to come and see you, and Kate," Finn said, nodding in Kate's direction. "It was a fine night, and I was going crazy at home. Anyway, I came over the path, past Mrs. Leach's—"

"You came by Morag's farm?" Kate's voice was keen.

Venus watched the two, her eyes shifting back and forth, not understanding the strangeness passing between them.

"Mrs. Leach, Morag, yes. She had a right blaze going too. I thought it strange, but after yesterday—well—"

"What do you mean?" Kate interrupted again.

"I was there, Monday afternoon, with Emily. Oh, Christ. Look," Finn gestured impatiently, "There's a lot I need to tell you."

"You were with Emily? At *Morag's*? You'd better start at the beginning, Finn."

"All right, all right, if you'd let me, I will."

"Can someone please, please, tell me what is going on?" Venus whispered. The room settled into clear, motionless lines. In the garden, Venus heard an owl, hushed, calling to its mate, signaling the moon. "Please, I'd like to know."

Venus sat at the bottom of the garden. The sea roared dimly behind her. The sun made its way up into the sky, an early dawn, the hopeful fishing light of summer's beginning. The solstice was less than three weeks away; the sun was climbing to its longest journey, the zenith of its life. Life, Venus reflected, how pale and insubstantial. Yet it surrounded her in the nodding crane's bill, the lichen and moss growing along the wall, the rose reaching up the side of the house. The birds were awake with the sun, chattering over the sod and in the new vegetables just emerging. Venus could not rise and admonish the birds from the garden. She sat, tired, eyes burning in the cool of the morning light. It was half-four. In a few minutes she must start the walk to the Mourning Dove cafe and begin her day. A week ago, minus one day, Gerard had died. Now another death marked their lives.

She needed Mary, couldn't wait to see her and melt into her friend's embrace of sympathy. But it was Emily who needed sympathy, not her. It had shaken her, this death, but did it affect her? Venus thought about the inevitable gossip, the questions from the villagers who would all be in early for their tea. For they would know already. Sergeant Crombie would tell his wife, and she would tell Mrs. Moore at the post office and it would be round the shops before the clock struck half-eight. The English girl, dead on McNeill's farm; the corpse found in the doocot. And the questions would begin. On the heels of Gerard's murder, Emily's death held special significance. Were they related? Lines would be drawn between the two of them, and eyes, Venus knew, would turn to her. As a killer, perhaps; as a victim, certainly.

But she knew nothing. Finn's story had been distracted. He had been defensive with Kate, whose own mood had seemed to alternate from sadness to anger and irritation with Finn's discovery. He had been patient with Venus, repeating again the details of the story, details that had flown from his mouth and dissipated like smoke. It had been hard for her to understand. But finally she had it: Finn had decided to come to visit—had wanted to tell them about being at Morag's —he had walked along the footpath leading to Morag's farm, had broken the stile, seen the bonfire. He had startled her on the path beyond her house, she had acted strangely—and on this Kate had quizzed him closely. What did she say? Where had she been? Finn couldn't answer her questions, and Venus could not divine her Gran's interest in Morag's doings.

Finn told her about passing the doocot, wondering about it, and being curious, suddenly, and having to go inside. And then, well, he had found Emily. He understood now that the place was Kate's meditation shelter, her place of worship, of solitude. He had been told that Emily was hidden there, from Matthew, to make her escape from Orkney the following day. Finn hadn't known that Kate was about to come down when he had knelt to feel for Emily's pulse. The place had rejected him; he was expelled by Emily's death, and he ran over the hill to find Kate readying to leave. He had been breathless, her Gran shocked and shaken. Finn dialed the police. He helped make the tea.

Sammy had arrived quickly, with Sergeant Crombie. The ambulance sped up from Kirkwall. Scene of crime officers drove in, filling the yard with strange cars, from Kirkwall, Stromness, one other man from a village two miles away. There was no more to be told. Finn supposed murder, Venus suicide. He said nothing about the body. Once again, Venus didn't even know how the victim had died.

The stones of the wall were cold. Venus pulled her hair back sharply. She twisted it into a tight bun and tied it there with an elastic band. It was time to go. Her skirt was moist from the ground. She brushed at the linen and straightened her sweater. Venus hadn't changed, had barely slept. She didn't care. She walked up the garden and out of the gate, followed by birdsong. Venus' steps were slow and her eyes grazed the ground as she walked, leaving her Gran tossing in the old bed in her corner room, and Finn snoring quietly on the sofa in the sitting room. She liked that he was there, but didn't know why. Venus thought of Matthew as she walked, and wondered where he was. Did he know that Emily was dead? Had he loved her? Venus touched her fingertips to her cheek. The long scrape was nearly healed. She would not allow the thoughts that squatted in the corner of her mind to take form, pushed away the image of Matthew abducting Emily's life as she had sat, unaware, on the beach not half a mile away. Venus walked faster, grabbing up crumpled folds of her skirt in her hand.

CHAPTER THIRTY

"Sammy's coming round now," Mary said, hanging up the phone. "Let's get some tea on."

Venus turned from the window and the table she wiped absently with a cloth. The day had been long, exhausting, and she felt the downward pull of her limbs from lack of sleep. All day the cafe had been busy and abuzz with gossip. Venus despised the smallness of the village at this moment, hated the morbid interest in death, the fascination with the hows and whys, the quickness to suspicion. Yet she knew that the same people who had come round the cafe at half-eight would have been up to New Farm by ten, bringing up a plate of scones, or a special packet of tea, or some embroidered thing, to comfort her and Kate as if it had been one of their own killed in some natural way, by the sea, perhaps. No one felt the loss of Emily's life, except, she supposed, Matthew, yet they each felt the shiver that another unnatural death brought to the village and their ordered lives. Venus knew the gossip was a testament first to the need to find explanation, and second to the whims of boredom. But that didn't help the throb in her head, didn't diminish her desire to be off, alone with Teke, walking across the green fields that meant no harm.

Venus knew that Sammy had come to talk, ask questions. She had expected him in the morning, but he had been detained in Kirkwall, Mary said, waiting for the word from the medical examiner—the results of the autopsy.

Mary brought a pot and three cups out from the kitchen. Her face was weary too, having spent the night awake after the call from Finn to the police.

"Has he talked with Gran, did he say?" Venus asked, sinking into a chair at the window table.

"He didn't mention it. I expect he went round there first, after going to Emily's flat to look for Matthew—who they haven't found, by the way. I know he gave Finn a lift into Kirkwall to give his official statement on finding the body. God, but it's strange that Finn has found them both. Bad luck, or . . . you don't suspect him, do you Venus? I can't figure any reason he'd have to kill either one."

Venus shook her head and sipped the strong, ginger tea Mary had prepared. No one had been murdered in Blackstone in her lifetime, and now there were two unsolved deaths right on her own doorstep. It was as if someone were trying to punish her and Kate. Or implicate them in something, but what, Venus couldn't fathom.

"I don't suppose I can tell him anything helpful," Venus mused. "I wasn't at home—"

The two women looked up as the bell rang over the door. Sammy entered, his face tired and his usually energetic walk subdued. He looked shaken and unhealthy. He came to the table and sat, kissing Mary on the cheek and shrugging out of his jacket.

"What's this, Mary?" he said, after a sip of the peppery brew. "More of your herbals, Venus?" Sammy tried a brief smile. "I'll take my PG Tips any day."

Mary half rose, but he put his hand on her arm. "I'm just having a go, don't bother." Sammy turned to Venus. "I know it's been a long day, but let's get this over with." He pulled out a notebook and flipped through several pages filled with his loping scrawl.

Venus laid her head on her arms and looked up at Sammy through her fringe. Her skin felt oily and she smelled of garlic and fish. Underneath the odors of the day's special she detected the musky aroma of her own sweat; she longed to strip off her clothes and plunge into the frigid sea.

"Now, can you tell me where you were last night, from about ten o'clock on?"

She sat up and pulled her hair down from its twist. "God, Sammy, I don't know. I mean, I do know, but not exact. You know Gran and I are hardly concerned with the time." She paused to pull her hair back up tightly. "I guess I went out for a walk about half-ten. Gran was getting ready to make a bonfire in the yard, because she couldn't go down to the doocot." Venus hesitated. "I went out with Teke and just walked awhile, toward Wickhouse Wood, then back up past the cottage toward the church. I couldn't go in the end, but went down by the cove. I was there until probably twelve or so—it was getting really dark. Then I heard the siren and I started up."

"We didn't get the call until 11:45, and the ambulance didn't arrive until half past midnight," Sammy stated.

"Well," Venus felt irritable, defensive, "I told you I don't know about time. I don't wear a watch. Time slips away . . ." She shrugged.

"It's all right. You didn't hear or see anything unusual in the time you were walking or at the beach? Were you alone? Where exactly did you walk?"

"Of course I was alone. Who would I be with? I was observing the full moon. I always have done, both Gran and I." She looked at Mary. "You know that."

Sammy put down his notebook. "Venus, I know it seems like these questions are pointless. But please understand, I need to ascertain the facts of what happened. Two deaths in the space of a week . . ." He smoothed his hand over the glossy finish of the table. "Emily died of heart failure. Her death could be accidental, but I doubt it. We don't know the exact cause—we've had to send blood samples and the like to the lab in Inverness. This is a very different crime from Gerard's murder, but I feel that so close together, they must be related. And we know there was a connection between the victims."

Venus shuddered and felt the bite of ginger tea surge in her throat. She hated people, humanity, the brutality of life that weighed like a stone against her chest. She felt that the sanctity of her home, her and Kate's land, had been defiled. And she was afraid.

"Look," Sammy went on, glancing between Mary and Venus, "it's probable that Emily was administered some type of poison. Either on purpose, or accidental . . . well, there's a limited amount of people who had access to her."

"What do you mean?" Mary's voice was sharp.

Sammy hunched in his chair. "I mean, Venus, that you and your Gran—in the police's eyes—are primary suspects. Both events occurred on or near your land; and only you and your grandmother knew Emily was in the doo-cot."

Mary grabbed Sammy's wrist. "You can't suspect Kate or Venus! Sammy, that's absurd. Matthew's the one you should be going after."

"Listen," Sammy snapped, "it does me no good to have you going off the deep end, Mary. I said *in the police's eyes* that is what makes sense. It doesn't matter what I feel as an individual. But I am investigating this case, and I can't ignore the facts, regardless if my friends are involved."

"That's bollocks!" Mary pulled away from him and shoved her teacup across the table. "You *are* the police, Sammy. Your Superintendent doesn't know anything about this village or about the people who live here. If you don't work with your intuition, what *you* know, how can you solve this crime?"

Sammy's face flushed red. "I don't need you to tell me my job."

"Sammy—" Venus took a deep breath. "Sammy, could Emily have killed herself? She was pregnant, her—her lover dead, her boyfriend was beating her . . ."

Mary looked fiercely at Sammy. "Have you ruled that out?"

"No," Sammy said, leaning back in the chair. "No, we haven't. But, depending on what we get back from the lab, it's unlikely that she had access to the particular poison. The ME wasn't familiar with the substance found in her blood. So it's not one of your 'usual' poisons."

"Well, what about accidental death? How do you know she was murdered?" Mary slapped her hand against the table for emphasis.

Sammy ran his hands over his hair. "It could be. But she was young, healthy. There was no sign of any weakness with her heart. So close to Gerard's death, and with a connection between the victims, I'd be more inclined to say she was killed. Or, as you point out, she killed herself."

"Did you talk to Gran this morning?" Venus asked.

"Aye. She was fair upset, she was. Jesus, you know I don't think you or your Gran killed Emily—*or* Gerard. But you have to see how it looks."

"Well, what about Finn?" Mary asked. "He found both the bodies. Does he have an alibi?"

Venus suddenly laughed aloud. She felt the dark bubbling inside her. Bodies, murder, suicide. Her life had twisted, in the short space of a week, into the stuff of television or bleak novels. Mary grabbed her hand, but kept her eyes on Sammy.

"Finn doesn't have an alibi for either death, although he did tell me he saw Morag Leach last night, as he was walking to the doocot. He said it was sometime before eleven, so I will talk to her next, see if she'll corroborate that, and find out where and what *she* was doing. Still, death occurs in a window of time, not a moment the ME can determine precisely. So Finn may be in it yet. But . . ." Sammy paused, thinking. "He has no discernible motive for killing either one. As for Morag, we know that she and Emily had an altercation, and Morag might have been on her way to see Kate, and sussed that Emily was in the doocot, seized an opportunity . . . But would she have been casually carrying an unusual poison? No," Sammy continued, nodding at Mary, "Matthew is still really our best hope, though as we all know, he couldn't have figured where she was. Unless the silly girl rang him . . . but there's no call to him last night on her mobile. Oh, I don't know. I wish you would press charges on the attack, Venus. It would give us something to haul him in for. If we could find him, that is."

CHAPTER THIRTY-ONE

Kate stood in the back garden watching the clouds race over the sea. She turned as she heard Teke bark, and saw Venus and the dog come in the kitchen gate. She raised her hand to wave. Venus walked toward her. She looked small and tired. Kate sighed. As much as she loved Venus and was proud of her, she knew how much the girl didn't understand about people and the world. She knew the last week had rocked Venus' previously peaceful life. The police had been swarming over the farm all day. The doocot itself was off-limits and she had spent the morning answering questions from Sammy Douglas and his sergeant. But she knew how to handle life. Venus was another story.

"How was your day?" Kate asked gently, as Venus joined her by the low wall.

"Tiring. God, so tiring."

Kate saw the circles under Venus' eyes. "You need sleep, girl. You should go on inside."

"I'm too tired to sleep, Gran. I want to hear about your day, anyway. Are you all right? Did you find out much?"

Kate leaned against the wall, turning her back to the sea. She looked at the rose climbing over the side of her house. That rose had been planted before Venus was born. How things grew, raced on. How time went, and things with it.

"Well," Kate said, "young Sam was here with that Crombie fellow, asking and scribbling for the better part of two hours. And they've been all over the path and the doocot of course. They talked to Finn too, they did, and put me right out of the house like a dog." She cackled. "Then Sammy left to take Finn to the station in Kirkwall, and Mr.—excuse me, *Sergeant* Crombie stayed and finished off the ginger biscuits and then slouched on along himself."

Venus bounced against the stone wall. Her arms were crossed and she looked absently out to the sea. "Sammy asked me some questions about you," she said finally.

"So they did, I'm sure. As they did me, of you. Don't worry about it," Kate said, at Venus' alarmed glance. "It's not as if we're suspects, love, but she was killed here and there it is."

"Sammy said we might be suspects. He says that Matthew—that they can't find him."

"Aye, I heard Crombie jawing away on his mobile to his wife, telling her all the details. They're on the lookout for him leaving the island. If he hasn't already." Kate looked at Venus. Her face was pinched and drawn with fatigue. Something else too . . . Kate felt goose bumps on her arm. "But it's not our worry. We just have to keep our heads down and move on."

"What does it mean, Gran? Why did—why do people . . ?" The sentence went unfinished as Venus brought her hands over her eyes.

Kate winced at the defeated tone in her granddaughter's voice. "The world's a violent place, that's all. And it's touched us here, finally. But the wind will blow it away, you'll see. I'm sad for Emily, but all the same, there was no hope for her." Kate shook her head.

"What do you mean? Just because she was pregnant—"

"Pregnant she was, but desperate too. That fellow of hers beat her regular and—" Kate stammered to finish the sentence. "And took his liberties with her as well, when it wasn't wanted." She felt the pricking of tears and turned her head away from Venus' puzzled gaze.

"What do you mean, Gran, that he—"

"For God's sake, girl, don't be such an innocent! He fucked her whenever he felt like it, whether she wanted it or not. And like as not, after a beating, too. As a way to make up. Oh, she told me all about it, pathetic little cow. It's one thing I'll never understand, how women will let a man like that trap them up." Kate's face flushed with anger. She stuffed her hands into the pockets of her overalls. She felt chastised by Venus' shocked look.

"Gran! When did she tell you all these things?"

"Oh, one time or another when she was here, some last night. I wanted to help her, but she was that far gone that she didn't want help, really. Kept saying it was her own fault." Kate paused and considered grimly. "Even last night, when I spoke to her. When she showed up, all teary eyed and bruised from his latest beating. Afraid he would follow her and kill her."

"She was that afraid of him."

It was a statement, not a question. Kate felt a shiver of alarm at the tone in Venus' voice. "Aye, she was. But then, she'd been raking up all kinds of trouble for herself, asking questions, getting people angry. You heard Finn's story about what happened at Morag's. She hadn't a friend among us. I wouldn't be surprised if after all the fuss they find she killed herself."

"Do you think so, Gran? Mary asked that too, of Sammy, but he thinks she was murdered. It would be better, wouldn't it, if she had committed suicide? But still sad." Venus' voice was small.

"Emily wanted deliverance. She'd gone and made a bed that she couldn't lie in. We all face that a time or two in life. You have to pick up and keep going, make yourself new circumstances. Even when things are very bad." Kate shook her head. "Emily didn't have sense. She was talking crazy last night. Aye, it's better she's dead. Her kind never can get along, need some-one to carry them all of their life."

"Gran! Don't say that."

"Sometimes people *are* better off dead, Venus. Oh, I find life sacred, as you do. But sometimes people aren't strong enough, and other times . . . well, other times they deserve to die." Kate pushed herself away from the wall. "Come on, girl. You're tired and should get to bed. I'll make you a nice cup of tea and off you go."

Kate started up the garden path. The air was quiet of birdsong, only the wind rushed over the wall. The wind knows, she thought, and will whisper down the years for justice. Kate stopped and closed her eyes, shivering as the sun disappeared behind roaming clouds. She turned to look behind her. Venus' gaze was far away, and tears made their way silently down her face.

Chapter Thirty-two

Venus lay splayed on the bed. Her thoughts drifted; the light from the moving clouds shone in and out of the window. The glass was wavy, distorting the clouds into plumes, feathers fanning in the blue. Venus swept her arm idly back and forth, letting the swish of her hand against the duvet lull her almost to sleep.

Venus heard Kate in the garden, through the slit of the open window, talking to herself—no, talking to Teke. He barked and Kate laughed. Venus stopped the movement of her hand. The light in the room seemed fragile; it hung suspended and fuzzy. She closed her eyes.

The phone rang and rang. Venus heard Kate's voice in the kitchen down the hall, muffled by the closed door. Silence, then Kate's footsteps in the hall, going into her room. Venus tried to make herself rise, but she was heavy, languid. She wanted to be alone. Kate's steps came again, down the hall and out to the back, pulling shut the gate. Venus was surprised to hear the sound of her Gran coaxing the engine of their old Morris into life. Kate almost never drove.

Venus was abruptly aware of the vastness of her Gran's own life, a life of motives and choices far bigger than she. Memories, events, circling outside the scope of her life. There was so much about her grandmother that she didn't know. Years of things, wells of feeling . . . Venus' eyes fluttered open and closed. She felt a puff of air from the window; it was fresh, carrying the sea and birds. And what of Morag? Or Mary? Or . . . Emily? What did one know of anyone? Venus let her head roll slowly side to side. She heard knocking on the door and a voice calling, "Hello, the house."

Venus rose unsteadily and went down the hall. On the edge of sleep she opened the little-used front door—but today so much in use, and yesterday—and fastened her gaze on the face of Finn.

"Can I come in?" he asked, after a moment of silence. He stepped to the door.

Venus opened it wider and moved for him to pass. "I've been sleeping," she said finally.

"Oh. Sorry." He seemed disconcerted.

But she was glad he was there. Had it only been this morning she had left him sleeping on the couch? "Come in." She rubbed her face with one hand. Her skin felt stretched, dirty. "Go on into the kitchen. I'll be right there." Venus went past him and down the hall to the bathroom. She stood at the sink and ran the tap. She filled her hands with cold water and splashed it over her face until the cold made her hands ache. She turned off the water and stood, pulling back her hair, running her hands wetly through the slippery strands. Her fringe was getting long. Impulsively she opened the cabinet and pulled scissors from a cup; she angled the scissors and began to cut. Fine, silky tufts fell to the basin. She stopped. Her clear forehead now half-exposed, she looked like a surprised and innocent child. Venus smiled, for what seemed like the first time in days, weeks.

"You've cut your hair," Finn said, when Venus entered the kitchen. "Well, I started the tea."

"That's fine." She sat down at the table, at the edge of her chair, hands resting on the scarred worktop. "It was in my eyes." She felt like she was at school, about to have an examination.

"So, how are you?" Finn rocked on his heels waiting for the kettle to boil. "Where's Kate?"

"She went out," Venus answered, hearing the surprise in her own voice. "She took the car. I don't know where." She looked up at Finn. He was tall. His shoulders seemed wide. He was a potential suspect, she remembered, and sat up straighter. Venus felt a spiral of fear in her belly. But his face was kind, she saw, as he gazed at her. Venus looked away, closing her eyes. She saw in her mind's eye a train station, the destinations and arrivals ticking over on a large reader board. There was a woman, with black hair, a child on her knee. Venus could almost hear the clatter of trains, the busy swirl of voices.

"Venus, I need to talk to someone. *You* need to talk to someone. That's what they say, in times of stress. Process." He smiled and pulled the kettle off the stove. He filled their pot.

Venus opened her eyes and the vision dissipated. She would tell him. But now he was talking . . . "Yes, I think that would help." She smiled back.

They prepared their cups a moment in silence. The kitchen door was still ajar. Teke lay on the mat just outside, panting and whining in his sleep. He twitched at the pleasure of his dream. Venus smiled.

"We need to discuss these murders. I don't have anyone to talk to about it," Finn said.

"But you're a suspect. Maybe that's why." She looked at him and laughed. It was ridiculous.

"As you may be." He returned her laugh. "No, I could be out of it; seems I may have an alibi. Old Mrs. Leach, with her flying hair, on the stile. If she can vouch for the time. And *I* didn't know Emily would be in the dovecote. But maybe she did . . .?" Finn tapped his finger on the side of his tea cup.

Venus focused on the small sound. Yes, Morag and her strange messages, her anger toward Emily. She knew that her Gran and Morag had once been friends, and yet there was no love lost between them now, and for as long as Venus could remember. She felt again the mystery of her Gran's days; saw herself small and insignificant in the sea of life. And what of Finn? Of his life, his motives? The black-haired woman flashed in Venus' mind. She was smoking and crying in the train station. The child sat, with a lamb, on the floor. Venus squinted at Finn.

"So, I looked at my mobile when I left Knowehouse. It was just past eleven, maybe ten past. I met her some minutes later. It's no distance from her house to the last stile. What a sight she was. Looked like a witch out of Shakespeare or something. With Wellies." His voice sparked again into an easy laugh. "But it's odd, sure, that she was out rambling the fields with a fire blazing in her backyard."

Venus looked at him, and in the meeting of his gaze she felt her mind shift into crystalline focus. His eyes were steady, and in that moment she felt a complicity with him.

"We need to figure out the links. What is the connection between Emily, Gerard, Kate, Morag . . . it seems clear to me, Venus, that someone is trying to implicate your family—one or both of you—in these killings. Why? Why?" He leaned forward.

"The police—," she began.

"The *police*," Finn snorted in disgust. "No harm to Sammy, like, but the police are showing themselves to be fucking useless. No surprise."

Venus shrank back in her chair.

"I need to get out of here, that's the truth of it. I'm in a right state. I can't leave Orkney until this is sorted, or unless I somehow become less important, less *suspicious*." He laughed bitterly.

"All right." She regarded him soberly across the table, then lowered her eyes to drink. "What do you want to do?"

"We need to look at the facts, ma'am, the facts of the case." Finn drew his face into a serious frown, but his mouth quivered. He raised his hand, pointed a finger. "The facts as we can ascertain them. Let's begin with what you know, about Emily."

Was he playing a game? Being detective? But his voice was serious. And he was a suspect, or, at least, held prisoner by the investigation as if he was. She thought of Emily. Yes, it would be good to have everything clear.

"All right," Venus said again, considering. She poured more tea.

"Start at the beginning. When did you first meet her, what do you know about her, did you talk, that kind of thing. Then I'll do the same. We'll compare."

"I'll try." Venus thought as she drank, wincing at the strength of the tea. "She came to Orkney, I don't know, a few months ago. To do research for her postgraduate dissertation in folklore and mythology. Specifically the northern isles. She stayed in Stromness a short time then went to Shetland. When she came back in—I don't know when it was, May?—the historian at Kirkwall sent her up here, because she was interested in Selchies and such. The village," she stopped, smiling at Finn, "has a reputation for these things. So does Sanday, but she hadn't gone out there yet. So," Venus paused, "she came up here with Matthew and they rented a flat off the High street for two months and then she planned to go on to the other islands. But she had run out of money."

"Did she tell you that? And when did Matthew arrive? Did he go to Shetland with her?"

"I don't remember who told me. Someone did—maybe Mary. She came in the cafe one day, and we talked a little. She asked me about Gran. And she had two or three meetings up here with Gran to talk about the stories and old things. Then she and I met, in her flat." And there were dead flowers, Venus remembered, and Matthew had come in as she was leaving. "Matthew arrived, I think, when she got back from Shetland. They came to Blackstone together, anyway. She was always a bit rude, a bit brash. She asked me about herbs and the calendar of the year—the pagan—and such and then she asked me about witchcraft."

"Did she, now?"

199

"Yes, I was irritated with her and she was implying—she had got hold of some old diaries—that Gran had been involved in some secret circle years ago—"

"Ah—the diaries again. What did they say?"

"I don't know what they said. I didn't see them. They belonged to Lorraine, an old friend of Gran's, who's dead. Her son, Mansie, gave them to Emily."

"Is that what she said? She told me that she'd gotten them from Gerard. In fact, I think she went to his flat to get them after he was—after he died."

"Why would Gerard have them?" Venus tried to remember if she had known this.

"Something about his parents, that he thought he'd found. That's what Emily told me Monday. That's why she wanted to talk to Morag. *She's* got them now, old crow. And, I imagine, they're gone. Up in smoke."

"What do you mean, gone?" Venus leaned forward, pushing her cup aside.

"The bonfire," Finn said. He tapped the table. He appeared to be enjoying himself. "Go on. We'll get back to the journals. You were at Emily's, and she was asking . . ."

"So, anyway, I told her that I didn't know anything about any 'circles', and that she had better ask Gran herself or mind her own business or something like that. And then I left. She called me Aoifa," Venus remembered. "My given name. But I don't use it."

"Why not?" Finn looked at her, his green eyes like warming, shallow water. He sat up. "You're charming, Venus. Aoifa is the name of a warrior goddess in Irish folklore. And yet you choose the name of another goddess. Of love." He smiled; his face was flushed.

Venus looked down at her hands. She felt cold, then warm. She was embarrassed for him; he had revealed his weakness for her. She wanted to extricate him from the well of intimacy he had flung himself down. Venus willed herself not to stand.

"It's after the planet, actually—Venus—the evening star. Aoifa," she smoothed her hand in a fan shape over the top of the table, "Aoifa belonged to my mother. It was her name for me." How should she continue? She wouldn't follow him down the well; she must pull the rope up. "But I don't know how Emily learned it or why she called me that. From Gran, I suppose."

Finn gazed at her a moment longer. He took a sip of tea, and seemed to gather himself. "So when did you talk with her next?"

Venus sighed in relief. "Well, of course I saw her around the village. There was the pub the other night. She came up here on Friday, and I overheard her tell Gran she was pregnant. She was crying."

"And that was the last you talked with her, or saw her?"

Venus looked out the window. The light waved through the tree by the gate; the wind directed the branches in and out of the frame of glass. The tap dripped, drops falling bulls-eye into the brown stain on the basin. The kettle burbled.

"Venus?"

"I saw her—heard her—last night. When she came to see Gran. We had been gardening," she remembered, seeing the faded colors of yesterday pass before her. "Peter came up to tea and then I took a nap. When I got up Peter was here and Gran had taken Emily down to the doocot to sleep. Peter went to move her car."

"Why did Kate want to help Emily? Why get involved?" Finn poured himself a fresh cup of tea.

Venus looked at Finn with surprise. It had not occurred to her that they had a choice to help Emily or not. It would not be like her Gran to refuse help to someone—especially a woman—in need. "She just did. That's what she does. She helps people."

"Did *she* know that Gerard and Emily—?"

"I—I don't know. She did after last night, because Emily told her the child was his. Oh," she said, her voice low with terrible wonder. "The baby. Well, of course, it's—"

"Aye, of course," Finn replied, looking at the wall. "It wouldn't have been viable in any case. You know that."

Venus looked at the picture of her grandpapa, smiling down from the wall. Life was fleeting; she had never known him. His life with Gran was the yellow stuff of the past.

Finn shifted in his chair. "I had quite a few interactions with Emily," he said. "For some reason she found me a safe person to confide in. She talked with me after Gerard was killed, because she wanted to get into his flat. I think that she wanted to get some letters she had written him and perhaps these diaries. She was worried. I advised her—well, that doesn't matter." Finn seemed flustered. "I went to see her after I told the police about her interest in the flat. After Matthew . . . I saw him hit her," he said slowly. "That was Sunday. They had a row. He knew then she was pregnant, I think." He pushed up the sleeves of his dingy Aran sweater.

Venus didn't want Finn to reveal Emily this way. Her indignities. Autopsy, medical examinations; she would have no privacy. *The grave's a fine and private place* . . . Venus remembered a line of poetry. But not for the murdered.

Finn nodded as if responding to a line of questioning in his head. "I went to see her again on Monday, like I say, after the police. She told me some things . . . Venus, can I be straight with you?"

"Yes." She put her hands flat on the table. She pressed into the wood.

"Emily told me that she had known Gerard for several years. That they had an affair back in London, years ago. She followed him up here. I don't know when they started up again—I mean, she hasn't been here that long—" Finn's eyes traveled again to the wall. "It was clear to me that he didn't care about her, and she was obsessed with him. I think she got pregnant on purpose."

"Why are you telling me this? What does it have to do with anything, now she's dead?" Anger swam inside her, lapping at her throat.

"Because it's all part of why they're both dead. I'm sorry. When I went to see her that day she was fair out of it. She lied to me about the bruise, as she would do, but when I started asking her questions she started talking right enough. She lied for Matthew. Neither one of them have an alibi for the time of Gerard's death. But, as far as she knew, Matthew found out about her pregnancy—from the letters she retrieved from Gerard's—after his death. Necessarily. But it's possible he knew before. It's a perfect motive." Finn crossed his arms and stared out the window.

Venus was silent. Matthew . . . she saw his white skin, dark hair against his cheek, the steel intensity of his eyes.

"But the really strange thing," Finn said, sitting up at the table, "is that she asked me to go with her to Morag's. I was trying to tell you both this last night, but I'm afraid I wasn't thinking too clearly. Emily told me that Morag knew something about Gerard's *parents*, and that he had been to see her—Morag—a few times. This is where we come back to the journals, and to what Emily asked *you* about when you talked to her. We went along to Knowehouse, and there she started asking Morag about what was written in the diaries. A ritual or something where Morag got a new name, where your grandma was present. Morag was furious, grabbed the diaries, told Emily off. Emily rushed out of the house, and that was the last time I saw her." He swallowed. "Until last night. After she left, Morag told me to tell Kate, said something like 'tell her I won't be responsible, not now.' I haven't a clue what that means, and in all the craziness last night, I wasn't able to ask her. Do you know?"

Venus sat quietly, looking at the table. She knew about the naming ceremony; her Gran had a special name as well, used only in ceremony and ritual. She couldn't imagine what Morag meant by her request of Finn. Venus' mind felt empty, clear of meaning or understanding. There was something in Lorraine's diaries, about Kate and Morag. But how would Morag know anything about Gerard's family? And what would it matter if she did? Venus realized again that she knew nothing of anyone's life but her own. Secrets flowed behind the familiar faces. She wanted to cry.

"Gerard was researching his family—he was born here and his mother was Orcadian. We didn't talk much about it. He had a picture, and an old note from his mother. That was all. He didn't even know her name." Venus frowned, trying to remember. "There was something written on the picture, but it may have been only Gerard's name or age."

"I wonder if we could get ahold of it. Maybe you could ask Sammy for it." Finn rubbed the stubble on his chin.

"But why? I don't see what this has to do with Emily's death. Or Gerard's."

"Aye, I know. In reporting you learn, though, that if something keeps coming up, it's important. These journals—who was this Lorraine?"

"She was a friend of Gran's a long time ago." Venus leaned back in the chair, closing her eyes. The room was warm and familiar, but underneath her skin ice was building, spreading.

"When I went by Morag's last night, she had that fire blazing. Well, I could just see pages of something burning in it. It could have been the journals. Must have been."

Venus let Finn's voice flow over her, smooth water over stones. All she wanted was her life back, simple and peaceful. Gerard's death, their relationship, was distant and black. It would recede into nothing, like the sun disappearing below the horizon. She closed her eyes. The black haired woman, a red haired child. A train, blurring fast through the countryside. The woman looked out the window. Her eyes were far away blue, lips a raspberry red. She was beautiful and very sad.

"Finn—"

"But there *is* the Neill connection. That's what I don't see. He could have killed Gerard, but why kill Emily? As far as I know, she knew nothing about the man. And there's still the fact that no one besides you and Kate knew she was in the dovecote. Unless—did she ring someone? Matthew? And then there's the whole method of Emily's death. Heart failure. Mystery substances." Finn let out an exasperated sigh.

Venus nodded, speaking past the vision of the black-haired woman. "Sammy told me that Emily died from some poison. They sent the—whatever, blood?—to Inverness. To identify it. I think she killed herself, but he doesn't. I mean, have you thought of that?"

"It's possible, aye. Go on, how would she have done it?"

"It's not that difficult. She could have eaten water hemlock—although that makes you sick right away. But there's tansy, that grows wild, or eyebright . . . she could have taken something to abort the child and taken too much. That could even have been an accident."

"Or she could have taken drugs of some kind. Antidepressants maybe. Because, why would she eat wild plants?" Finn was skeptical.

"I suppose you're right," Venus mused. "I gather wild plants all the time, but it doesn't make sense that she would. Plant compounds might be harder to identify, though, than some regular drug she might have had."

"What about Morag?" Finn asked, leaning toward her again.

"What about her?" Venus looked away. There was a shrinking inside her she didn't want Finn to see.

"Would she know about plants and such?"

"She might. Yes. But why would she give Emily poison?"

"She was angry with Emily. She warned her off. And I saw her coming from that direction when I was on my way over. Aye, it fits. It fits. What do you know about Morag?"

"You can't think that *Morag*—"

"Why not? The manner of the death, the location—fits better with Morag as a killer. Emily was obviously on to something in these journals. You didn't see her that day; she was furious with Emily. All the wrath of the devil himself. Aye, there's something about this Lorraine, something *she* knew—"

"Lorraine was a silly woman who lived in her daydreams. She was my friend, I loved her, but she never could cope with the real world. She made things up."

Finn and Venus both turned with surprise to see Kate standing in the kitchen door.

"I didn't hear you drive in, Gran."

"No, I expect you didn't. Had to roll on down the lane," Kate cackled. "Ran out of petrol, fool that I am. Barely made it into the yard." Kate reached into the cupboard and got a mug. She poured herself tea from the pot on the table. She grimaced at the color. "You Irish do take your tea strong."

"So you don't like my idea of Morag as a suspect, Kate?" asked Finn.

"She's an old woman. Bitter, unpleasant—that I won't deny. But she's got no reason to kill anyone over something written down in a book. This isn't the city; we're simple folk here. There's been more killing in the last week than in the last forty years, that's no exaggeration. No," Kate wagged her finger at Finn, "this is the work of an outsider. Or, I imagine we'll find that Emily killed herself on purpose or accidentally. That Matthew is missing, isn't he? He's responsible for Gerard's death. Mark my words."

Kate sat with them and they talked of other things. Relief suffused Venus' body as Kate took over their conversation. The black haired woman, with her small red-headed child came again into her mind's eye.

"Oh, Finn," she sighed.

Kate and Finn stopped talking, and looked at her, Kate with an unusually guarded gaze.

"Aye?"

"Finn," she said again, summoning strength of voice. "Your family—your wife and baby—they're on a train. I'm afraid . . . I don't know why. I'm afraid of what she will do."

CHAPTER THIRTY-THREE

Finn stood in the wide parking area where the bus had left him off, squinting in the sun. A raft of clouds stood off to the west and south; rain would be upon them again soon. He strode over the lot, avoiding the knots of tourists headed for the ferry terminal behind him. He crossed the street and turned left, wandering into a wide courtyard that led to the High street. Finn had his groceries to buy, but at the moment the pub straight ahead was what he needed. A combination inn with pub below, and they had a nice bit of lawn in front. It was good to be in Stromness, the big city, and away from the maddening confines of his cottage and Blackstone.

Finn pulled open the door of the pub. *Just one, now. Keep yourself straight.* The gloom was inviting. He stopped for a packet of cigarettes from the machine, enjoying the cheery lights that displayed each brand name, the American cowboy that graced the front panel of the dispenser. High mountains, the horse and sky. That would feel good now—freedom.

From the lobby he went into the main lounge. He walked to the gleaming copper and wood bar and ordered a pint of Guinness. The woman pulling the pint was young and pleasant; they chatted while they waited for the beer to settle. He bought a packet of crisps and, glass in hand, he went to a cozy corner table. Finn arranged the ashtray, cigarettes, crisps, and beer in front of him. Thus organized, he began to think.

He was wound tight, stressed, but it was essential that he remain clear-headed. Whether or not there was anything to Venus' second 'vision,' he knew right enough that it was time to leave Orkney. He opened the crisps and began to munch, not tasting them, thoughts far away, sorting through his afternoon yesterday with Venus.

In many ways she reminded him of Nuala. He realized that must be the attraction, yet she was utterly different. Not only were Venus' faintly Asian features and skinny, girlish body completely unlike Nuala's classic Irish beauty and voluptuous curves—here he paused, wiped a hand over his thigh—but Venus was an innocent. It was an old-fashioned description, and he applied it not to an unlikely virginity but to a purity, a childlike quality of attitude and thought. Venus seemed beyond the world, untouched by it; she was vague and dreamy, even obtuse. It was her vagueness, her way of shutting a curtain over herself, appearing blank, like a seamless surface that reminded him of his wife. Nuala had the same ability to become opaque, but in her case there was a gritty echo, a calculating gleam reflected behind the neutral expression.

Finn took a gulp of beer and gathered fragments of crisps on his finger, licking them off absently. Venus had been willing to discuss the murders, but she was keeping something back, he was sure. His keen reporter instinct, honed over fifteen years in the business, buzzed with the certainty of background, of story, details beyond his reach. He was clear that she trusted him, and he was absurdly flattered. Why? He was a suspect; they had laughed about it. That laughter had burned in a way—she didn't take him seriously. And he had embarrassed himself. She had skated over his foray into intimacy, but he wasn't surprised. He didn't care if she knew he fancied her. The main thing was that he continue to earn her trust, and that they find a way to—what? Solve the mystery? He laughed out loud.

"Inspector Ross, on the case," he said grandly, lifting his glass in salute.

His discussion with Venus and Kate had really raised more questions than answers. Matthew was a viable suspect for Gerard's death and had the opportunity. But though he might have motive for killing Emily, there really was no way he could have known she would be in the dovecote. Whereas Morag was a perfect suspect for Emily's death, but less so for Gerard's. Kate had defended Morag in the end, suggesting that bitterness alone wasn't a motive for murder. And she wouldn't have known of Emily's presence in the dovecote either. Kate was confident of suicide; after all, Emily's life was caving in around her and she was none too stable emotionally.

Finn finished the last of his beer. He opened the packet of cigarettes with ceremony. Lighting one, he reflected that Kate had a point. Suicide was more plausible, given all the circumstances. Why would Morag be involved at all? The connection there had to be with Neill. It was more likely that Neill had killed Gerard and that Morag knew about it; more likely that Emily had died in desperation or grief. But why had Matthew disappeared, and where was he?

"Mind if I join you?"

Finn looked up into Matthew's smiling face. His face was red, his eyes bleary, his hair hung lank and greasy to his shoulders. He had a pint in his hand.

Finn's heart accelerated. He squinted up through his smoke at Matthew, wary. "Aye, please yourself."

"I'll get you another." Matthew turned to wave at the barmaid before he sat.

Finn offered Matthew a cigarette. "Where have you been keeping yourself?" he asked, trying to keep his tone light.

Matthew tapped the top of the table. "Right here. Nice place, isn't it? Thought I deserved a little rest." His face distorted into an ugly frown. "That fucking cow—had to get away from her. Cunt." Matthew downed half of his pint.

Finn froze, his cigarette halfway to his lips.

Steady now, take it slow.

"Thought I'd give her a little time to realize how much she needs me. Give her a couple days to worry, to get perspective. She has no idea how fucking lucky she is I put up with her shite. She'll be in a proper state by now." Matthew laughed and drained his glass.

Finn set his cigarette carefully in the ashtray. He watched the smoke rise. The bartender brought two fresh pints and took their glasses away. She flicked a keen eye on Matthew, checking to see how far gone he was, no doubt.

"So, you have been *here* for two days? Just staying at the inn, like?"

"Aye. Using her card, too. I'll make her pay. You have to, you know." Matthew nodded sagely, gesturing with his cigarette. "Keep the cunt in line." Matthew's face creased again in anger. Redness bloomed in his cheeks. "I'll tell you, it's all over between us anyway. She's a whore. I've been thinking about it. She's no good to me anymore. Should've got myself shut of her long ago."

Finn cringed. Was it possible that Matthew did not know that Emily was dead? Finn didn't have television, so he didn't know what had been reported there. Nothing had appeared in the *Orcadian* about Emily's death; the police must be working hard to keep the story down. But why hadn't the police found Matthew here? Wouldn't they have checked the hotels? "I'll just be a moment," Finn said, rising. He headed toward the bar.

"More crisps, please," Finn said to the girl at the bar. "Have you seen my friend there these last two days?"

"Oh, aye, he's been full of the drink every day. Sits in the small lounge usually, playing the machines. My manager told me not to serve him last night, but I did. He got angry with me when I tried to refuse him." She giggled nervously. "He's a bit scary."

"Aye, he is that." Finn tried to smile. "Have you been putting up with him alone, then?"

"No. I've got help in the evening. I go off shift at eight anyway, then Willy is here. He just works seven to closing."

"Well, he'll be away soon. He does this sometimes. Girlfriend trouble," Finn smiled conspiratorially. "Hope it hasn't been a burden for you."

"No worse than others," the girl said, smiling.

Finn walked back to his seat. Matthew was lighting another cigarette. Finn tossed two packets of crisps on the table. How would Matthew take the news of Emily's death?

"What's Emily been doing without your car?"

"I didn't take the car. I was that mad, I just walked out of the flat. The bus was right down the road at the stop, so I got on. Didn't know where I was going till I got here. Came straight to the pub."

"Aye. And you haven't left?"

"No. What concern is it to you?" Matthew's eyes slitted.

"You should know, Matthew, that Emily was found dead two days ago. Tuesday night. The police have been looking for you."

A wave of expressions crossed Matthew's face: surprise, anger, fear—and finally, wariness. "Did you know I was here?" he asked.

"No."

"Well, well, well." Matthew took a long drag then exhaled. "Fuck. Stupid fucking cow. What happened?"

"Don't know." Finn didn't want to reveal too much. Let the police fill Matthew in. "I found her, in the McNeill's dovecote. She was a mess. If you've been here, and you've got witnesses, I'd get on to the police."

"You'll be on to them yourself, I imagine." Matthew smiled at Finn. "Well, it's no odds to me. I've got nothing to hide."

"You're a rare man, then," Finn stretched a smile over his face. "Even the innocent have secrets."

CHAPTER THIRTY-FOUR

The wind was against her today, blowing into her with such great gusts that Venus could barely walk up the hill. Her head down, hands in her pockets, she made her way up from the village. Today she would visit the church-yard. It had been one week since Gerard had been killed. Almost a week since Matthew's attack on her. It was time to visit her special place and re-claim the peaceful energy that had always resided there. Her heart beat in her ears, roaring with the wind, but she was determined. Matthew was missing— but he wasn't in the churchyard, she was sure of that. Venus felt protected now, safe. She looked out to the sea. Two seals floated, watching the shore. She took them for companions, for a sign that she should con-tinue on.

Chop whipped up the water as the wind increased. It wasn't storm sea-son; islanders liked to joke that they took no notice of the wind unless it was over 120 mph. Deep, dark clouds punctuated the sky. It would rain anyway and most likely the wind would come and go as it always did. Venus searched in her pocket for an elastic for her hair, brushing the edge of the picture Sammy had given her. Something of Gerard's, not important to the investigation, he thought she'd like it. Venus hadn't even really looked at it, just squirreled it away to unfold later, like the treasure it was. She secured her hair in a tight ponytail as she approached the gate to the churchyard. Venus paused here, noticing the grass still mashed in places from the police vehicles, the cigarette butts that were disintegrating into the soil. She pulled up the latch on the gate and went in.

The flowers seemed to have grown tall since her last visit, undulating pinks, yellows, and purples. The upright headstones were nearly covered. Venus glanced at the sycamore. It waved in the wind, a greeting, not a warning, and she made her way over. She looked all around her, but the atmosphere was one of emptiness, of loneliness, but in that, safety. She paused as she reached the tree. The area around the tree was tidy, swept clean. Her shells and rocks were gone. Sammy had warned her of this; everything was checked and analyzed and searched for the invisible DNA, that storyteller that could reveal a universe in one cell, one piece of hair. It was a new start. That was fine. Venus crossed her arms. Where exactly had Gerard's body lay? She found herself looking for blood and bone, knowing that the police would have taken it away, or it had been washed into the earth by the rain.

Venus took a tentative step into the shelter of the tree, bending to avoid the waving branches. She realized she was holding her breath. She reached out a hand to touch the stone wall, solid and cool. She turned and sat on the flat stone that she had liberated from weeds and grass years ago. It was a gravestone, unreadable, under the tree, and it was her sitting spot. The rock was cool beneath her legs and bum; the jagged edges of the stone wall pressed into her back. She breathed. Her eyes traveled around the churchyard, then closed. She began the prayer, the ritual that Kate had taught her to cleanse a place of evil or disturbed energy.

Some time later, Venus swam up from the depths of her meditation, her conscious contemplation of love. She blinked open her eyes. The light was yellow and green, moving fast in the wind. Her legs tingled and she stood awkwardly and stretched. She moved away from the tree to the sanctuary ruins. The nettles greeted her, a thick patch of dark iron-green. She walked around the ruin counterclockwise and returned to the nettles. Here the sun shone and warmed her. She stood against the wall and pulled the picture out of her pocket.

The image was faded black and white. A woman with bobbed blond hair turned away from the camera, displaying a blurry profile. Venus recognized Gerard's nose and forehead in his mother. Gerard himself was only a baby, chubby and solemn, staring into the camera. It was a small picture, informal, a snap taken by a friend perhaps. Gerard had showed this to her once or twice. She knew that he had been searching for his family, but they had so rarely talked about it. Venus turned it over. A woman's sloping writing spelled out 'Gerard' and the number one. In pencil someone had jotted a list of names and a question mark. Was it Gerard's writing? She squinted at it. It appeared to be, but the writing was light. The first name was 'Tille,' followed by 'Matilda,' and 'Clotilde.' Venus' heart jumped, and a clear picture fell into place, like tumblers in a lock. Clotilde. Her Gran's friend. Venus' mind raced back to their conversation, days before. Her Gran telling the story of Anne, and Pierre, all the friends of her youth. And how Kate had closed up so strangely at the mention of Clotilde, at Venus' questions of what had happened to her. Could Clotilde be Gerard's mother? Venus struggled to think of how old she would have been in her pregnancy—sometime during the war, was it? She couldn't remember the details. She would have to ask Kate. But it could be . . . Kate had said her friend Anne went to France with her husband. She had a child . . . the child came back. It *could* be.

Venus slipped the photo back in her pocket. Had Kate known who Gerard was? Why would she have been silent about his parentage, when she knew he was looking for his family? And why, if Kate had been so fond of Anne and Clotilde, would she object so to Gerard and she being lovers? Of course, Gerard had revealed himself to be unkind, but in the beginning . . . Venus' head whirled with ideas. She remembered what Finn had said the afternoon before, about Emily's conviction that Morag knew something about Gerard's family. He told her of his and Emily's visit to Morag, Emily's questions about witchcraft and secret names. What did the circle of women that Emily so doggedly searched for have to do with Gerard's family? Finn had been confused at Emily's line of questioning that day, and by Morag's venomous anger. How did *Morag* know about Gerard's family? Who had his father been? A final question loomed, dark behind her spinning thoughts. If Kate or Morag knew who Gerard's family was, then why was it a secret they felt compelled to keep?

CHAPTER THIRTY-FIVE

The garden was alive with birds, chattering, screeching in the wind. Though there were hours and hours of light left to the day, the dark-bellied clouds had finally coalesced to promise a soaking rain. Drops began to spatter as Kate stared out the window. Her heart beat in her chest, and she found her breath coming in uneven gasps. She glanced toward the telephone on the wall. Sammy's news had shocked her. Trails of wind infiltrated the kitchen through the open door, bringing the beguiling scent of rose. The past, like a shadow under the summer sun, cast its darkness over her. Emily, dead by poisoning. The light and noise of the present faded. Kate's thoughts spiraled in, the voices of time pulling her back.

The four of them had gathered, anxious, in the kitchen. Kate had watched Clotilde hide the bruises from Thierry long enough; the tragedy of his assault on Lorraine was the final blow. Their men were in the sitting room, setting the stage for a normal evening of late tea—beer and bread and cheese. Kate looked at the women around her. They watched and waited.

Sweat sat on Clotilde's upper lip. "I can't do it. I can't," she whispered. Her eyes were bright.

"You must," Kate hissed. "Think of your child."

"I can't," the girl pleaded. "What if it doesn't work? He'll find out, he'll —"

The women fell silent. From the other room the men's voices rang in discussion, Thierry's accent thick, voice loud. Kate moved away from Clotilde to the icebox and removed three bottles of her husband's strong, homemade bitter ale. She removed the corks and poured into tall waiting glasses. The low ceiling and thick heat from the cooker enclosed the room. Morag shivered, though the sweat ran down her face, and under the collar of her woolen sweater. Clotilde stood miserably by the counter. Lorraine sat at the kitchen work table, bruised face bent into the heat from the stove. Her breath was heavy.

"Kate? We're in want of a drink, my love." Hamish stood in the low door, stooping to avoid the lintel. "Shall I fetch it?" He met her eyes with a probing gaze.

"No, I'm bringing it out. I just need to slice the bread and cheese."

"All right." Hamish withdrew and the male voices continued the discussion of the day's work.

"We have all decided," Kate said. "Let us each pour from the bottle." She pulled a small vial from her skirt pocket. "No one will bear the full responsibility. We have decided." She set aside one glass of beer in the center of the table. "Lorraine, you will be first." Kate gave the bottle to the woman seated near her.

Lorraine looked up at Kate. One eye was swollen shut, bruises marked her neck. Two fingers were broken and wrapped together. She struggled with the lid of the bottle while the three other women watched. Lorraine removed the cap and poured a few drops of amber oil into the beer. Her lips moved soundlessly.

"Now Morag."

Morag swallowed, her young face awash with fear. She looked at Kate, a plea in her eyes. Kate waited. Morag took the bottle and added to the beer.

Clotilde came next. Her hand shook violently. Kate took the hand in her own and together they poured the remaining contents of the vial into the beer.

"Morag, see to the cheese and bread," Kate commanded. "Clotilde, take Thierry's glass and I will bring the others."

The women silently obeyed. Kate and Clotilde moved into the main room of the house. The men were comfortable around a peat fire in the grate.

"About time. You women waste too much time with your gossiping." Thierry laughed and pinched Clotilde's arm as she handed him the glass.

Kate handed round glasses to her husband and Peter. He caught her eye and she gave him a grim smile.

"To our luck today, with the catch." Hamish lifted his glass. "To getting what we all deserve."

The three men lifted glasses high and drank. Thierry shuddered as he set his down, empty.

The memory of that night, so long ago, washed over her, fading as it pulled away, a wave drawn by the tide. Kate clutched at the counter, gagging into the sink. She looked at her hands, once strong and smooth, now spotted and cramped with age. Her hands, her choices. She had delivered babies, laid out the dead for burial. She had been a participant in both life and death. The room swayed. Kate moved to the table and sat, cradling her head in her hands.

"Gran!" Venus burst into the kitchen, calling. She stopped, hesitated. "Are you all right?"

Kate looked up at Venus, dabbing her tears with a tea towel.

"Sit down, Venus. Come and sit down."

Venus grew pale. Kate watched a spectrum of emotions cross her face; fear stayed in the girl's wide eyes. She seized the back of a chair and sat.

Kate took a deep breath. She rubbed her forehead rhythmically, feeling the softness of her hair at her temples, the dryness of her own skin. She realized she felt very, very old. Where was she now, between past and present? Venus looked at her expectantly, hands clenched. The phone call. She must tell Venus, prepare her. Kate summoned strength, looked her granddaughter in the eye. "I've been on the phone with Sammy just now. He called to say a few things. I've a mind he's doing me a favor, letting me know."

"What? What are you talking about?"

"First off, they've found Matthew. Or rather, Finn found him—"

"No! Not dead? Poor Finn!"

Kate leaned back in her chair, letting her hands fall to her lap. "No, not dead, girl. In a pub." Kate let out a cheerless laugh. "Seems Matthew has been on a two day drunk in Stromness. He could not be responsible for Emily's death."

"Oh."

"He didn't even know, I guess. That she was dead. Finn told him."

"So who—?"

"Aye, exactly. Well, the autopsy has come back, or whatever they were waiting for. Sammy said that Emily died from heart failure. There was something called Thujone found in her body, quite a lot of it from what he said. It's contained in wormwood."

"So . . . did she take some? For abortion after all?" Venus paused. "Wormwood isn't the most common abortificaent that lay people would try."

"Aye. Aye. Well, she didn't know she was taking it. We—I—there was wormwood in the tea, to help her anxiety, with the lemon balm. And I burned an incense that had wormwood too. For her protection, to banish the anger and despair."

Venus' face grew even paler. She did not speak. Her eyes were fastened to Kate. The question, the trust . . . like so many faces from the past.

"I told Sammy what I had done," Kate said, breathing back tears. "Aye, I was up front and honest. But I didn't mean to harm her. I can't understand it. Wormwood in small doses is not harmful. There couldn't have been enough there to kill her."

"Did you tell Sammy that?"

"Aye, I did. He said he'd check with the doctor and ring me back." Kate glanced at the phone on the wall. "He wanted to know how much I had on hand. Just the usual peedie packets, I told him. I went to check, because I thought I had some oil of wormwood too. But I didn't."

"You did have some oil, Gran, because I just used it for Teke's ringworm, last week. There was a whole vial of it. Labeled and marked. I just used a little, on his skin, and put it back."

Kate looked at Venus sharply. "Well, it's not there now. You must have left it out."

"I didn't," Venus protested. "Anyway, how would she have gotten it? She wouldn't know to look in your room for the herbs. Did you tell her about it before?"

"No. We didn't talk about specific herbs. She didn't outright ask for help with an abortion either. Last we talked," here Kate paused, struggling, "she wanted to keep the child."

"But if she changed her mind and drank the oil by mistake?"

"It would kill her before it would have time to work on her uterus." Kate felt like she was talking from the bottom of a well. Venus seemed far away, unreal. She watched her granddaughter, saw the thoughts passing swiftly through her mind. Venus was an innocent. A child, she shouldn't be a part of this thing—

"Who else would know wormwood oil was a poison?" Venus demanded.

Kate was surprised by the force in her voice. "I—I don't know, girl. Anyone might. It isn't for us to find out."

"Gran—if Sammy suspects *you*, it is!" She paused again, thinking. "Morag would know."

"Aye. So she would. But . . ." Kate felt anger, red and black, rise inside of her. Anger toward herself, toward the arrogance of her youth. "Justice will come down. For whomever needs it. Aye . . . I've had enough of passing judgment."

Venus looked at her oddly. She bit her lip, started to speak and stopped. Kate waited.

"Gran—I saw Sammy today too, at the cafe. He gave me a picture of Gerard and his mother, when he was a baby." Venus fished the photo out of her pocket and pushed it across the table toward Kate. "Do you know who this woman is?"

Kate pulled the picture to her, bent fingers caressing the edge. She brought her hand to her forehead again, shielding her eyes. The anger dissipated and she was filled with a biting sadness. "That's Clotilde. Dear Anne's girl. Aye." She looked up to meet Venus' gaze.

The sounds of the house were thundering in the silence that followed. Kate could hear a tractor in a neighboring field, a momentary buzz before the next blast of wind carried the sound away. Rain began to lash the windows.

"You knew. Does Morag know?"

"She does, indeed. I told her when I realized it."

"Why?" Venus gripped the table with her fingertips.

"It's an old, old story, and one that doesn't concern you." The past was cracking open, flowing, touching everything. Venus was an innocent. She mustn't know. Kate pushed on the table with her hands, feeling the strength of the wood.

"It does concern me, Gran, and I think it concerns Emily's death too. Maybe even Gerard's." The cold, logical words dropped like steel from her mouth.

"Emily thought so too. Emily pursued it, and now she's dead. Does that not tell you something? To leave well enough alone?"

"Gran, I don't understand the secrecy. So Clotilde was Gerard's mother. What harm can there be in anyone knowing? Did she—did something bad happen?"

Kate watched Venus' face change, her eyes turning opaque, almost glassy. Venus saw things, knew things. Kate shuddered, gripped the table.

"Clotilde had made a poor choice of husband. He was a bastard, through and through. Worse than Gerard, oh, so much worse. But he—disappeared before Gerard was even born. It was just after the war. Strange things happened; people often just . . . went away."

"What does Morag have to do with it?"

"Oh," Kate struggled for nonchalance, willed her voice to be calm. Voices from the past mixed in her head with Venus' questions. What to tell, what to secret away? "She was involved with protecting Clotilde, that's all." Kate focused her attention on a loose stitch in her jumper. She examined the sweater closely. "You see, Clotilde's husband had beaten another woman. And raped her. She was a widow, with two small children. We had to protect her, protect ourselves. Thierry knew he had to leave. We wouldn't stand for it."

"Thierry? Was that Gerard's father?"

"Kate!" Peter's strong voice called from outside. "Kate! You're boat is off it's mooring. The tide's about to turn and there's a fair gale already blowing." He stepped into the kitchen, hair windblown and jacket shoulders soaked with rain.

"Did you walk, Peter? You're drenched." Kate looked up at him without standing.

"I've just been outside. But we've got to fetch the boat."

Kate felt Venus' eyes upon her as Peter reached and took her hand.

CHAPTER THIRTY-SIX

Finn watched Matthew weave his way toward the men's loo. He exhaled, realizing that he had been holding his breath. An uneasy tightness held his throat; his mouth burned from too many cigarettes. Fresh air seemed imperative, and Finn rose, leaving a few pound coins on the table. What Matthew did now was of no concern to him. He was not surprised that Matthew indeed had an alibi for Emily's death. Certainly Matthew could have killed her, and maybe would have, given more provocation. Finn doubted now that Matthew had killed Gerard, although he wasn't out of it as far as the police were concerned. No, Emily would have been Matthew's first victim, and Gerard would have been the afterthought. Besides, Finn didn't believe that Matthew had known about Emily and Gerard's affair until the Sunday following Gerard's death.

Wind and sun greeted Finn as he exited the pub. He breathed a sigh of relief, trying to relax the tension in his throat. He needed to call the police and he wanted to talk to Venus. At least Matthew should be charged with attacking her, despite his innocence in Emily's death. Who *had* killed Emily? Who could have? Finn stood on the steps outside the pub, letting the noises of the busy town flow around him. Were the deaths of Emily and Gerard related? They had to be; but if not Matthew, then who? Neill

Leach's face popped into Finn's mind. Yes, there was still the connection there. Sammy had been going to talk to him, but Finn hadn't heard, of course, the results of that conversation. Neill had a clear motive for killing Gerard, but not Emily. Still, it wouldn't hurt to go round and have a chat with Neill himself.

Neill lived on the opposite end of the High street from where the pub lay. The street was narrow and cobbled in places, slim sidewalks fronting the typical shops. A chemist, snack-grocery, dress shop, Red Cross thrift store. It was mid-afternoon, and the streets were busy, the tea shops full of young mothers with prams and grannies greeting each other with exclamations and kisses. Finn walked through it all, dialing Sammy's office number on his mobile twice before getting through to Sergeant Crombie. The Sergeant informed him that Sammy was out of the office, so Finn told him of his meeting with Matthew. Crombie seemed excited by the news, and Finn was gratified. He rang off as he approached the side street leading to the housing estate where Neill lived.

The day was warm, and sweat formed on Finn's neck, damping his collar. Anxiety began in his belly, a soft drumbeat of pain to match his pulse. What approach to take with Neill? What information did he hope to gain? He breathed in, recognizing fear. And on the other side, a welcome rush of adrenaline.

"I'm ready for something," Finn muttered. He ran his hands over his hair and continued up the street.

Neill's house looked identical to the others. One-story bungalows, neat patch of grass in front, with tile roofs and a bit of dark wood detail about the windows. Finn almost mistook the house—he'd visited Neill only once, in February—but remembered Neill's Ford Escort in a putrid shade of yellow. Finn heard the murmur of the television through the open window. Neill would be at home then, still whiling away his days with mind-numbing talk programs, getting comfortable on the dole.

Finn stepped up to the front door and rapped twice. The tightness had returned to his throat but blood hopped in his veins. Neill opened the door and stared at Finn.

"Wha'?" he said, voice slow.

"Hello, Neill. It's Finn Ross—I came to interview you before, a way back in February. And you'll remember I was at your ma's just the other day."

Suspicion dawned with comprehension. Neill moved to push the door closed but Finn, used to this response, stepped through the doorway, positioning himself in the way.

"Don't mind if I come in for a bit, do you? There's a few questions I'd like to ask."

Neill's brow furrowed. "What d'ya want, then?"

He had grown bigger, more slothful in the months that had passed since he'd lost his job. Finn had seen it before, with friends of his: the ambivalent despondency of unemployment. Finn shoved his hands in his pockets and moved into the room. The place looked a mess, with overflowing ash trays and lager cans cluttering the tables. A pizza box sat half open on the table, and a fly buzzed over the congealed grease and cheese in the box. Finn sniffed, the air stale despite the open window. "Morag not coming round to clean for you anymore? Why's that?"

Neill scowled. "Look, I don't know what you're here for, but you're not welcome. What my mum does is none of your business anyway." His hands gathered into fists.

Finn felt exalted by the energy moving through his veins. Every aspect of the room stood out in detail. Neill's heavy features were distorted by his weight gain, and the spark of intelligent anger that Finn had seen before was absent. There was a dullness, a throb of surly petulance instead. And, as Finn had sensed at Morag's, a stink of fear.

"I'm doing a little . . . investigation, on the side, like, into the question of some old diaries. I'd like to know what you could tell me about them. Emily

Haworth was asking Morag about it that afternoon we were there." Finn strove for an air of confident nonchalance.

Neill crossed his arms. "Don't know anything about it. Why don't you ask my Mum?"

"For obvious reasons—you can see for yourself she's a bit bitter on the subject." Finn rubbed his jaw; he needed a shave. "Look, Neill, between the two of us, things are getting complicated with this business of Emily. Your ma . . ." the memory of Morag, meeting her on the stile that night, stopped his speech. Yes . . . it had to be . . . "She's right in it, and she'll take you down too unless we can help the police figure out what actually happened."

Finn paced to a side chair, watching Neill. The man didn't alter his stance, but a strange look shuddered over his face.

"I don't know what you're talking about," he sneered. "I don't know any Emily—"

"Sure you do. And I know you were burning those diaries in that bonfire Tuesday night," Finn took a chance, still watching Neill's face.

"What the fuck are you on about?" Neill's voice rose. "I don't know anything about Lorraine's diaries—"

"Then how did you know they were Lorraine's?" Finn suppressed a smile. The classic catch-out.

"Listen," Neill tossed his head and moved toward Finn. "You've got no rights. You're not police and I'm not suspected of anything. I don't know any Emily, and I don't know about any fucking diaries."

Finn was reminded of a belligerent bull. He moved slightly toward the door, to counter Neill's approach. He knew Neill had information about the diaries, but he hadn't gotten the reaction he expected regarding Emily's death.

"Where were you Tuesday night, Neill? Because if you can't tell me and you can't tell the police, then depend upon it, your ma will let you take the blame."

Neill roared. "I don't know what you're fucking on about! There's nothing to take blame for. I've had enough of taking the fall for someone else! My mum took those diaries and if they got burned, well it's her own fucking doing! It's none of mine and I won't let her drag me into it, not this time. If you want answers, take yourself off and ask her. Now fuck off!" Neill flung his hands up as if to banish Finn from the room.

Finn's thoughts whirred. It seemed almost that Neill didn't know that Emily was dead. But he knew his mother had the diaries, so he must have some idea of what was in them. Neill obviously harbored a deep-seated anger towards Morag, and no wonder. What else had she gotten him into?

Neill swept the cans and ashtrays from the coffee table in one gesture. He sat, head in his hands, grabbing fistfuls of hair. The television buzzed in the background. Finn crept back to the side chair. Despite the layer of dust, it was covered in expensive fabric and had once been nice. Finn wondered at the change in Neill from a professional man doing all right for himself to this slow, angry slob.

"Listen," he said again, sitting, "You have got to tell me what you know about those diaries. Why would Morag want to burn them? Emily was asking her about them, and now Emily is dead. And I *saw* your mother coming from the scene of the crime. Jesus, she's right in it, man. Do you know what that means? If you don't tell—"

"What? What are you saying, Emily's dead?" Neill's face took on a look of horror.

"I mean, someone's killed her. Tuesday night. It's Thursday, Neill, have you not heard about it? Has your ma not been on to you? Or were you involved all along and now keeping it cool, keeping it quiet?"

Neill's face went blank, and Finn saw his eyes darken to black. He beat the coffee table in front of him, startling Finn to the edge of his chair. "No fucking way. No fucking way she's getting me involved with that! Now you listen," Neill jabbed his meaty finger in the air. "She took those sodding diaries—you saw her do it. Right out of that fucking cow's hands. She told me it would end with that. 'Burn and be gone,' she said. I told her I wouldn't do any more. I pulled up her floor and chopped those sodding boards and built the fire heap. But if she—"

Finn leaned forward, his voice hissing through his lips. "But what was in them that she was afraid of? Why steal them, burn them at all? And why pull up the floor?"

A sly intelligence transformed Neill's face. "Well, she'd been a part of it, hadn't she? Lorraine had written it all down and people were reading it, taking an interest."

"A part of what?"

"A killing," Neill said, suddenly thoughtful. "A killing. But Kate McNeill, she led them to it. She and Mum and Lorraine and some others, maybe. I don't know—I didn't care! But Mum was crazy. She said she couldn't have it coming out." Neill's voice was high and shrill, filled with the anger of the years. "What did it matter, now? Nothing would happen to her, I tried to tell her. But *he* knew, and wanted money to keep quiet. Profiting from his own father's death! And then there was Kate, you see, Kate had to be punished, didn't she? That was Mum's mind. And what about me, I asked her, and what that fucker Gerard had done to me? Justice for both of us, she said—" Neill stopped, shoving his fist into his mouth in an almost comical gesture.

Alarm bells rang in Finn's mind. Could he mean that Kate and Morag had actually killed Gerard's father? But when? And how or why? There was no time to puzzle it out; the conversation had spiraled into confession, and Finn realized he wasn't ready for the consequences. After the fire of Neill's anger was spent and the need to talk gratified, the fear would set in, and then Finn's own life would be in danger. Finn stood, and Neill with him.

"Neill, it doesn't matter what happened—what happened before." Finn edged toward the door. "I've got no stake in it," he lied. "I'm away to home, and . . . and . . ." He scrambled for thoughts. "Do you have an alibi for

Tuesday night? Do you?" He had to make Neill focus on Emily's death instead of Gerard's.

Neill sprang over the coffee table, fear making him agile. Finn turned for the door. He grasped the handle and pulled down as Neill made contact with him, twisting him onto the floor. The carpet was soft against his face. He smelled Neill's stale breath. The man was heavy, and a muscle twinged in Finn's low back. Pain cramped in his belly. He struggled. Neill's face came up with a roar and their eyes met. Finn pushed against his throat.

"Don't make it worse!" he cried. "For fuck's sake, man, were you a part to Emily's death or not?"

"No! I won't be blamed for that, I won't—"

"Then don't fuck yourself by killing me!" Finn almost laughed; the ignominy of lying underneath this bear of a man, begging for his life. "I've no stake, I tell you. I don't care. I'll walk away and forget I heard any of it. But if you didn't kill Emily, then don't let your mother blame you. Again. Matthew's out of it, I'm out of it. But you'll be right in the middle if you harm me."

Neill beat his fists into Finn's gut and chest. Finn grunted in pain, the force of air being knocked from his lungs. Gasping, he struggled against an overwhelming feeling of suffocation. Finn brought a knee up and pushed with all his strength. The edge of his keys and mobile phone in his jacket pocket dug into his ribs. Neill grunted with the push of his knee but remained on top of him. Memories of the streets, the fighting, the police harassment flowed through Finn's mind. With a roar he raised his head and torso and butted Neill between the eyes. Neill cried out and rolled back. Tremors of pain ricocheted through Finn's head. He scrambled to his feet, sending a kick to Neill's stomach before stumbling out of the house and down the street.

Outside the birds called and Finn smelled the sweet fragrance of roses. His nose began to bleed. He ran down the lane, adrenaline replacing pain. He heard his phone ringing in his pocket but Finn was concerned with only one thing. Finding the police and getting to Venus and Kate. If Morag had killed Emily—and he was convinced she had—and if she had made Neill kill Gerard, Finn didn't think she would stop there. His vision blurred as he finally reached the High street and staggered into an old woman and her husband, pushing their grandbaby along the cobbles.

CHAPTER THIRTY-SEVEN

There was a scrabble for jackets and Wellies, then the three of them were outside. The wind had become strong and the already receding tide pulled and roiled in white-capped chop. The small fishing boat had started to drift, mooring line snapped or worn through. It had been a long while since anyone had been out in the boat. Venus walked a little behind Kate and Peter. They were headed toward the small beach and the dinghy that rested there on its own short mooring line. Rain pelted down and the field was mucky, tall grass leaving trails of wet on her clothes. Venus' thoughts were churning. Something was happening, something she didn't understand and that was beyond her control. Venus was sure that whatever had happened to Gerard's father had affected Morag and Kate's relationship. And Lorraine . . .the journals . . . what had Lorraine recorded there? Kate turned suddenly and commanded:

"Get up to the barn, Venus, and take care of the cows."

"What?" Her voiced roared away with the wind.

Kate turned to walk back to her. "The cow needs milking and the calves fed. They are more important than this old boat; we don't need you anyway. Get on up to the barn."

Venus stood rooted in the field. Lapwings mewled in the air above them, hovering in the belligerent wind.

"Go!" Kate cried and gave Venus a little push. She walked back to where Peter waited.

Venus turned to the barn uncertainly. She felt out of control, pulled by forces beyond her. She wanted suddenly to talk to Finn, to hear his rational voice parceling out the facts. Hampered in her Wellies, she began a jolting run to the house. He had given her his mobile number only yesterday. Perhaps he would come for dinner, for tea. He could help with the boat.

Venus entered the kitchen and rummaged in the counter basket for the paper she had put his number on. She found it and went to the phone. His voice was soothing, even on the voicemail, and she was surprised at her own voice, calmly leaving a message. An invitation. But she was frustrated that she couldn't reach him, frustrated by her Gran's strange behavior. Kate had retrieved the boat before, albeit in better weather, when the mooring line had snapped. Venus was the better swimmer, she should be the one to row out to the boat. But Venus knew nothing about how the vessel ran, even how to start the engine. Peter was strong and smart. It would be all right.

Venus left the house again and headed to the barn. The cow and her calves were inside, out of the weather. Lunette lowed from her pen. Venus had to milk Lunette and bottle feed the calves. She went about fixing their milk replacer, filling bottles and attaching them to the stand that Kate had built. The babies were there instantly, greedily sucking down the food. The wind howled around the impervious stone of the barn. Venus grabbed the milking stool from its corner and climbed over the gate to Lunette's pen. She next filled Lunette's grain bin and latched her to the wall. Lunette was happy to feed and be milked. Venus felt for the heavy teats, laid her head against the cow's humid flank. She could hear the gurgles of Lunette's stomachs, and the cow's slow, soothing heartbeat. Venus was soon lost in the rhythm of milking. The spray of milk into the bucket, Lunette's chuffing pleasure, the distant slobber of the calves upon their bottles. It didn't seem that there was anything else, any other unfolding, unstoppable drama in the outside world. There was the smell of hay and manure.

The bucket full, she hurried to unlatch Lunette and put the stool away. She carried the bucket to an old refrigerator on the other side of the barn. The wind was a persistent dragon. Venus checked the calves again and left the barn. She was surprised to see Morag's Mini parked in the yard. She had not heard the car. Venus felt acid panic rise in her throat. She went to the house, calling Morag's name. The woman wasn't there, and Venus came out again and crossed to the field. From the top of the sloping hill she could see Morag and Kate arguing on the beach. Peter was halfway to the drifting boat, the dinghy rising up and down with the waves. It was much too choppy, she realized. The dinghy would be awash in no time.

Rain slicked down Venus' hair, slipping down her neck and underneath her clothes. She was freezing cold and gusts of wind threatened to knock her over. She wished for Finn and started down the hill. Before her, as if in slow motion, Venus watched Morag drag Kate into the ocean. Kate was screaming at Morag, her face distorted and full of pain. Morag's hair was loose and flew up in a crazed tornado around her face. She pulled Kate further into the water. Venus froze, grasping at the soaking, waist-high grass that surrounded her. It was wet and slipped through her hands. Kate's tiny body was deluged up to her breasts. Morag was in front of her tugging at her jumper. Why didn't her Gran struggle? Venus felt her mouth open, tasted rain on her tongue. Peter pulled with the oars toward the women, against the tide and pummeling chop. He called out, but Venus could only see his mouth open and shut. The wind escaped with his words.

Morag had Kate now and shook her with both hands. Taller and younger, she seemed to tower over Kate, like a mother over a child. Venus saw Kate clawing at Morag's hands. Morag lunged, or lost her balance, and sank with Kate into the water.

"No! Gran! Gran!" Venus' words tore from her throat and she began to run down the hill. Her boots slipped in the boggy grass and she fell painfully onto her tailbone. Her breath left her in a single gasp. She doubled over, unable to get her breath. Black, treacly panic melted into her arms and legs. She couldn't breathe. Venus forced herself onto her hands and knees. Then her lungs worked again, and she drew in a breath of rain and air, coughs scraping her throat. She stood up, ignoring the dull pain in her low back, pushing her streaming hair away from her face.

Venus focused on the water. Peter had reached the two struggling women. It was a bleak comedy; Venus wanted to laugh at the spectacle of these three withered, aged bodies fighting against the torrent of the ocean and themselves. The inky hysteria washed over her, and she heard a high laugh fly out of her throat. Confused with her Gran's name, the sounds had the quality of language never heard before. Venus reached the small beach. Her feet squelched deep into the water-soaked sand. She struggled with her boots; she knew that she must go into the water but that the boots could pull her into drowning. Venus flung them away and ran into the sea.

The water was icy, but it was her friend. She swam so often; this was just swimming. She could walk to where Morag and Kate were still struggling. Against the backdrop of leaded tails of rain—Rousay now completely obscured—Peter rocked in the small blue boat. Morag and Kate had stumbled out further, and Kate was now reaching desperately for the side of the boat. Peter pushed Morag hard in the chest with his oar. She bellowed; Venus heard her cry in the wind. It was an animal cry. The tide sucked at Venus, threatening to pull her down. The ebb tide through this channel was murderous. It went out in a flash, hurrying to rejoin the North Sea. Venus saw Morag tear the oar from Peter's hand as she fell forward, gulping in a mouthful of salty water. Venus choked and flailed for the bottom; it was still shallow here. She mustn't panic. A wave receded and she abruptly found the bottom, jabbing her hand on a rock. She stood and wiped her stinging eyes.

Peter held fast to Kate's hand as she flopped and bobbed against the side of the boat. He was struggling to pull her aboard; the water was over Kate's head. Morag beat upon his helping arm with the oar and Venus could hear her cry.

"Let her die! Let her die! It's what she deserves. She's ruined our family! Let her die, you bastard!"

Peter grimaced at each blow. Kate's other hand scrabbled at the side of the boat. He cried out as the heavy oar smashed against his hand. Kate slipped from his grasp and went under the boat. Venus slogged towards them. She could not get closer; the tide was pulling them away. Morag was afloat now, her long arm draped over the side of the boat. How could she be so strong? Peter rocked in despair and Venus could see his arm hanging useless by his side. Where was Kate?

Venus saw her Gran at last, choking to the surface a little distance from the boat. Morag's head whipped round to find her. As she turned from the boat, Peter grabbed her arm with his left hand, crooking his elbow in hers. Somehow he pulled her half into the boat. The dinghy was pitching dangerously in the waves. Morag was half in, half out. Her free hand lashed at Peter's neck and head. Venus saw it slowly, the seconds pulling into an hour, an eternity. She heard her own voice, disembodied, screaming Kate's name. Kate's head bobbed in the water; the tide was taking her. Venus dove forward into the chopping waves, propelling herself like a seal in her Gran's direction. When she surfaced, gasping, she was in deep and began to tread water. The sea lapped over her head. She saw the dinghy, overturned, floating away from her. There was a false sense of darkness; she couldn't see, the clouds were low and the rain streamed like fountains into the sea. Then she saw a bit of white—Kate's jumper. Kate was struggling feebly, trying for the dinghy. Venus dove under again, using her instinct to guide her toward Kate. Once more to surface; she was closer and strode out with bold strokes in her Gran's direction. In a moment she had her, grasping the featherweight body under the armpits.

"The dinghy, Gran, we've got to hold on. Help me."

Kate scrabbled on her back like a child and Venus began to swim. Every muscle ached. Kate was murmuring. Venus thought she might be losing consciousness. The tide brought her the dinghy and she grasped it, hanging on to a rope lashed in the side. She could not see Morag or Peter, but she had an icy fear that Morag's hands would reach up to grab her.

"Gran, can you get off me? Can you hold on? I want to try and drag the boat in." It would be impossible, she knew. But she had to try. She moved so that Kate was facing her, holding the old woman in a watery embrace. "Hold on, Gran. Feel the ropes. Put your hands around them and hold on. Keep your head up." Somehow Kate understood, found the strength. Venus felt her way to the prow of the boat, using the rope to hang on against the chopping waves. The shore was receding, the hungry tide sucking them toward the main channel and the sea. If they floated into Eynhallow Sound, they would never make it. Venus began to swim with her right arm, kicking with her feet and pulling the dinghy behind her. Her back and neck screamed with pain, her feet were numb with cold. Please, she prayed, please, please, please. She fixed her eyes on the shore. She saw a figure there, absurdly waving and running down the field. It was Finn—was it? Her eyes closed for what seemed like a long time. The prow of the dinghy banged the back of her head. Her hand, striving through the water, touched clammy, slippery skin.

Venus screamed, and her throat filled with water. Her hand felt welded to the rope of the dinghy. A seal emerged in front of her. Venus began to laugh. The rope slipped through her cramped fingers. She held out her arms, laughing, as the sea slipped over her head.

CHAPTER THIRTY-EIGHT

The hospital was small and old, smelled of antiseptic and the vague sweetness of urine. They always smelled the same. Finn exited into a narrow courtyard, covered from the rain and wind. He paced and lit a cigarette. He glanced at his mobile. Half eleven. Hours had passed since he had run into the High street in Stromness, bleary from Neill's attack on him. After a frantic call to the police emergency number, Finn had, out of pure luck, caught the last bus back to Blackstone. On the way he had checked his voicemail; the call from Venus was the only message. With some coercing, the bus driver had agreed to drop him at the top of McNeill's drive. He had started running, screaming Venus' name, when he recognized Morag's Mini. He shivered, remembering his terror at seeing the drifting boat, the overturned dinghy, searching the water for Venus' head. He had seen the seal first, and it had let out a low, keening sound. The seal dove and surfaced, pushing up Venus' torso. He had struck out for her, horrified by the cold of the water and the certainty that she was already dead. The seal had stayed close until he reached her body, and then had darted darkly away.

"Finn! Finn, you are here." Sammy's voice called from the orange light of the hospital corridor. He waited for Finn to reach the door, holding it open.

Finn chucked his fag onto the brick paving of the courtyard. He looked into Sammy's worried face.

"Is she all right? I mean, will she *be* all right?" Sammy asked.

"Aye. Took a lot of water into her lungs. Bit hypothermic. Gashes, bruising here and there. She'll be fine. I think she's asleep; at any rate the nurses won't let me near her."

"And Kate?" Sammy's voice shook.

Finn looked at the scarred lino flooring. "I don't know. She was unconscious when I fished her out, and she hasn't come out of it." Finn sighed. "She's old, Sammy. It's a miracle that—"

"Aye, aye." Sammy looked away.

The silence was painful. Finn touched Sammy's elbow and motioned him toward the miniscule waiting area, the inevitable hard plastic chairs.

"It's a crime about Peter," Sammy muttered, as they sat. "What were they doing, anyway, trying to save that old boat? He should have known better."

Finn nodded. Morag and Peter's bodies would be drifting in the North Sea by now. He sat back, stretching his arms overhead. The edge of the chair dug into his back. "So, Morag . . . Neill—did you arrest him?"

"Aye, well, the constable in Stromness went straightaway you called. Neill was packing a bag. Didn't put up much fuss, though. Didn't say anything all through the caution, I guess, and they took him in to the station there. Let him stew awhile, until Crombie and I could make it in. By then, of course, we'd heard about what had happened, on the scanner." Sammy snorted. "Didn't know what to do first—tell him his mum had died or start questioning."

"How did he take it?" Finn was curious. Although he had harbored a well of anger towards his own father, when the old man finally died he had been surprised by the powerful grief that had filled him.

"Broke right down. Seems he was fond of her after all. Anyway, he started talking and didn't stop for the better part of two hours. But we got a confession out of him."

"For Emily's death as well?"

Sammy hesitated. "No . . . he's well accounted for that night, it seems. Spent the evening at the pub with his mates, playing darts. We've confirmed it with the barmaid and the two friends we could reach. So Morag must have been in that alone. It fits, you know. She had a good working knowledge of the old time herbal lore. She would have known wormwood was poisonous in large doses."

"Did Neill tell you that?" Finn rubbed his eyes, still gritty from the sea. His head ached.

"Aye, he did. But Kate had told me that as well." Sammy leaned back in the chair and folded his arms. His eyebrows drew into a frown.

"Beyond the embezzling angle, what did Neill have to say? I don't understand why Morag got involved—killing the man, for fuck's sake—especially months after Neill lost his job. Neill gave me a pretty confused story when I talked to him. He said something about a killing that Kate and Morag and Lorraine had been a part of. Did he tell you about that?"

Sammy nodded. "Well, first he told us about how Gerard was forging checks, embezzling money right and left. Neill got sacked for confronting Gerard—stupid sod, should've gone to the board, or the police—and then cried on his mum's shoulder. Put her in a right fettle, it did. We'd had that story out of him before, as you had, the first time we questioned him. Then it seems that Gerard paid Morag a few visits, asking questions about his mother and father. Venus had told me Gerard was born here, and that his mother was Orcadian, so that made sense to me."

"Aye. Neill said something about Gerard 'profiting from his father's death,' but I didn't understand what he meant. What would Morag know about Gerard's father? Was he from Orkney too?"

"I don't know," Sammy said. "But Gerard had figured out something about his father from these diaries he had and thought Morag could tell him more."

Finn shook his head. "I can't figure how Gerard knew there had been any crime involved. Surely Lorraine hadn't written the story down in detail—how she'd *killed* a man? What a stupid thing to do."

"I'm sure she never thought anyone would read it. Surprisingly, Lorraine's son gave the journals to the History Center library instead of tossing them out. Gerard came across them by accident as far as I can tell—they were full of songs and stories too, her son told me. Gerard must have spoken of them to Emily, because of *her* studies." Sammy shrugged and rubbed his eyes.

"According to Neill, Lorraine had written down the whole story of how Gerard's father was killed by a circle of village women. The names that she mentioned were Morag and Gerard's mother's, and someone Neill didn't know—Faola, I think it was. Gerard had figured out who his mother was by this time, so that's how he knew his father was the victim Lorraine wrote about. He recognized Morag's name, of course—her age was right and she'd been on the island all her life—and thought he could blackmail some information out of her. And he also threatened to bring suit against Neill."

"But Neill said Kate was involved. How did he know if the diaries didn't mention her?" Finn asked.

Sammy sighed heavily. "Morag told him the story one night, and said that the killing had been Kate's idea. Morag was fifteen when it happened, and had never forgotten—or forgiven. Morag convinced Neill to help her kill Gerard. She had so far not paid Gerard any money, but she was getting scared. She was trying to make him back down, saying that she had evidence to prove that he had been the embezzler, not Neill."

"Huh," Finn said. His stomach growled with hunger. He hadn't eaten since the crisps in the pub.

"Tricky, I know." Sammy leaned forward again. His jaw was shadowed with stubble. "We had a hard time getting a coherent story out of him. It seems clear that Gerard *was* embezzling from the Festival, and positioned Neill to take the blame if he was ever found out. Neill's not smart enough to have carried the scheme off. As a sideline, Gerard thought he could make a little more money blackmailing Morag." Sammy grunted. "From Neill's description, Gerard didn't seem too bothered about the fact that his dad had been murdered by a bunch of women, including Kate. Venus' *grandma*, for Christ's sake. I can't believe it of her! Not that there's any proof now anyway."

"But how—why—the churchyard?"

Sammy's face flushed crimson. "Aye. Well, seems they killed him at Morag's and then Neill drove him up to the churchyard in his car, while Morag took Gerard's Mercedes down to the Wickhouse Wood." He grimaced. "We should have sussed that a vehicle had been driven down that track, but—well—"

"Och, there was no reason to think it. That makes sense with Neill tearing up Morag's kitchen flooring, and them burning it. I never thought of it myself, Sammy. But were there no prints in Gerard's car?"

"No. She was smart about it. There was mud, and various clothing fibers, but she was careful—must have put her hair in a hat. They wanted suspicion to fall upon Kate or Venus, as being the main frequenters of the churchyard, that's why they took him up there. And it's more difficult to gather forensic information in an outdoor scene."

"Och, but they'd have to drive right through McNeill's farm. Taking a chance, like." Finn watched the nurses come and go from their station. A worried looking couple joined them in the waiting area. He tried to catch the duty nurse's eye; when their eyes met she shook her head. Finn looked back at Sammy.

"Morag knew that Kate and Venus would be at the bingo. Or it was a good chance at least. She went there later herself, cool as you like."

"So that's why Morag killed Emily in the dovecote? To make it look like Kate?"

"I don't know. Jesus, I just don't know. We can't prove Morag killed her, even though you saw her coming from the scene. I believe Neill when he says he didn't know she was planning it. But that doesn't mean she didn't do it." Sammy shook his head, his mouth drawing down. "It seems likely she did, and that's better for me than an unsolved case."

"But what will you do about this killing of Gerard's father? If it happened the way Neill says—Kate was directly involved." Finn didn't like the thought of Kate ending her days in some court battle leading to prison. Unlikely as it was that she would emerge from her present coma.

"There's no one to bring a charge, no proof. We don't even know when it happened, *if* it happened. I'm inclined to let it go as Morag's delusions from some other wrong done, some other axe to grind."

Finn nodded, although he felt Kate, for all her humor and common sense, held a deep pain and an infinite well of strength. She could kill, for the right reason, and with the arrogance of youth inside of her. "What about Matthew?"

"There is nothing we can do to hold him. Venus won't press charges for the attack and he's innocent of any other crime. At least he's got the decency to wait for Emily's people to come up from London, see about the funeral arrangements." Sammy rose wearily. "I'm headed home to check on Mary and the kids. Will you call if anything happens? I don't think I can stay awake much longer."

"Aye, will do. I've got nothing else to do but wait." Finn watched Sammy leave, before he stood and went back out to the courtyard for another cigarette.

"Miss McNeill is awake and asking for you, Mr. Ross, if you'd like to come in."

The soft voice of the nurse broke through Finn's bleak thoughts of the afternoon's events and home. He pushed past the nurse into the corridor and strode to Venus' room. She lay pale on the sheets, her hair a stain of black on the pillow. Her eyes were open and very clear.

"The nurse told me about Gran."

"Aye. She's in a bad way, I won't lie. But she's strong. She might make it." Finn mustered a confidence he didn't feel.

Venus' eyes flicked to the window, the rain streaming down the pane. "What about Peter?" her voice was small. "And Morag?"

Finn shook his head and she looked away again.

"I don't understand what she was so angry about. She wanted to kill Gran. *Kill her.*" Venus' voice was still a whisper. "I don't . . . what happened?"

Finn pulled a chair close to the bedside and sat. "I found Matthew, you know, in a pub in Stromness. After I realized he hadn't killed Emily, I started to wonder. I decided to go round and visit with Neill Leach. I found him in, my luck, and he was nervous, like. Afraid. I started pushing him pretty hard. It's funny, you know," Finn said, rubbing his jaw, "how people forget that the press doesn't have any power. I mean, not like the police. But if you take the right tone questioning people, they fall like cards. Especially if they've something to hide, something they feel guilty about."

Venus' eyes opened and shut.

"Are you up to talking now, Venus? It might be better to rest."

Her hand gripped his. "I want to know. I want to know."

Finn looked at her hard, feeling his heart begin to ache. He told her about his and Neill's fight, his anxiety-ridden journey to New Farm, and Neill's confession to Gerard's murder.

"But I don't understand," Venus whispered. "Why was Morag so angry? So crazy? Why did she want to kill Gerard?"

Finn licked his lips. His mouth was dry. "Well—apparently, Morag and—and—some others had been witness, or party to, Gerard's father's death. And covered it up. But someone had written it all down—"

"Lorraine," Venus whispered. "Lorraine's journals."

"Aye. Gerard tried to blackmail Morag, but she wasn't having any of it— he was the criminal, after all—and she came to Neill wanting the evidence that Gerard had been embezzling. She told him that she was going to catch Gerard out in a stalemate. Of course, Neill didn't know what she was on about at the time." Finn sighed, felt tiredness wash over him. "Anyway, at the end of the day, Morag told Neill the story of this man's death, and Neill told Sammy. Morag, Lorraine, and—" Finn hesitated to say what he knew: that Kate had been the ringleader.

"Gran," Venus murmured. "Gran and, I don't know—maybe Clotilde."

"Clotilde?"

"Gerard's mother. He had figured out her name," Venus whispered. "I saw it on the picture. He never told me." A tear slid down her face.

"Aye, so Sammy said she was involved. Do you know about this story?"

Venus closed her eyes, waiting a long moment before she spoke. "Gran told me that Thierry, Gerard's father, had beaten and raped a woman with two small children. I think maybe it was Lorraine, but I don't know. He was dangerous, she said. I suppose he beat Clotilde too. Gran said he disappeared. That they had to protect themselves."

Venus' voice was so quiet that Finn had to lean down to hear her. He smelled her, a mix of salt and disinfectant soap. "He didn't disappear, Venus. They killed him."

"Ahh . . ." She closed her eyes.

"Venus," Finn squeezed her hand. "Morag confessed the whole story to Neill. Told him that it had ruined her life; she had been only fifteen and Kate had made them do it. That's why she was so angry. She never got over it. Neill told her it was ancient history. The man deserved it. No one had come looking for them then, why worry now?

"But Gerard had come looking. He had pieced it together and confronted Morag with accusations of murder, and she tried to match him with threats to reveal evidence that would surely put him away for embezzlement. It was a game of tit for tat, like, but Morag panicked." Finn felt himself separate, heard his voice pouring out the remaining facts as if it were someone else. "They—they killed him there in Morag's kitchen, then brought him up to the churchyard in Neill's car. Left him there, for you to find. Cruel, like."

Venus moved her head from side to side on the pillow. Finn watched her, her face so childlike but so wise. She was beautiful. He felt the absence of sexual attraction, only warmth as he looked at her.

"So Matthew . . . what about Emily? Did she kill herself?"

"I don't know. I do know that Neill had nothing to do with it. He was at the pub with his mates. Sammy's confirmed that. Sammy thinks Morag did it, because I saw her that night, and she was so angry with Emily."

Venus nodded faintly. "Sammy said Emily was poisoned. With wormwood oil. I thought Morag must have—because—oh . . . Peter." Venus' voice sank to a whisper.

"What?" Finn leaned toward Venus, drawn by the light of recognition that burned in her eyes.

"But no one knew Emily was in the doocot. Just Kate and I. And Peter." Venus' look was far away.

"What do you mean?" Finn searched her face, but the veil closed, her gaze opaque once again. "Venus?"

"Nothing. Nothing." Venus closed her eyes again. "I'm tired. I want to see Gran."

"There, you can see her after a wee bit more rest. Do you want the nurse?"

Venus nodded, her eyes drooping. "Some water."

"All right." Finn rose and moved out into the hall. He flagged down a nurse and asked for the water. He returned to Venus' room; already she had drifted into sleep. He hesitated, holding his breath, then bent to kiss her cheek. He took in her smell, the softness of her skin, her raspberry mouth, lips open with soft breath. Finn left the room. He went down the hall to where Kate rested, in an unconscious, critical fugue. They would not let him in. He wandered back down the hall. The ring of his mobile penetrated his ears. He pulled it out; his ma's number.

"Ma," he said walking out to the courtyard once again.

"They're gone, Finn. Nuala never came back to work and even her mother is worried now. Nuala left a message, something her mum couldn't understand. She's not been back to the house, I don't think. They're gone."

Finn breathed through his mother's voice, on the high ascent into hysteria. He held his stomach, waited for the pain. "I'm coming home now, ma. I'm away tomorrow. I'll be home as soon as I can. I'll ring you from the ferry." Finn pocketed his phone and strode back inside to the nurse's station. He demanded pen and paper, and, with a shaking hand, wrote Venus a note.

Venus, I've got to leave. My baby—my wife has taken her and I'm afraid. I know you understand; you've seen them. I'm sorry about all that's happened to you. I'm not much of a praying man, but I ask whatever God there is to pull Kate through, and to give you peace from all that's happened. I'll ring you, I promise, as soon as I can get things figured out at home.

He hesitated. Warmth surged through him at the thought of Venus' innocent face, her pale skin. *With love, Finn.* He read the note through quickly and took it back to Venus' room. As an afterthought he wrote down his mobile number and his mother's telephone at the bottom of the note. *If you need me*, he scrawled. He left with a last look at her face.

Finn hurried through the maze of the small hospital, out into the quiet street. He gazed at the sky, dimming into the perpetual twilight of summer. The moon had started her waning journey; beside her burned the fragile spark of the evening star.

CHAPTER THIRTY-NINE

Venus flew over New Farm in her dream. She saw Emily, hands shaking, preparing the blankets in the doocot. She saw Peter, the flask of tea in his hand, tears on his face, striding down the path to Emily. She turned away from the house and dove, free, toward the shimmering sea. Venus swam there, with a seal. He was sleek and beautiful, and held Venus within his flippers. The seal whispered an old song, a lullaby her mother used to sing. They let the water carry them into the sound. Eynhallow gleamed like a jewel in bright, rain-glazed sun. Kate stood upon the shore, her knobbled fingers waving. Venus raised her hand effortlessly and returned the wave. The fin-folk were in their summerland; her Gran had gone home. Venus turned to find the seal, but she was alone in the shifting, sliding midnight of the sea.